The Art of Falling

Also by Danielle McLaughlin

Dinosaurs on Other Planets

The Art of Falling

DANIELLE McLAUGHLIN

JOHN MURRAY

First published in Great Britain in 2021 by John Murray (Publishers)
An Hachette UK company

3

Copyright © Danielle McLaughlin 2021

A CIP catalogue record for this title is available from the British Library

Hardback ISBN 9781473613669
Trade Paperback ISBN 9781473613676
eBook ISBN 9781473613683

Typeset in Monotype Bembo by Manipal Technologies Limited

Printed and bound in Great Britain by Clays Ltd, Elcograf S.p.A.

John Murray policy is to use papers that are natural, renewable and recyclable products and made from wood grown in sustainable forests. The logging and manufacturing processes are expected to conform to the environmental regulations of the country of origin.

John Murray (Publishers)
Carmelite House
50 Victoria Embankment
London EC4Y 0DZ

www.johnmurraypress.co.uk

For John

I

To be, rather than to seem. The school motto was carved in stone in the arch above the entrance. It was in English on the way in, and in Latin – *Esse Quam Videre* – on the way out, presumably, Nessa thought, to reflect the learning aspired to by the girls who passed through these gates. Meanwhile, Jennifer, her daughter, was struggling with lower level French.

Nessa had taken several shortcuts, the traffic light gods had smiled on her, and now she was only seventeen minutes late for her meeting. She pulled into the visitor's car park, between an Audi and a BMW station wagon. It was April and the school playing fields were fresh and green. Beyond the playing fields was Cork city, the grey slate rooftops silvered with recent rain. She walked past a two-storey block of 1970s construction to the new glass and steel annex where she was to meet Ms Johnson, Jennifer's Year Head. She was unsure why she'd been asked to come in. Jennifer's grades had improved since last term. And she was a polite girl, not counting interactions with her parents.

Ms Johnson was waiting in an empty classroom, correcting papers. Her blonde hair fell forward as she bent over the desk. 'You must be Jennifer McCormack's mum,' she said, looking up and gesturing to a chair. 'Nessa, isn't it?'

'That's right.' She sat down, tucked her dark hair behind her ear. She liked Ms Johnson, who was little more than a girl and had always been kind to Jennifer.

1

Whenever she ran into Ms Johnson outside school hours, in the coffee shop or at the hairdressers, the teacher always spoke to her as if they were friends. 'I'm sorry I'm late,' Nessa said.

'Not to worry,' Ms Johnson said, indicating the pile of student compositions. 'I have plenty of reading material to keep me occupied.' She picked up a ruler and began beating a rhythm against the desk, a low-grade, irritating noise, *twack, twack, twack*. It was like something Jennifer might do, and Nessa had to fight an urge to tell her to stop.

'Have you noticed Jennifer seems to have gone into herself lately,' Ms Johnson said, 'that she's become more withdrawn than usual?'

Than usual? Jennifer was quiet, certainly, but withdrawn was different, wasn't it? 'She's a teenager,' Nessa said, 'withdrawn is the factory setting.'

Ms Johnson frowned. 'It seems to me that Jennifer's social circle has contracted. It could be nothing, of course, but we watch for these kinds of changes. She's not running with the same gang anymore. I was wondering if you knew of anything that might have happened.'

Nessa shook her head. 'Not that I've heard.'

'So you can't think of anything that might be impacting on her?' Her stare was bordering on defiant.

Nessa understood that they were not, in fact, friends and never would be. 'No,' she said. 'I can't.'

Ms Johnson sighed. 'How can I put this . . . I understand that there may be problems at home?'

Oh, Jennifer, Nessa thought, *as if I haven't got enough to deal with.* 'There are no problems,' she said hoarsely, her throat tightening.

Ms Johnson put down the ruler and sat back in her chair. 'I see,' she said. She looked toward the window, out to the green of the carefully tended playing fields. 'There's also the problem that has arisen concerning your daughter and Mandy Wilson.'

Nessa felt the blood rush to her cheeks. 'I haven't heard of any problem with Mandy.' *Please don't do this to me, Jennifer,* she thought. *Please.*

'They were such good friends, weren't they?' Ms Johnson said. 'Best friends, I would have said, though of course that's something of a movable feast among girls that age.' She smiled, as if to compensate for her brittleness earlier, but Nessa was no longer capable of smiling back. Her hands of their own accord had dropped to grip the plastic edge of her chair, and she brought them back to her lap.

'Lately,' Ms Johnson continued, 'it's clear that they are no longer friends and . . .' She paused. 'There's no nice way of saying this, but Jennifer is bullying Mandy.'

'No,' Nessa said. It was impossible. Her child was not a bully.

'Yes, I'm afraid,' Ms Johnson said.

'What exactly . . .' Nessa stopped, swallowed a couple of times. It *would* be the Wilson girl, of course. Several times in recent months, Nessa had reached what she thought was peak hurt, only to be sideswiped by some new humiliation. It was bad enough Cora Wilson going about as if nothing had happened, running for re-election to Parents' Council, and getting it too. Only last week, Nessa had picked up the school newsletter to find Cora's round, jovial face beaming out at her. She glanced at Ms Johnson, tried to gauge how much she knew, but the young woman's expression was opaque. Nessa cleared her throat. 'What has been happening?' she asked.

3

'They used to be inseparable,' the teacher said. 'You never saw one without the other. They sat together in the cafeteria every day. Now, Jennifer eats lunch with some other girls she has recently taken up with – a girl in particular from the year above, one of the Sullivans, you may know her?'

Nessa nodded. 'The name is familiar. I think she might be coming over today.'

'Mandy now eats alone,' Ms Johnson continued. 'Mandy, even more so than Jennifer, has become isolated within the class. She's more introverted, doesn't seem to have adapted to the whole . . .' She glanced quickly around the classroom, as if willing a suitable word to present itself. '. . . situation.'

Nessa experienced a twinge of guilt. Part of her was secretly glad to hear that her daughter's friendship with the Wilson girl had cooled. It was too difficult, looking at Mandy only to be reminded of the girl's mother. And if Jennifer and Mandy had not been friends, then perhaps Cora Wilson would never have got to know Philip and might have confined her affections to her own husband.

'It's not the sort of thing parents can intervene in, is it?' Nessa said. 'They're sixteen. We can't make them hang out if they don't want to. And eating lunch with new friends hardly counts as bullying. Maybe you could speak with Mandy's parents?'

Ms Johnson's gaze was steady. 'I believe this is hurting Jennifer as much as Mandy,' she said. 'She's missing their friendship, I can tell. It's a classic case of misplaced anger, like she's lashing out. And it's more serious than Jennifer simply having new lunch friends, I'm afraid.' She paused. 'A number of stationery items belonging to Mandy have gone missing.'

Nessa sat straighter on her chair. 'So my daughter's a thief now?'

'I never said that.' Ms Johnson's tone remained neutral. 'Please listen carefully to what I am saying.' She got up and went to the water cooler, came back with a glass, which she offered to Nessa.

Nessa shook her head. 'No. Thank you.'

Ms Johnson set the glass down on the desk. 'I'll leave it here in case you change your mind.' She picked up the ruler again and this time began to tap it against her knee. 'Jennifer has also stopped playing hockey. She says she refuses to play on a team with Mandy. I have heard her, on more than one occasion, remark on Mandy's physical appearance – Mandy's weight, Mandy's hair, for example. And I've noticed that when school finishes, Mandy walks home alone.'

It was true that it had been a long time since she'd found Mandy Wilson sprawled on their couch after school, or, more often than not, on a beanbag on the living room floor, watching YouTube videos. 'When did this start?' Nessa asked, though she could guess.

'A few months ago. But things have deteriorated in recent weeks. I fear the other girls in the year may begin taking sides.'

Nessa swallowed. 'How come we're only hearing about this now?'

The teacher's gaze flickered again to the inviting green of the outdoors. 'I did discuss it with Jennifer's dad at the parent-teacher evening. I take it he hasn't mentioned it to you?'

When Nessa said nothing, Ms Johnson said, 'I guess this brings us, in a roundabout way, to what I was getting at earlier – the question of whether there might be problems at home . . .'

Nessa stood up abruptly, banging against the desk and upsetting the glass of water.

'Please sit down,' Ms Johnson said. She lifted the pile of papers out of the path of the encroaching water and dabbed at the spill with a tissue. 'I appreciate that this must be awkward for you. In the circumstances. But we need to think about Jennifer. And Mandy. I assure you that I'm not here to judge you in any way . . .'

'Good,' Nessa said. She straightened her shoulders, took a deep breath. 'Because we pay fees to this school to have our daughter educated. Not to be judged. Not to have our private lives dissected.'

'I have precisely zero interest in your private life.' Ms Johnson threw the wet tissue in the bin with a certain degree of force. 'I'm interested only in the well-being of the pupils under my care, specifically in this instance the well-being of your daughter and Mandy Wilson.'

Nessa remained standing. She gripped the back of the chair to stop her hands from trembling. The teacher got to her feet also, smoothing down her skirt before she spoke. 'As a first step in these instances, we usually invite the parents of both girls in for an informal chat. Everyone around the table together. In most cases, we find that to be very helpful.'

Nessa shook her head. 'No,' she said. She and Philip sitting across the table from Cora Wilson and Mr Wilson? It was unthinkable.

Ms Johnson placed a hand on her arm. 'As I said, I know this must be awkward . . .'

'How old are you?' Nessa said, shaking off her hand. 'Twenty-three? Twenty-four? You know nothing.' Fat treacherous tears began rolling down her cheeks. She turned and walked out of the classroom and down the corridor, ignoring Ms Johnson, who stood in the doorway looking after her.

Nessa waited twenty minutes in the school car park before driving home. She wasn't one of those women who cried well. Hers was the puffy-eyed, graceless kind of crying. She watched Ms Johnson come out of the building and leave in a 1995 Toyota, one quarter panel a different shade of blue from the rest of the car. Nessa took a stick of concealer from her handbag and dabbed at the worst of the red blotches on her skin, then set off for home.

They'd inherited the house, or rather Philip had, from his mother, who'd paid off the final instalment of her mortgage a year before she died. Philip had managed to remortgage it for almost a million, all of which he'd sunk into property investments that had crashed. The house was in Sunday's Well, mid-nineteenth century, with big sash windows, the ones at the rear looking out onto a sloping garden that ran down to the river.

In the hall, she found the usual muddle of shoes and coats and bags. Going into the kitchen, she heard a snuffling from beside the table. Bailey, a blind Labrador also inherited from Philip's mother, had upended a plate containing the remains of a sandwich and was licking mayonnaise from the floor. 'Out!' she said, picking up the plate, but he nuzzled against her legs until she took him by the collar and dragged him to his blanket by the back door. In the living room the curtains were drawn and the room was in darkness save for the flicker of the TV in the corner. Jennifer was sprawled on the couch with her headphones on. Nessa switched on the light. 'Hey, Jen. What's up?' The girl was tall, like her father, and her legs dangled over the end of the couch. She'd cajoled her mother into taking up the hem of her uniform by several inches, and Nessa could see where the sewing was already coming undone.

Jennifer blinked, rubbed her eyes. She had the same strong brows and hazel eyes as her mother. 'Nothing,' she said, and yawned. She took out her earbuds.

Nessa had expected to see the Sullivan girl too. She glanced around the room – perhaps some lithe thing was sunk in a beanbag, but no, there was only her daughter. 'I thought you'd a friend coming over?'

Jennifer shrugged. 'She had to cancel.'

Before today, before her conversation with Ms Johnson, Nessa would have thought nothing of this. Now she said, 'Why? Was she sick?'

'Yeah. I think so.' Jennifer's eyes were fixed on the TV, which was showing cartoons. The sound was off.

'You *think* so? What did she say?'

'She said her mom thought it would be better if she waited until her sore throat had cleared.'

'But she was at school? With her sore throat?'

'Yes.' Jennifer picked up the remote and began scrolling through channels.

'Was it the Sullivan girl?'

'Sorry?'

'What was her name? The girl who was supposed to come over.'

Jennifer frowned. 'Deirdre Sullivan.'

Nessa remembered now that the Sullivans lived on the same road as the Wilsons. Were the parents taking sides? She knew Mrs Sullivan slightly, wouldn't put it past her to meddle in her daughter's friendships as a show of loyalty to Cora Wilson.

She positioned herself between her daughter and the TV screen. 'You know who I was thinking of on the way home this evening? That girl, Serena, who used to be in your piano class? We haven't had her round in a while. We should invite her over.'

Jennifer sat up, swinging her feet onto the carpet. 'Why?' she said suspiciously. She was in the process of putting her earbuds back in, but stopped.

'You seemed to get on well together.'

Jennifer made a face. 'She's all right.'

'Maybe someone else then. One of the other girls.'

'Deirdre Sullivan will come over next week when her throat's better. Doesn't she count?'

'Of course she counts, but I just thought it might be nice for you to have someone else round.'

Jennifer shook her head. 'What's the matter with you, anyway?'

Nessa sighed. 'Is anything wrong at school, sweetheart? Is there anything you want to tell me about? Because I went to see Ms Johnson this afternoon.'

Jennifer frowned. 'Why did you do that? Ms Johnson is such a ditz. What's she been saying?'

Nessa sat on the arm of the couch. 'You used to like her, if I remember.'

'Yeah, well, not anymore. What did she say?'

'She said that you and Mandy Wilson don't hang out any-more, and . . .' Nessa held up a hand to silence her daughter's protest, because Jennifer was already on her feet, eyes flash-ing. 'I know there are reasons for that, and I feel bad about it, believe me, you have no idea how bad I feel about it. Your father does too. But just because things went wrong between us adults isn't any reason for you to be unhappy.'

'I'm not unhappy. Mandy Wilson is a dope, Mom. I don't know why I was ever friends with her in the first place. She's a dope, and her mother's a tramp.'

'Jennifer!'

'Well, they are. Or are you going to tell me that Mrs Wilson is a really nice person?'

Her daughter's bitterness shocked her. She attempted to keep her own voice even. 'Ms Johnson said you've started to bully Mandy.'

'Well, I haven't. Mandy has been feeding her a pack of lies.'

'She said you and Mandy don't sit at the same lunch table anymore. She said you left hockey because you refused to be on the same team as Mandy.'

Jennifer rolled her eyes. 'I left hockey because I wasn't any good at it, okay? I left because I'd rather be in choir and the times clashed. And, last time I checked, there is no obligation on me to be anybody's friend if I don't want to be.' She paused. 'I don't see you being friends with Mrs Wilson.'

Nessa stared at her daughter. She felt tears rising and blinked them away. She would have to revisit this later; she didn't have the strength for it now. 'Is your dad home?'

'He's in his den.'

On her way out to the hall, Nessa paused in the doorway. 'Your father and I are okay, Jennifer. You do know that, don't you?'

Jennifer glanced at her mother, a pink blush rising on her cheeks. 'Yes,' she said, before looking away.

A room off the hall had been fitted out as a studio for Philip. On the walls were framed sketches of various buildings he'd worked on, and a cork bulletin board, on which he had tacked correspondence from local authorities, cost engineers, builders. An architect, he sometimes held meetings in this room, but mostly he preferred to meet his clients in hotels. The studio, or den as Jennifer called it, had been his mother's 'good room', crammed with fussy furniture, rarely used. Nessa had cleared it out and painted it white. Along one wall was Philip's drafting table, an antique Fritz and Goeldel mechanical table she'd found years ago during a trip to London, when they'd had money for things like that. He was at the table now, a set of plans in front of him.

'New gig?' she said when he looked up.

'A kitchen extension.' He said it the way one might say 'dog turd'. 'For the woman who owns the florists on the corner. I could hardly say no.' He was sallow-skinned, tall and sinewy, with dark blond hair that had begun to recede and was cut short at the back and sides.

'Will you get paid, do you think?'

'I don't know. But she seems to be doing well enough, so here's hoping.'

Nessa sat down on the sofa, took a deep breath. 'I met Ms Johnson after school this afternoon.'

He frowned. She could see that he was trying to work out who Ms Johnson might be; perhaps he thought he was about to be accused of doing something with her.

'Jennifer's Year Head,' she said.

'Ah, yes,' he said, 'I remember her now.'

Ms Johnson was the sort of woman men tended to remember, Nessa thought. She felt a twinge of jealousy, pushed it aside. 'It seems that Jennifer's having some problems at school. Her social circle has changed, contracted. Did Ms Johnson mention anything at the parent-teacher meeting?'

He shook his head. 'Nope. I'd have remembered.'

'Are you sure?' She swallowed. 'Because she asked me if there were issues at home.'

'I'm positive.' He had a way of saying things that convinced his listeners utterly. There was a time when it had even worked on her. It was partly why they were in so much debt.

'Apparently Jennifer has started bullying Mandy Wilson. Ms Johnson said she told you about it.'

His expression became more guarded. 'She did mention something about Mandy. It didn't sound like much, to be honest.'

'And you didn't think to tell me?'

He looked away. 'I didn't want to upset you. On account of it being the Wilson girl. I thought it was one of those things that kids sort out best on their own. I still think that. Us getting involved is only going to make things worse, particularly when it's . . . well, you know. The Wilsons.'

'Ms Johnson wants both sets of parents to meet,' Nessa said quietly.

'What?'

'She wants you and me to sit down with the Wilsons to talk about our daughters.'

He sat up straighter. 'Well, that isn't going to happen.'

'That's what I tried to tell her. But . . .' In spite of herself, her voice shook. 'She *knows*, Philip. Ms Johnson knows. She knows about everything.'

He got up and came to sit beside her. He wiped away a tear that was sliding down her cheek. 'She'd have to be a simpleton not to,' he said. 'You didn't really think we'd be able to keep it quiet, did you?'

There was a time you *thought you'd be able to keep it quiet*, Nessa thought, but didn't say. He put an arm around her shoulder, but she shook it off. She took a tissue from a box on the table and blew her nose.

'How were things left?' he said.

Nessa felt her cheeks grow hot. 'Up in the air.' He didn't need to know about the crying, or the storming out. 'She said we'll talk about it again.'

'Maybe we can encourage the girls to . . . I don't know . . . sort things out themselves.'

As if it were that easy, she thought. As if the mess their lives had become would magically resolve itself, just like that. She stood up. 'I know,' she said. 'Why don't we invite Mandy Wilson for a sleepover? We used to do that before, remember? Before you started having sex with her mother.'

'Please, Nessa,' he said. 'Come on now, that's not fair. This is about Jennifer.'

'Maybe Cora Wilson could come too. Maybe you, me, and her could, I don't know, play Scrabble or something, while the girls hang out.' She shoved her feet back into her shoes. 'You know why Jennifer is taking things out on Mandy Wilson? The same reason she takes things out on me. It saves her blaming you.' She banged the door behind her as she left the room. In the kitchen she took a bottle of wine from the fridge. The thing was, Jennifer really had been good friends with Mandy Wilson, before Philip did the dirt with Cora. Let him think about that for a while.

As she struggled with the corkscrew, she heard a familiar low hum from across the river. There was a public park along the opposite bank, and the park attendant often cut the grass at this hour. He had a ride-on lawnmower that was stored in the maintenance building during the day and in the evening she would hear it stirring out of silence like an animal disturbed, a whimper first as the engine ignited, then a steady growl as it began its looped journey in and out between the trees. The dog knew the sound too, and now he responded, not with annoyance but like it was a call to vespers, rising from his blanket and pawing at the door until she let him out into the garden. He stood snapping at insects in the long grass while his eyes trailed the machine across the river, as if he could see it.

13

She poured a glass of wine and sat at the kitchen table, listening for any sound of Philip coming out of the studio to her.

She got out her laptop, opened the Progress Report that she was required to submit once a month to the gallery where she worked. The gallery, in turn, filed the report with the EU cultural agency funding the acquisition she was currently curating. All the boxes had to be filled in. If she didn't fill in one box, it wouldn't allow her to proceed to the next, and she stared at it for a while as she drank her wine, then closed it again. She thought that if Philip met her halfway, if he came out of the studio now and came as far as the kitchen door, then she would be the one to apologise. There hadn't been another woman since Cora Wilson, she was reasonably sure of that.

Possibly there hadn't been another woman before her either. There had, perhaps, been an occasional, discreet straying, evidenced by a temporary distancing when he got home from a business trip, a restraint in the way he touched her. But nothing like those months when she thought that she'd lost him. Then, even the nights he was home, asleep beside her, she'd get up and walk the house in the small hours, touching things, trailing her fingers along walls, the backs of chairs, as if trying to hold down everything that was slipping away.

There were nights she'd taken things out to the garden, things singled out for destruction earlier in the evening: ornaments, serving dishes, a shell brought back from their vacation. She'd go to the end of their property, where Philip wouldn't hear, and she'd smash them against his mother's rusty fence. One night, glass littering the ground at her feet, she looked back up the hill and saw a light come on in the house next door, saw the blinds raised and Mrs Moriarty, their neighbour, at the window. She'd been an old, dear friend of Philip's mother and for a split second Nessa had feared that the woman would go running to her mother-in-law with tittle-tattle tales, before she remembered that her mother-in-law was dead. She began to laugh then, right there in the middle of the night in her penguin-patterned pyjamas; she stood there and laughed at herself and at the old woman watching her.

When she'd discovered his affair with Cora Wilson, Philip had offered to leave. 'Don't think that you get to be the one to leave,' she'd said. 'If anybody's going to leave, it's going to be me.' It was spoken in anger, but in retrospect, it was the best thing she could have said. He was still in contact with Cora then, and she'd seen immediately how unnerved he was at the prospect of being left to manage both the house and Jennifer. Cora, who had two younger children as well as Mandy, was unlikely to jump ship and come live with him. And if she did, she'd bring her whole brood with her. Nessa had often thought since that if his mother had been more of a feminist, if she'd raised her son to cook and clean and take an interest in child-rearing, they might have divorced.

In the event, when faced with the prospect of running a household, he'd broken with Cora Wilson. When next it was Nessa's turn to host the monthly fundraiser for the school orchestra, she'd walked up to Cora at the school gates and handed her an invitation. Cora had turned up that Friday afternoon, Mandy shy beside her. She'd accepted a glass of elderflower cordial, complimented the cut of the crystal. And then she and Nessa and the other mothers had engaged in shrill, giddy conversation, laughed, even, if a little hysterically, while their daughters hung out in the living room, tapping at their phones. After that day, Mandy never came to their house again.

2

The day after her meeting at the school, she and Philip had an appointment with the marriage counsellor. They'd chosen a therapist in a small town twenty miles east of the city, where they weren't known, or at least she had chosen the therapist and Philip had, grudgingly, agreed to go. 'I don't see why we must pay a stranger in order to talk to each other,' he said.

'Because we don't talk to each other,' Nessa said.

'Yes we do.'

'No, not properly. Not now.'

For several months they had unpeeled their lives in this room. It was, Nessa thought, like undressing in front of a stranger. That morning she wanted to raise the unfairness of Jennifer continuing to adore her father while becoming increasingly distant from her mother.

'It's like she's blaming me for his affair,' she said. They were seated around a table in a small, chintzy room above a dry cleaners.

'That's ridiculous,' Philip said.

'Is it?' she said. 'Children blame the wrong parent all the time. When my sister and I were young, we made a voodoo doll of our father and whenever he burned the dinner, or made us wait in the van while he was on a job, we'd stick pins in it. It makes me sad now to think about it, because our father was doing his best. It was our mother who was to blame, decamping to her relatives whenever the mood took her.'

'How old were you,' the therapist said, 'when you played that game?'

16

She considered for a moment. 'Ten. Maybe eleven. It wasn't a game. I kept the doll. I never did anything with it afterwards, but I kept it, and for a while, when I was about fifteen, I used to take it to school with me.'

Philip glanced, in an obvious way, at his watch. 'I think we're getting off the topic.'

'I'd like to stay with this a little longer, if we may,' the therapist said. 'Carry on, Nessa.'

She saw that he was looking at her expectantly. What more was there to say about the doll? 'I remember wondering why it never worked for us,' she said, 'when it always worked for the people on the television.'

The therapist steepled his fingers. 'Well . . .' he said.

'Hang on,' Philip said. 'Is that the cloth doll with the bamboo legs? The one I found in your sock drawer?'

'Yes,' Nessa said. 'That's it.'

'You told me that doll belonged to your grandmother. A family heirloom.'

'I'm more interested in the fact that you kept it,' the therapist said. 'Why was that, do you think, Nessa?'

Philip held up a hand to silence him. 'You lied to me,' he said, turning to Nessa.

She reddened. 'What was I going to tell you? It was years ago. We didn't know each other that well back then.'

'We were married.'

She felt her temper rise. 'After all the hurt you've caused,' she said. 'After everything you've done, you have the nerve to sit there and accuse *me* of lying. Me choosing not to talk about a doll, Philip, does not equate to you choosing to sleep with Cora Wilson.'

Philip looked to the therapist, as if to say *Rein this in*, but the man said nothing. 'We drive all this way,' Philip said, 'to talk about us, and all you do is bring everything back to Cora. Cora, Cora, Cora.'

'That is not fair,' she said.

'Maybe we should park this for the moment,' the therapist said, 'and get back to your relationship with your daughter.' But for the remaining half hour, Philip was curt to the point of rudeness, and it was a relief when the time was finally up and they left in their separate cars, Nessa for Tragumna in West Cork, where she had an appointment on behalf of the gallery with the family of the acclaimed artist the late Robert Locke.

'I'm afraid we're running behind,' Loretta Locke had said on the doorstep, 'my mother took a bit of a turn.' The first time she'd used that phrase, 'a bit of a turn', Nessa had been alarmed, but it turned out that Loretta used it to mean anything from a mild stroke to a fit of bad temper.

'Is she all right?' Nessa stepped over the leaves of an encroaching plant and onto the porch. Things grew with lush vulgarity here. Maybe it was the sea air: all those tiny particles of seaweed, all those hapless microorganisms blown inland to fertilise reedy fields.

'Oh, Mother is absolutely fine.' Loretta inclined her head to the small room at the end of the hall where Nessa usually spoke with Mrs Locke. 'I've left you the newspaper.'

They were standing outside the studio where Robert Locke had worked on a number of his better-known pieces. Before the Lockes came to the house in the late sixties, the room must have been a sitting room. It was wide and bright, with two tall windows looking out to sea, another smaller window to the side, a ceiling with subdued cornicing and one bare lightbulb in the centre. *Gravity*, nominated for the Turner in 1985 and now in the National Gallery, had been conceived and shaped in this room. *Venus at the Hotel Negresco*, known locally as 'the Chalk

Sculpture', was here still. Over seven feet tall, it commandeered the room, part human female, part abstract. The 'chalk' wasn't strictly speaking chalk at all, but a soft gypsum Locke had experimented with, fleetingly, in his middle years. Come September, the sculpture would move to a more fitting space in the gallery in the city, and the studio would move with it – the door, the floor, the ceiling. Even the dust would be transported. 'I'll be in here, if that's all right,' Nessa said, indicating Locke's studio. 'I've one or two things to check.'

'Of course,' Loretta said. 'We won't be long.' Locke's daughter was in her late forties, tall and lean with close-cut auburn hair. She wore the kind of clothes that elicited politeness from shop assistants. That day it was tailored navy trousers, a striped blue and white shirt under a camel-coloured sweater.

It was humid, dull, save for a dazzle of light miles out at sea, and Nessa hadn't worn any tights. She noticed that her legs, pale, and dappled here and there with old bruises, complemented the floorboards. She'd already measured every inch of this floor on her hands and knees, photographed it, sketched it on gridded paper over a series of afternoons in preparation for the gallery's acquisition of the studio. She'd marked in pencil the exact location of Robert Locke's chair; his workbench still with its rasps and chisels; the cast–iron statue, half stoat, half man, that had stood so long in one place that when she'd moved it, she'd found two perfect imprints of its clawed iron feet on the floor. She had liaised with the conservationist, commissioned the survey and the elevational drawings. She had tagged; she had devised a computerised archive. Already some things had been packed into boxes with typed labels on the outside, a catalogue number in the top right-hand corner.

The Chalk Sculpture stood in the middle of the room. It had achieved notoriety some years before when it came to be regarded as embodying fertility powers. The public had sought it out in their hundreds; they came in a spirit of supplication, less to marvel at what critics had described as the piece's 'gritty transcendence', its alien, unsettling beauty, than to plead their case.

Nessa walked over and touched a hand to the swell of the figure's belly. The sculpture had once languished for a period in a disused cowshed in Clonakilty, before the farmer, reportedly tired of it, delivered it by tractor and trailer back to the Locke women, Robert Locke being dead by then. Nessa touched a finger to the indent in the centre of the chalk-white belly. A groove had formed from the already water-damaged gypsum being eroded by the hands of pilgrims. Nessa wondered about these people, who'd flocked not to consider Robert Locke's genius but to beg for babies. She had rescued the sculpture from such indignities. But when the gallery had set about acquiring it, parts still had a dung-ish tinge from the years in the cowshed. The conservationist had spent days with a small brush engaged in the complicated process of cleaning without erasing.

When she was younger and a student of art history, Nessa had written her thesis on Locke. There were many theories on why the sculpture didn't have a face, and she had critically analysed all of them. Looking at the figure now, she was no nearer to understanding why Locke had left the head as a block of unchiselled stone, and yet made one foot so miraculously detailed that even now, all these years later, after all the erosions of air and cow breath, all the indignities of Loretta's cleaning solvents before she knew better, it was still possible to see the trace of a hair on the big toe and the amphibian webbing of the two smallest ones.

Outside, beyond the patch of gravel where her car was parked, an untended field sloped to the seashore, with the ghost of an old pathway, a tiny modulation in the tilt and shading of the reeds, running down the centre. She imagined Robert Locke walking that path after a morning spent chiselling and shaping.

She'd met him, decades earlier, at college when she was a star-struck student. To be here, in his studio, his former home, still felt, on occasion, as if she were taking liberties, as if she were becoming privy to things that she shouldn't. What sort of man had he been? What sort of father? Or husband? One who wouldn't have made a fuss about a bloody doll, she thought; one who understood the necessity to transfer our emotions to forms and shapes outside ourselves, lest our feelings rise up and destroy us.

'Everything all right?' She hadn't heard Loretta come back, but there she was, standing in the doorway, head quizzically to one side. 'I'll bring you down now. My mother's ready.'

In a smaller room at the back of the house, Mrs Locke was seated at a circular table. She was eighty-four, small proportioned, with white hair pinned in a French twist. There was a smattering of broken veins on her face, which she liked to disguise with a dusting of powder, always that little bit too much powder, so that fine grains of it sat on her cheeks, on the tip of her nose. She was wearing a black suit cut from a fabric that Nessa's mother might have rubbed between her fingers before pronouncing good. She might also have pronounced it old-fashioned. The afternoon was overcast, and Nessa reached for the light switch.

'I never need the lamps in the daytime,' Eleanor said, 'not in summer. Artificial light is a sacrilege in a place like this. We moved here for the light. Didn't I ever tell you that?'

'You did.' Nessa went to a lamp in the corner, switched that on too.

'Do you know what Robert would say if he could see us now? With all these lamps on? He'd say what a pity. What a pity to squander the lovely soft light.'

Nessa imagined that Robert Locke, if asked, would not call the light 'soft'. The light here was glorious, but it was blade-sharp, unsparing. There were days, as she drove along the coast road, when she thought the darts of silver coming in off the water might slice her in two. She glanced at Loretta, but she had already sidled away with a book to an alcove at the side of the room. This was where she hid out on the afternoons Nessa interviewed her mother.

'Is that thing on?' Eleanor said, pointing to the Dictaphone.

'Not yet.'

'Well, turn it on, would you? I've remembered something I must tell you about Robert.'

3

Robert Ethan Locke was born in a small village in south-west Scotland in 1932. The story told was that his father was a coal miner and his mother a seamstress. These were facts he'd often pressed into service when describing his early life, though how much mining or sewing was done depended on whom one spoke to.

His father, as a young man, had worked a summer in the mines at Muirkirk, but the family had a sheep farm near Priesthill where Robert spent most of his childhood. And his mother did make shifts and petticoats, but mostly as a charitable effort for the local Women's Aid Committee. Robert had one sibling, an older brother who died in a drowning accident as a teenager, an incident he could never be drawn to discuss. In interviews, he'd spoken about how he spent a year at the Slade studying fine art in his early twenties, then dropped out to travel to India and South America before settling in Cambridgeshire, where he married Eleanor. In 1968 they moved to West Cork.

All of this Nessa had known from her undergraduate days, and none of it was what Eleanor wanted to talk about now. What she wanted to talk about was how badly Robert had treated her that time he disappeared for several weeks in 1972. This was also well known; Nessa had already heard it from Eleanor herself several times.

Eleanor had her mouth to the Dictaphone. 'He was like a beggar when he came back that time,' she said. 'A beggar you might find sleeping under a piece of cardboard in the street. The filth of him. His hair sticking out like he'd hacked it off with a knife. His shirt torn.' She sighed. 'If he had to go away,' she said, 'would it have killed him to take a change of clothes? If you saw him then, you'd have offered him the price of a cup of tea.' She turned toward the alcove. 'Wouldn't you, Loretta?'

Loretta put down her book. 'My father never took much interest in his appearance,' she said. 'It wasn't important to him.'

'And he brought nothing home for the child,' Eleanor said. 'Washed up on my doorstep in the same clothes he was wearing the day he left, and nothing else. Not even a small trinket for his daughter. Remember, Loretta?' she said.

'It doesn't matter, Mother,' Loretta said. 'It makes no difference.'

They sounded, Nessa thought, as if they were discussing something that had happened only the week before.

'How difficult could it have been to find something small?' Eleanor said. 'Some little souvenir for his own child. A knick-knack from a stall, a plastic donkey. You know the sort of thing. Anything would have been better than nothing.' She paused. 'And he wouldn't even tell us where he'd been.'

Nessa was aware that Loretta had gone back to her book, but her expression was strained, and she wasn't turning any pages.

'Quite a man for the vanishing acts,' Nessa said. She managed a polite smile.

'Vanishing acts!' Eleanor said. 'You make them sound like something delightful. He ran away, that's all. Ran away like a little boy to hide. But young women like you, you always come wanting to give him medals.'

'I didn't mean it like that. It must have been terrible for you, not knowing where he was.'

Eleanor glared. 'You have no idea,' she said. Then, as if the Dictaphone and Nessa were two separate audiences, she dipped her head low again to address the machine: '*You have no idea.*'

Corralling Eleanor's thoughts was never easy, and that afternoon, still raw from her fight with Philip, Nessa found the job slower and more difficult than usual. She'd had an idea to write a paper, perhaps a newspaper article, to be published at the time of the gallery's unveiling of the studio: Robert Locke through the eyes of the women who lived with him. Loretta had refused outright. Eleanor had taken to the idea when Nessa explained that it would, in part, be about her, but cracks had begun to emerge as to the precise nature of that part. Nessa was on the point of packing away her Dictaphone when Eleanor said, 'You're missing a button.'

Nessa looked down at her blouse. 'So I am.' She shrugged.

'You must let me fix it.'

'It's fine. I have to go. I'm giving a talk on Robert's work at the gallery later.'

'My mother won't be able to attend that talk,' Loretta said quickly. 'I'd prefer that she got some rest.'

'I understand,' Nessa said. 'It's just that I need to be on my way. The button doesn't matter.'

'No,' Eleanor said, 'go and take the blouse off. Loretta will fetch you something to put on while I'm sewing. It won't take a minute.'

Nessa hoped Loretta would interject, but she put her book down on the floor and came over to the table. 'Come on,' she said, in a tone that suggested *We might as well get this over with.* She beckoned Nessa toward the stairs.

She had been in the house half a dozen times, but had never got further than the studio, the back room, the downstairs toilet. If she hadn't been running late, she realised, she would've been grateful for the missing button. In curating the life of Robert Locke, what little she had learned so far of these women's personal lives was confined to their roles as wife and daughter. Of their personal day-to-day existence she knew very little. And it was no small thing to know that Locke himself had slept in one of these very rooms, albeit almost two decades ago. Her student self would have blushed at the idea; now she thought that she'd like to settle herself, even briefly, on his bed. In some ways, Nessa thought, she was not that different from those people who came to paw at the Chalk Sculpture.

The landing was wide, with one wall shelved floor to ceiling and stuffed with all kinds of oddities. On closer inspection, she saw that many of them had gift tags or handwritten notes attached. It reminded her of Jennifer's bedroom, but with varnished shells and boxed soaps instead of eye shadows and celebrity-endorsed perfumes. Loretta caught her staring. 'Mostly they bring her ugly, sentimental things,' she said, 'things my father would have hated.' She lifted a box from a shelf, grimaced, put it down again. 'What use they think a statue might have for embroidered hankies I can't imagine.'

'Are people still coming to see the Chalk Sculpture?' The house was no longer meant to be open to visitors. This was something on which the gallery and the Lockes had had extensive negotiations. The publicist was busy whipping up excitement about the planned unveiling of the sculpture in its new home at the gallery. These home visits were diluting the brand.

Loretta flushed. 'These are from before. I used to toss everything out as soon as people left, but then I came to an arrangement with a woman who owns a souvenir shop further up the coast. If she needs extra stock during the regattas, I give her a box of things to sell.'

Loretta unlocked a door to a room that might once have belonged to a lodger or servant: a bed, a wardrobe, a desk and chair. 'Take your blouse off. I'll get you something to wear while you're waiting.' She went off, and Nessa heard another door opening, the metallic ring of hangers sliding across a rail. Loretta returned with a blouse that was most definitely Eleanor's: a chiffony thing with a froth of lace around the neck, mother-of-pearl buttons at the cuffs. 'Come down when you're ready,' she said, in the same kind but brisk tone the nurse at the GP's practice used when leaving Nessa to undress before examination. Nessa looked around. Finally she was in the sleeping quarters of the house where Robert Locke had once lived. This room was so bare, though, that it was hard to imagine it had witnessed much living.

The blouse, being Eleanor's, was much too small. Having failed to do up more than three buttons, Nessa clutched it closed at the front. She sat on the edge of the bed, not wishing to go downstairs. She would be late getting home to cook dinner, and she would have no time to go over her notes for the lecture. After what felt like an eternity, and holding the blouse closed with one hand, she stepped out onto the landing. She paused in front of the shelves stuffed with oddities. Loretta was right, what need had a sculpture for hankies, or lace doilies or paperweights or pincushions, for that matter? But then, the pilgrims were paying a visit; they could hardly have come, as her mother might have said, with their hands hanging. Perhaps they did not wish to scupper their chances

27

by appearing mean. Ten years previously someone claimed to have become pregnant after touching the Chalk Sculpture, and for a while it did a brisk trade in superstition. It became an object of pilgrimage for the desperate, the ones who'd spent all their money on IVF, who'd said their last prayer, and whose only remaining hope was to push their last tenner into the donation box placed discreetly to one side. Then they'd rub the Chalk Sculpture's magnificent belly, cry a bit, and leave a box of scented candles, say, or a string of rosary beads, on the floor by her feet. Nessa had read all about it in a newspaper at the time, back before she'd ever known Loretta and Eleanor, when Locke himself was just the brilliant man she'd studied at college. The day she got the letter from the gallery confirming funding had come through, that she was to be contracted to work on Locke's studio, Philip had cracked a joke about keeping well back from that statue, how one child was quite enough. How they'd laughed! That was over a year ago, before Cora Wilson. Proof that they'd been happy once.

Downstairs, she found Eleanor struggling with the blouse and a needle, the fabric held close to her face. Loretta was in the chair that was usually Nessa's. 'Don't get up,' Nessa said, but Loretta was already drifting back to the alcove. Eleanor paused, needle mid-air. 'I used to get shirts sent over from London when we moved here first,' she said. 'It was hard to get well-made clothes back then. Much better selection now. For those that want them. For those that have an eye.' Then, with a flourish, she brought the thread to her mouth, bit it, and handed over the blouse.

Nessa wondered if she should go back upstairs to change, if they would consider it improper if she whipped the borrowed blouse off in front of them, exposing her greying Marks &

Spencer's bra, but she was in a hurry. She compromised by changing in the hall.

When at last she could get away, Loretta waved goodbye to her from the porch. Nessa walked to her car, sidestepping the wild rhubarb plants that protruded onto the path, their giant leaves heavy with rainwater.

She had never found nature comforting. Even as a child, the cultivation of watercress in cotton wool had held a peculiar terror, the stealthy colonising while she slept. A smattering of fuchsia blossoms dappled the car windshield. She frowned, and pulling her sleeve down to cover her hand, she swept them off before getting in.

A thing that she would later learn: Robert Locke spent those lost weeks in 1972, the weeks that had so pained Eleanor, in a small fishing village in the Inishowen peninsula, boarding with a fishing family who didn't usually take boarders. She imagined him turning up on their doorstep, not bothering to cajole them into friendship, simply placing himself in their midst, whether they liked it or not. There was a photo of him with that family, the men ruddy-faced, their hands hanging in front of them, fists clenched, not to fight, but as if hauling imaginary nets. And Locke in the middle of them, looking like a colonel who'd happened upon a tribe in the jungle. When she found out later where the photo had been taken, she kept it to herself. It no longer mattered by then.

4

It was a quarter past four when she drove, a little too fast, down the narrow lane that linked the Lockes' house to a minor road, a minor road that after some miles led to a road that was slightly less minor. She had wanted to do the weekly food shopping, discreetly, in an Aldi store in a country town on her way home, it would save her fifty euros, but now, thanks to Eleanor and her button, there wouldn't be time. Still she had to pick up ingredients to cook dinner before going to the gallery – Jennifer had texted to request tacos. She stopped at a mini-mart attached to a petrol station in Skibbereen and went directly to the fruit and vegetable aisle. The ready-to-eat shredded lettuce was all sold out. An assistant directed her to a box of unwashed whole heads, and she grabbed one and put it in her basket. She was at the meat counter, about to ask for minced beef, when she spotted, too late, Katherine Ferriter.

'Hello, stranger,' Katherine said, placing a hand on her arm.

'Katherine! What a lovely surprise!' The last time they'd met was more than five years ago at a wedding in the Hudson Bay Hotel in Athlone. Years before that, as students in London, they'd shared a flat. Katherine's makeup was subtle, apart from her lip pencil, which was too stark, too high above her upper lip. Her hair was darker and glossier than Nessa remembered, and she had on a very nice jacket. She took Nessa by the other arm, as if there were a chance that she might abscond. 'You haven't changed a bit.'

'You neither.'

Katherine took a step back. 'I can't believe it,' she said, 'it's been so long. What are you doing down here?'

'Just work. You?'

'We have a cabin out at Lough Hyne.'

Nessa had been there once, a secluded marine lake, popular with water sports enthusiasts because of the tidal flows that rushed in from the Atlantic. Cradled in a fold of hills, it had salt marshes, cliffs, beaches, and was a mecca for marine biologists. She recalled how, after the cabins were built, she had laughed with Philip and one of his architect buddies about how very un-cabin-like they were, and also, how expensive. 'It's very beautiful there,' she said.

'We think so,' Katherine said. 'And Dublin's got so crazy, you know? It's not like it used to be. So I'm down here a lot. It's harder for William to get away, but he comes down when he can.' All the time she was talking, Nessa could see that she was doing the social arithmetic – jacket, shoes, hair – taking in Nessa's red Ecco flats, the coffee-coloured skirt Nessa had borrowed from the floor of Jennifer's room, the Dunnes Stores blouse, now with one very expensive button. 'So what are you doing with yourself these days?' Katherine asked.

'I'm project managing an acquisition for the Elmes Gallery. We're in the process of buying Robert Locke's studio. You might have heard about it?'

Katherine stared blankly.

'The sculptor Robert Locke?' Nessa said. 'The Chalk Sculpture?'

'Ah. Of course. The *Examiner* had an article about him recently. Did you see it?'

'I wrote the article.'

'Did you? Goodness. Well. That's marvellous. Well done, you!'

'I'm really sorry but I have to rush,' Nessa said. 'I've got to get home and cook dinner. It's so nice bumping into you like this. Tell William I said hello. Tell him I send my love.'

'Do you know who contacted me recently?' Katherine said. 'Luke.'

Now it was Nessa's turn to look blank. 'Luke?'

'Amy's son.'

'Oh, of course. Gosh, yes. Luke. Sorry.'

'He's twenty-one. Can you believe it? He friended me on Facebook. He's living in Manchester, with his father, and studying digital media.'

'I'm glad,' Nessa said. 'I mean, I'm glad that things worked out for him.' She'd felt herself flinch at the mention of the father, and wondered if Katherine had noticed.

'He's over here for a few weeks,' Katherine said, 'he's staying with Amy's Aunt Gretta in Tipperary. I've invited him to spend some time with us at the cabin.'

What would the word 'cabin' conjure up for a twenty-one-year-old Manchester lad? 'You know him?' Nessa said.

'No. And that's what William asked too.' A flicker of doubt crossed Katherine's face. 'But Luke's really keen to meet anyone who knew his mother. It's understandable, I suppose.' She paused. 'Maybe you'd like to come to supper some evening?'

'I don't know that I'd be much help. I don't think I've anything to say that you couldn't tell him.'

'He asked about you,' Katherine said. 'He had your name.'

There was a Frida Kahlo painting called *Wounded Deer* in which a stag with Kahlo's face was depicted in a forest clearing, its hide pierced by nine arrows. The way Nessa saw it, standing there in the mini-mart, she had been hunted down and cornered.

'So you'll come?' Katherine said. 'Philip too, of course. And your little girl. Jennifer, isn't it?'

'She's not so little anymore. She was sixteen last birthday.'

Katherine shook her head. 'Where does the time go?' she said. 'It seems like only yesterday that we were all running around London like mad things.'

In fact, Nessa thought, Katherine had never been a mad thing. That year in London, when Nessa – and Amy Corrigan – had grudgingly taken Katherine in, she had set her alarm every morning for 6.30 a.m. to use the bathroom before anyone else got up. The Irish nurses in London had partied harder than the art school crowd, but Katherine had ironed her uniform every night while watching *Coronation Street*.

'He's arriving in a couple of weeks,' Katherine said. 'How about we say supper on a Friday evening? Are you still at the same email?'

Nessa looked down at the lettuce in her basket. She needed to get minced beef; she needed to get home in time to make dinner and give her lecture. 'Yes,' she said, 'okay. I mean, thank you.'

'Wonderful!' Katherine said. 'It will be so much more special with you there. We're the third cabin along, but . . .' She faltered. 'It won't be hard to find us. Things are quiet there. It's just us most of the time.'

Nessa watched her leave, noted her neat, confident walk. Katherine had always been middle-aged. They used to mock her for it: the way she put out the garbage, the way she read the council notices that came in the mail. Now that her actual age had caught up with her, it suited her.

While the butcher fed the meat into the machine, Nessa stared at the steaks laid out on their fields of chipped ice. There was a day in London over twenty years ago when Amy had decided that she needed animal parts for the piece she was making for the end-of-year art college exhibition. She had persuaded Nessa to go with her to an abattoir on the edge of the city. From the outside it could have been a clothing factory, or a toy warehouse, or any number of innocuous things. Inside, there was a long cavernous room, carcasses strung up on hooks. Amy had handed money to a man whose white overalls were spattered with blood, and listed her requirements. The man had looked them both over with his butcher's eyes and Nessa could almost see his mind going: ribs, brisket, shin. She had pictured herself sliced open, innards labelled, like a diagram of a cow in an old-fashioned cookbook, the kind that wasn't shy about where meat came from. 'I need some air,' she'd said, and she'd gone outside, vomited behind a stack of wooden pallets. Amy emerged carrying a blood-streaked plastic bag. 'You're going to have to toughen up,' she said scornfully. 'That's life, in there.'

When they lived in London, she and Amy used to joke that an honest epitaph for Katherine might read: 'Here lies Katherine Ferriter, who never caused any trouble.' It could probably also add that she was a loving wife and daughter. She would have made a good mother, Nessa thought, given the chance, but there had been no child when they'd met that time at the Hudson Bay Hotel, and she'd have heard if one had arrived since. Katherine was harmless but she was a reminder of London, and of Amy, and now there was this boy to think about. Luke. And Stuart, his father.

Nessa paid for the groceries and hurried out to her car. As she drove back to the city, even the ordinary fields were beautiful, with yellow bursts of furze in the thick green ditches and everything overrunning its boundary, the grasses on the shoulder toppling long and heavy onto the roads. To the other side was the sea, grey and solidly forbidding, none of the shallow turquoise tomfoolery that passed for sea elsewhere.

Robert Locke had made a series of six thematically linked pieces titled *Sea Urchins*. In compendiums of his work, they were usually attributed to his first year in West Cork, and images of them were often included in coffee-table books, perhaps because the delicate sea-hedgehog spikes were so pretty. They weren't his best work, in Nessa's opinion. He'd discussed them at length in an interview he gave to *Frieze* in 1991. He talked about wave shoaling and refraction, and amphibious life-forms as a metaphor for human existence. It had impressed her the first time she read it, but now she thought it smacked of gobbledygook. She occasionally tutored undergrads – there was a time when it was the only work she could get and she didn't like to relinquish it entirely – and it struck her now that Locke's 'amphibious life-forms' was the sort of thing the students came up with when they'd made something whose provenance eluded them.

There was nothing of this place in those dainty *Sea Urchins*. Her own view, one she never expressed publicly, was that Locke didn't make those pieces during that first year in West Cork. There were indications from his personal life that he was not well at that time. He may have been suffering a nervous breakdown. His work was how he measured out his life, and it wouldn't have been beyond him, she thought, to have decided to attribute something to that time, because he was a man who was uncomfortable with gaps.

5

The lecture Nessa was to deliver at the gallery that evening was one of four scheduled in the lead-up to the installation of the studio. The gallery was a renovated Venetian-style building on the north quays of Cork city, with windows reminiscent of Grand Central Station, though it was nowhere near as large. It had once been a seed merchant's warehouse, and toward the back of the downstairs exhibition space a section of an old silo ran floor to ceiling. Nessa momentarily took cover behind that silo, sipping a glass of wine to steady her nerves. It was a rare sunny evening in April and light was pouring through the high windows onto the gallery floor, forming honeyed pools on the flagstones.

Gerard P. Henchy, the gallery director, was stocky and in his early forties. Damp-faced, he came barrelling toward her in the jacket he always wore to public events, tweed in a weave of mustard and browns. She noticed how he never made any effort to suck in his belly, not even when he was being photographed, never felt the slightest need to make himself smaller. 'Remember to mention Cambridgeshire, won't you?' he said. 'That would be important. And don't forget to thank the Lockes, they need humouring. Especially the widow.' He looked around. 'Are they here?'

'No,' she said. 'Eleanor took a bit of a turn.'

'Turn?'

'Yes.'

'How shall I put this?' he said. 'There's no . . . immediate danger, is there? Because, ideally, Mrs Locke should be there for the main event.' The official unveiling of Locke's studio was scheduled for September, on what would have been his eightieth birthday.

'She'll be fine,' Nessa said. She watched him root in his pocket for his car keys.

'Cambridgeshire is easy to talk about,' he said. 'The early works, the influences. Stick to that and you'll be grand. Read out of the brochure if you get stuck.' She must have appeared sullen, because he winked then and said, 'Good girl. It'll look well on your CV.'

When he'd gone, she went over to a nearby table and picked up a copy of the brochure. There had been a tussle between her and the publicist over the content, and thumbing through it now, she wondered if perhaps the publicist had won. It was a glossy affair, erring on the side of bland – lots of fragments of things that could only be appreciated in the whole; lots of close-up shots of pieces best viewed from ten feet back. 'You can see Cambridgeshire in Locke's early work: the elongated figures, low and flat and stretched, the 1950s geometry of fear softened by the round of myriad water mills.' The director had insisted on that; it was, of course, the interpretation currently favoured. Eleanor herself trotted it out regularly: the late 1950s were all about Cambridgeshire, she'd say, Cambridgeshire and the Venice Biennale boys, and she'd affect a humble-brag weariness, as if she'd hung out with those boys every weekend, when the reality was she'd met Paolozzi once or twice. Word was he didn't care for her much.

Nessa was standing in the space that, come autumn, would be home to Locke's studio. The sculptures that usually occupied that part of the gallery had already been moved to another wing, after much negotiating with a man from the union who kept calling her 'love' until she thought she'd prefer to strap everything to her back in the dead of night and move it herself. She walked to the podium in the centre of the room, taking a copy of the brochure with her. The crowd was mostly drinking free wine and chattering. Nobody was paying much attention to the six pieces that were the focus of that evening's talk, apart from one woman who was looking at them closely, practically sniffing them. 'Good evening,' Nessa said. She'd attended a hypnotist once for help with public speaking. He'd advised her to visualise the microphone as a penis, something she'd never found the slightest bit helpful. She waited for the audience to notice she was there, but they carried on drinking and talking. She tapped the microphone, tapped it again. Then, in the way that a flock of sheep might suddenly, as of one mind, intuit a presence in their midst, they all looked together. First they looked at her, then they gave little furtive glances to the left of her and to the right. A couple of them looked over their shoulders, hoping, she supposed, to spy a more interesting person making their way to the podium.

Behind her were the six sculptures, two in granite, four in marble. They were good work, but they were also the work of a man early in his career. There was a hint of the populist about them. Just the faintest hint, but it was there. *Love me*, they whispered, *or at least throw a few pennies in my cap.* She'd spent a lot of time arranging the pieces in a way that she thought suggested motion, so that if viewed from left to right, very quickly, they would read like a short piece of animation. She'd walked back and forth in front of them many times in the preceding week, to check this. Now, as she cast an eye over them, she saw that the second piece was out of alignment by a couple of inches and the effect was slightly off.

'Good evening,' she said again. She hadn't yet decided exactly what she would say next. The thing was, despite what the director said, Cambridgeshire was not entirely flat; there were hills too, chalk hills called the Gog Magogs, where there once lived a giant of that name who died when he was thrown from a cliff by Corineus. And nowhere in any of the pieces exhibited tonight could she discern the influence of water mills. There was undeniably a fluidity in the joints, but she saw nothing of water there. It was more a restlessness, the way the pieces sat on the cusp of motion. This was no peaceful turn of a mill wheel, more a want to be away, as if they might run off at any moment. She had gone to Cambridgeshire with Philip once. It was just over two years ago, before all the ugliness happened with Cora Wilson. They'd had a pleasant, if unspectacular, weekend. She remembered a nice dinner in an inn that had a stag's head above the fireplace. And a small hotel with an expensive brand of body lotion in the bathroom. They didn't fight that weekend; they may even have had sex. At the very least, neither of them had sex with anybody else.

The audience was looking at her expectantly. 'There are chalk hills in Cambridgeshire,' she said. 'Cambridgeshire is not entirely flat.' She was so close to the microphone that it brushed, briefly, against her lips, and when she swallowed she got the fleeting taste of metal. She took a step back. And then she told them how an archaeologist by the name of Lethbridge claimed to have discovered ancient figures beneath the hill's surface, though his findings were not accepted by the majority of his peers. There was evidence that he and Locke were friendly, and this, she suggested, was the real influence of Cambridgeshire on Locke's work. Chalk, giants, the conversations he and Lethbridge must have had, Lethbridge not long back from eating polar bears in the Arctic Circle.

6

The lecture was over and an intern was going around with a brush, haphazardly sweeping up litter. Nessa was in postmortem mode. She was reasonably sure that she'd got something wrong about one of Locke's better-known works from the mid-1960s, a celebrated work called *Mute*. It was a severed tongue, over four feet long, carved from Kilkenny limestone, the detail remarkable: the raised papillae, the dorsum, the palatoglossal arches rising to meet the roof of a mouth that wasn't there. How she'd ended up mentioning it, she couldn't now remember; it had nothing to do with Cambridgeshire. It was in the Corkin Gallery in Toronto, and she'd said it was in the Albright-Knox.

The over-earnest woman from the audience had not yet left. She was going from piece to piece, squinting, brochure in hand. She dragged a chair from the side of the room into the middle and settled herself in it. Nessa was about to ask her to leave, when it occurred to her that this woman was possibly the only person who'd taken a proper interest that evening. She'd decided to let her sit on a little longer, when Sam, the security guard, went up and said, 'We're closing now, madam.'

The woman made no effort to move. She had brown hair run through with grey that was tied in a knot at the back of her head. Her nose turned upward at the tip, so that the nostrils were slightly too pronounced, and her eyes were large and unusually wide set. She turned to Nessa. 'I lived for a while in Seville and the galleries used to stay open all night, one night a week. It was a Thursday, I think.' Her accent was difficult to place. Sam, who'd gone out to the foyer, returned now with something in his arms. A rucksack. The woman sighed and stood up. Wordlessly, she took the rucksack and slung it over her shoulder.

'I thought you were hard on Cambridgeshire,' she said, as Nessa accompanied her to the exit. 'I had a friend who lived there for some years. He was quite happy. It's not exactly L.A., but it's a good place.'

Nessa wanted to go home. She could no longer properly remember what she'd said about Cambridgeshire, which was possibly a small mercy. She shrugged. 'It's only my opinion.'

The woman nodded. 'Yes,' she said, 'that's all it is. You know, my friend who lived in Cambridgeshire used to say that the air there was heavier than the air everywhere else. That there was always this sense of something bearing down, pressing you back into the earth, like a seed. Even when one was walking there, my friend said, more effort was necessary to achieve forward momentum than when walking elsewhere. Otherwise there was a sensation of tilting.' She looked at Nessa. 'That might have something to do with the flatness, don't you think?'

On the footpath directly outside the gallery, a visiting artist had made a mosaic out of antique manhole covers set into the footpath. Anytime Nessa stepped on it, felt the raised patterns beneath her feet, she had an urge to get down on her hands and knees and trace over them using a soft lead pencil and baking parchment. It was the sort of activity that if Jennifer were younger, they could do together, and she thought what a pity these ways to be a better mother were always occurring to her ten years too late. 'Well,' she said kindly, 'enjoy the rest of your evening.'

The woman was still holding her copy of the brochure, and she opened it now, began turning pages. 'You got something wrong, although I'm sure you know that already.'

Nessa was about to say that *Mute* had once been on loan to the Albright-Knox, even if it wasn't currently held there, and anyway what did it matter, when she saw that the woman's finger was resting on the text accompanying a photo of the Chalk Sculpture.

'My name should be there,' the woman said.

It wasn't the first time Nessa had heard that kind of thing. Usually people said it without any regard to historical period. They would stand in front of her in that season's Penneys raincoat and claim to have been the muse for a Walter Osborne.

'The Chalk Sculpture, or, to give it its proper name, *Venus at the Hotel Negresco*, was inspired by the sculptor's wife, Mrs Eleanor Locke,' Nessa said lightly.

'Huh! Venus indeed,' the woman said. 'What sort of a name is that for anything? But that's not what I meant. I meant my name should be there beside Robert's. I helped him make it.'

Nessa raised an eyebrow. 'You *helped*?'

'My assistance was an integral part; I believe that's an accepted definition of "helped". Anyhow, I think you know what I'm referring to.' She gave an arch smile.

'I have no idea,' Nessa said.

'I'm glad we have this chance to speak,' the woman said, 'because you're going to have to fix this. You can have all the opinions you like about Cambridgeshire, but you're going to have to put my name on there.' She stabbed at the brochure with her finger, as if targeting an insect that had flitted across the page.

Sam appeared in the doorway. 'Call for you,' he said, 'line four.' 'Line four' was code for *There isn't really a call*.

'I'm sorry,' Nessa said, 'but I have to go.'

'Huh,' the woman said again. She unzipped her rucksack and shoved the brochure in. She walked away with a strangely ambling movement, like someone more used to matching her stride to animals and the forgiving softness of grass, than city pavements. When she'd gone a few yards, she stopped, took a map from a side pocket of the rucksack, and shook it open. Nessa saw no more of her after that because Sam, anxious to get home, was already closing the front door, and she hurried inside to fetch her bag and coat.

Back home in Sunday's Well, Philip had ordered a Chinese takeaway. He put it on a plate and microwaved it. They hadn't spoken since that morning's counselling session. 'I'm sorry about that business with Dr Freud,' he said. 'Sometimes I think we'd get on better if that guy wasn't there. If we just went into a quiet room by ourselves for an hour.'

'Then it wouldn't be counselling,' she said, as casually as she could manage.

'True,' he said. 'Anyhow, I'm sorry.'

Jennifer was watching TV in the living room. Nessa put her head around the door. 'How was school?'

'Fine.'

'Anything good on telly?'

'No. It's a documentary. Part of my homework.'

On the screen, women in cheerleader costumes were gathered around a boy playing guitar. Nessa opened her mouth to say something, but closed it again. She went back into the kitchen, took the glass of wine handed to her by Philip. 'Has she had any friends round?' she said.

'I don't think so,' he said. 'There wasn't anyone else here when I got home.'

'At least Ms Johnson hasn't been back in touch. But she will be.' She ate at the kitchen island, with Philip sitting across from her. She told him about the speech and how she'd said *Mute* was in the Albright-Knox when it wasn't.

'But no one will know any different.' He placed his hand over hers. It was a gesture that always calmed her, and she left her hand where it was, even though she hadn't finished eating. Jennifer came in to get a glass of juice and her face lit up. She was constantly on the lookout for evidence that her parents weren't about to leave one another, and had been so pleased to see the roses arriving for her mother on Valentine's Day. This year's bouquet was beyond large, a size that the floristry trade referred to as 'guilty', and Jennifer had been ecstatic.

'I should just have read from the brochure,' Nessa said when her daughter had gone back to the TV.

He squeezed her hand. 'I'm sure what you had to say was much more interesting.'

'I got into that whole thing about Lethbridge and the polar bears.'

He frowned. 'Bears?'

'Lethbridge was an archaeologist and he and Locke were contemporaries in Cambridgeshire. And so I got talking about Lethbridge being lost in the Arctic Circle and having to eat polar bears. Seals also.'

'No harm in mentioning it.'

'You think so?'

'Absolutely,' he said, but she could tell that he was losing interest. Any minute now, he would take his hand away, and because she was too tired to weather even the smallest of rejections, she slipped her hand out from under his and picked up her fork. She took another mouthful of curry, but her appetite had gone. 'I think I'm going to take a bath,' she said.

When she got like that, the water helped. There was something primitive that happened to a body in water, something to do with the urge to stay afloat. She took a book upstairs with her, one from childhood called *Flight of the Doves*. In primary school, the headmaster had read that book aloud, one chapter a day, and whenever she returned to it, which was often, this was how she reread it. She heard her daughter's step on the stairs, heard her pause outside the bathroom door. 'Good night, Mom,' Jennifer called.

'Sleep well, darling.' In the warm fug of the bathroom, Nessa read one chapter of her book, then put it down on the floor.

She sank deeper into the water and thought about her husband. He was a handsome man, educated and ambitious. On the other hand: he wasn't a man much concerned with security, his or his family's, financial or otherwise; his tactlessness, his insistence on pointing out undusted shelves, had cost her several house cleaners, and he'd slept, on various dates and in various locations, with Cora Wilson. Nessa didn't touch herself in any way while thinking about him; it was not that sort of thinking. In any event, these days when the mood took her, she preferred to summon an image of the new security guard the temp agency had taken to sending, a young Scandinavian man with closely shaved blond hair, a good-looking man who had not, to her knowledge, slept with Cora Wilson, but given that this was Cora she was talking about, one couldn't be entirely sure.

She stayed in the bath until the water grew cold, then wrapped herself in a towel and went to the bedroom. Philip was already in bed. She saw his eyes flicker over her, and he lifted the duvet, patted her side of the bed by way of invitation. She pretended not to see and busied herself finding a nightdress, a thick blue cotton one. When she climbed in beside him, his hand travelled across the bed, found the side of her breast. He began a gentle, rhythmic stroking. She supposed that she should make an effort. Otherwise what was the point in spending all that money on counselling? She shuffled across the bed until their bodies were touching. He kissed the side of her neck. She lay still while he opened the buttons of her nightdress, slid a finger inside, and began to caress a nipple. She turned her face to his and let him kiss her. She simulated enthusiasm as best she could, closed her eyes and thought hard about the blond security guard, but that night he was of no use. As she lay there, she had a sense of being utterly alone and unreachable. The archaeologist, Lethbridge, in all his blizzards of blinding white could not have felt more alone, and yes, as Philip began to thrust she was thinking of Lethbridge again, because it had all come crowding back: the lecture, the Albright-Knox mistake, that eccentric woman, everything; the good of bath and book entirely undone. She thought of the oversized *Mute* tongue that had caused her such bother, and then she thought of Robert Locke. What sort of a lover had he been? Had he been gentle? She didn't imagine so. She imagined he was to his women what he was to the things he called forth out of stone, all those magnificent oddities that he handled with a very precise ruthlessness. And as Philip moved on top of her, she remembered, or perhaps deliberately called to mind, a story that Eleanor Locke had told her. It was shortly after Nessa had begun visiting them, an afternoon in late February, and a preacher woman, a Jehovah's Witness, had come to the door. Loretta had recognised the car – the woman evidently had called before – and had gone out to the porch. Nessa had expected that the woman would be sent packing, and was surprised to hear the back-and-forth murmur of conversation on the doorstep.

And it was then, while her daughter was being instructed in the finer points of Genesis, that Eleanor recounted how Robert had made love to her backstage at a festival in Munich once, with four hundred people only a velour backdrop away, how he'd pushed her against a props cupboard, lifted her dress. It had been quick, she said, but even so, a stagehand had happened upon them and had turned away when he realised what was going on.

Nessa had wondered if Eleanor was trying to shock her. Or perhaps taunt her. Had she caught the whiff of famine, sensed that Nessa was floundering in her own love life? She'd believed for a while that anyone could smell it off her, the putrefaction of her marriage. The cupboard had rattled a lot, Eleanor said, and she was sure the noise must have been heard in the auditorium. Afterwards, when Robert had gone out front, the stagehand had come back, mistaking her for, in her words, a common tart, and had tried to have a go himself.

As Philip came, Nessa imagined the roughness of the props cupboard against bare skin, and Robert Locke, a determined lover, rough, selfish even, the friction of his chest with its fuzz of dark hair against hers, because he'd been a young man then, as in that photo of him in swimming trunks she'd seen hanging in the Lockes' hall, bare-chested, his hair in those days to his shoulders, the glory of the hands that touched the Chalk Sculpture touching her, making her, making her Eleanor, making her faceless, fucking her.

7

Her office was a small room on the second floor of the gallery. It had a view of the River Lee, grey and silty, and of the comings and goings of shoppers on Lavitt's Quay opposite. From a certain angle, she could see, upstream, the glass facade of Cork Opera House. She'd stopped at the newsstand on the way to work and bought the papers, to see if last night's event had been covered. She was relieved to find that there was no mention of her, or of anything she'd said. Neither was there much mention of Robert Locke, apart from a photo of one of the sculptures, wrongly captioned. Henchy would be happy, though: there was a picture of him, arms folded across his chest, grinning beside the head of the Chamber of Commerce.

She switched on her computer and answered some emails. Shortly after ten, one of the interns, a nervous dark-haired girl, put her head around the door. 'There's someone here to see you.'

'Who is it?'

'I don't know.'

The intern didn't look much older than Jennifer. She might or might not have been new; with the interns it was difficult to keep track. Behind her, in the corridor, was the odd woman from the evening before. Today she had on a long blue mohair coat. She smiled at Nessa over the girl's head, gave a little nod as if to say *Yes, it's me*, as if she were expected. Nessa looked at the intern and frowned. 'She doesn't have an appointment. Why didn't you keep her downstairs?'

'I tried. I said that that would be best.'

The woman stepped forward, placed a hand on the girl's shoulder. Very gently, as if manoeuvring a farmyard animal, she pushed her to one side and sat down in a chair opposite Nessa. 'Thank you,' she said, to the girl, who slunk away, mouthing 'Sorry.'

'I'm afraid I was just on my way out,' Nessa said.

'We weren't properly introduced last evening,' the woman said. 'I'm Melanie, but of course you'll have read Robert's papers, so you'll know that already.' She reached across the desk and shook Nessa's hand.

'I don't recall a Melanie—' Nessa said slowly. 'Perhaps you can remind me?'

'Oh, please!' the woman said. 'There's no need to be coy.' She unzipped a canvas shoulder bag and took out a copy of the brochure. There were pieces of paper slotted into it, not Post-its or bookmarks, but strips torn from supermarket flyers. 'Now,' she said, 'first things first.' She set the brochure down on the desk between them. 'This recognition of Robert's work, late as it is, is a noble enterprise. I don't wish to detract from it in any way. That is the very last thing I would want to do. That's not why I'm here. And I agree completely with your analysis of the work he produced while in Rotterdam. Goodness, I don't think anyone ever got Robert as well as that.'

'Thank you,' Nessa said. There was an alarm button on the underside of her desk and she wondered if she should press it. But what would she say? *I have an old lady here, talking art?* And it would only get the intern into trouble. 'What did you say your last name is, Melanie?'

'I didn't say, but it's Doerr.' She leaned forward. 'Our Mr Locke would have liked this, all right. He was a fool for praise. You couldn't praise that man enough.'

'I've heard him described as modest,' Nessa said. 'Self-effacing is a word that comes up a lot.' She didn't know why she felt a need to defend him. Habit, perhaps, from all the times she'd taken his side against Eleanor, or the old veneration of her student days asserting itself. She remembered her dalliance the night before, the way she'd pressed the man, almost twenty years dead, into posthumous service in her bed, and felt the colour rise in her face.

'All an act,' Doerr was saying. 'All subterfuge. He was the vainest man that ever walked this earth.'

'Did you know him?' Nessa said, though she was fairly sure the woman couldn't have known Locke well, if at all. She'd already gone through all the old address books and notebooks provided by Loretta. She knew all the names by heart. Nowhere was there a mention of a Melanie. *Oh dear, Melanie,* she thought, *oh dear. Did you oblige him once backstage, against a different props cupboard, and now you've come looking for your footnote?* Mentally, Nessa scolded herself. The woman, deluded as she might be, didn't deserve that kind of malice. Nessa adjusted her expression to the same dispassionate one she adopted whenever she passed Cora Wilson on the street.

'Sometimes I think that I regret knowing him,' Doerr said. 'It's not fashionable to have regrets nowadays, but most people have far more regrets than they admit to.' She sat back in her chair. It struck Nessa that the woman, far from appearing embarrassed or nervous, was relishing the theatre of it all.

The silence that followed was not so much awkward as combative, and as Nessa returned the other woman's stare, she thought again how very striking her eyes were. 'I was a student of Robert's once,' Doerr said, 'as you will be aware.'

'I'm not aware of that at all. How could I be?'

'I hear that the gallery has acquired Robert's archives. You'll have read all his papers.'

'Yes, but I'm afraid I don't recall mention of a Melanie. And Locke preferred to work alone. He wasn't given to collaborating with other artists.'

'There are none so blind as those that will not see,' Doerr said. 'That's from the Bible. Or maybe you haven't read that either?'

'When were you his student?' Nessa said. It wasn't entirely impossible. Locke had visited many universities during the seventies and eighties. He'd taught a semester at the Royal Academy of Fine Arts in Ghent in 1975, and there was something in the way the woman pronounced her *v*'s that reminded Nessa of a friend from years back whose family had been from Flanders.

'It was in the seventies,' Doerr said. 'It was an informal arrangement.'

'I see,' Nessa said.

There was a flash of temper in Doerr's face. She opened the brochure, ran a finger down the left-hand column. She wore no rings, no jewellery of any kind other than a plain silver bracelet. 'I have thought long and hard about this,' she said, 'and I can't allow it.' Her finger had settled on a paragraph at the end of the page. 'I have turned a blind eye to many things over the years, but this is the last straw. That they should stoop so low as to attempt to sell it without a mention of my name. I cannot let that happen. Robert, if he were alive, would not stand for it.'

Nessa knew the brochure's layout, could picture it with her eyes closed. She knew that the woman's finger, sliding back and forth like a metronome, had reached the section about the

Chalk Sculpture. 'It's quite straightforward,' Melanie Doerr said. 'I require to be credited for this. My name deserves to be there alongside Robert Locke's. Instead, every art magazine I pick up I have to read about Venus and Eleanor Tomlin, while my name is nowhere to be found. I was Robert's inspiration as well as his helper. I sat for him sometimes; the Chalk Sculpture would not exist without me.' She leaned closer across the desk. 'Put my name beside his, that's all you have to do.' She indicated the brochure. 'I am not asking you to pulp this, although I could, you know. I could. But you will amend all subsequent publications, and of course, my name will appear in the catalogue. Between us, we will make Eleanor tell the truth. Loretta too. If this is put right, this one small thing, I will even tolerate the ridiculous title.'

Nessa sat straighter in her chair. Eleanor Locke never once after her marriage had referred to herself as Tomlin, and was quick to correct anyone else who did. It was strange to hear this woman call her that now; clearly, she had done her homework. Eleanor's family had been silversmiths from Devon, who'd moved in the 1930s to London, where they'd set up a shop in Kensington. Not much else was known about them, though the shop seemed to have done well; well enough for the young Eleanor Tomlin to have been sent to finishing school for a year at the age of seventeen, something she'd refused to talk to Nessa about. Perhaps it hadn't been a pleasant experience, being tossed into the lair of her betters. She was, after all, the daughter of a craftsman who'd turned his hand to grubby commerce. The Tomlins had money, but it wasn't old, and it mustn't have been enough, because in later years the shop appeared to have been taken over by a cousin, and Mr and Mrs Tomlin made a discreet return to Devon, while their daughter remained in London.

'I know what you're thinking,' Doerr said. 'What could he have seen in me?'

'I'm thinking that he was always very clear about the inspiration behind the Chalk Sculpture. He has always said that it was Eleanor.'

'And that makes it so?' She sat straighter in her chair. 'Because he said it?'

'He modelled it on a photo of Eleanor taken in Nice when she was pregnant with Loretta. That is well known.' Nessa had seen the photo many times. Loretta had shown it to her, but it had also appeared in a number of art journals. A hugely pregnant Eleanor leaning against a railing at the Hotel Negresco, below her the Nice seafront with its trees and promenade, a quiet contentment in her face. One arm was resting on the railing, the other on the swell of her belly. It was a portrait of a woman serene in impending mother-hood. And in the stance of the Chalk Sculpture one could see indisputably – Nessa had observed it a hundred times – the same stance of Eleanor by that railing, the unmistakable jut of her left hip angled to the camera, one leg ever so slightly in front of the other. The difference, apart from the scale and the unsculpted head, was Eleanor's right arm, which in the photo was sure and firm in its grip of the railing, but in the sculpture reached so vulnerably into nothing.

'You're referring to the interview in *Flint*, I suppose?' Melanie Doerr said.

'That, and others also.'

'He was at his least truthful in interviews. It was almost as if he felt compelled to lie.'

She pushed the brochure across the desk. She had scrawled notes in the margins, though 'scrawled' was maybe not the word, because the handwriting was neat, and sufficiently unadorned to be legible. 'I am not the sort of person to claim more than she is entitled to,' Doerr said. 'Ask anybody who knows me and they will tell you that. I am a very straightforward person. I make no claim about any piece other than this one.'

Perhaps it was the repetition of the word 'claim' that did it. 'Melanie,' Nessa said. 'Have you come here looking for money?'

Doerr stood up. 'How dare you,' she said. 'Money is the last thing on my mind. You think you know everything, but you don't. And the things you do know, you don't have the courage to say.' She paused. 'You're supposed to be the expert on Robert Locke. But all you are is his wife's foot soldier.'

Nessa frowned. 'I'm sorry,' she said. 'I have no idea what you mean.'

Doerr began to fidget with the edges of her mohair coat, and when she spoke again her words came faster, more erratically. 'You accuse me, falsely, of the thing that you yourself are guilty of,' she said. 'You ask if I have come looking for money. Huh! It's you – you and Eleanor and Loretta – who are plotting for money. You realised it would not be so easy to sell the Chalk Sculpture with me in the picture, so you have chosen to rub me out. Well, here I am. I am not that easily erased.'

A speck of spittle landed on the brochure, and Doerr extended a finger swiftly, the way a frog might shoot out its tongue, and wiped it away. 'I cannot stand idly by,' she said, 'while Eleanor Tomlin inflicts this sham upon us all, flaunts it, glories in it.' It was a strange choice of word, Nessa thought – 'flaunt' – especially when applied to an eighty-four-year-old recluse, though it was easy to see how a younger Eleanor, Eleanor of the Hotel Negresco, might have been guilty of it.

'I'm happy to look at any evidence you might have,' Nessa said.

In hindsight, perhaps it was the wrong tone. 'You're the one with all the proof,' Doerr cried. 'He wrote everything down. I watched him write it down with my own eyes. We worked side by side. It's in his notebooks.'

Nessa shook her head. 'There's nothing of the sort in his notebooks.' In an attempt to placate the woman, she said, 'I'll check again with Eleanor and Loretta in case there's anything they may have forgotten.'

Doerr gave a short, hard laugh. '*Forgotten*,' she said. 'Oh, those two are good at forgetting, all right.'

Nessa opened a drawer in her desk and took out one of the director's business cards. 'Maybe you'd like to put your thoughts in an email,' she said. As she held it out, she felt a surge of pity. This woman opposite her, for all that she was deluded, was also intelligent, handsome, articulate.

Doerr waved the card away. 'It's not right,' she said, 'after all these years, Eleanor Tomlin and her lies and now this very *public* lie. A lie that is to be feted and celebrated and put on display. It's too much, I won't have it. I can't.' She put the brochure with its fluttering strips back into her handbag, but still she stood there.

'I'm going to have to ask you to leave now,' Nessa said gently.

'It was never meant to last.'

'Excuse me?'

'The Chalk Sculpture. Why else do you think it's in gypsum? Do you see anything else of his in gypsum? It's designed to self-destruct. Grain by grain, year by year. Then gone' – she threw her hands in the air – 'nothing. It's an act of perpetual subtraction. To talk of the arms or the legs or the belly is to cheapen it, it was always about the *process*, the disintegration. And now you want to halt this process, and you call it *preservation*? Huh! Can't you see that by preserving it, you are destroying it? You're no better than a common vandal.'

Nessa picked up the phone and dialled reception. 'Can you send Sam up, please?'

Melanie Doerr slung her bag over her shoulder and took a step toward the door. 'You've disappointed me,' she said. 'When I heard you last night, I thought that you might be persuaded to take an interest. I mistook you for an ally.'

Nessa followed at what she judged a reasonable distance to the top of the stairs. Doerr descended three or four steps, then turned. 'I hoped it wouldn't come to this. I had no wish to get proprietorial about a work designed to be impermanent. I'm not blind to the contradiction. But I must tell you now: I worked on it, he promised it to me, it's all written down. If you are the expert that you claim to be, you will know this. I read in a newspaper that you spent years studying Robert's life, his work. I should not have to spell it out. That statue is mine.'

'No,' Nessa said quietly. 'It isn't.'

'I thought that you and I would have more in common,' Doerr said. 'But at least you share a not insignificant trait with the Chalk Sculpture. You're both bound for self-destruction.' Her hands were tugging at the front of her coat again. 'I could have saved you from yourself, from your . . . your . . . *mistake*.' Her lips curled around the word. '"Mistake" is so much nicer a word than "lie", is it not? And I believe in being nice where possible. But you don't want to listen. Careful how you go with Eleanor Tomlin. That's all.'

'She wouldn't like to hear you calling her Tomlin.'

'I know,' Doerr said, 'that's why I use it.' She turned then and carried on down the stairs.

Nessa watched until she reached the bottom. Back in her office, she returned the director's business card to the drawer.

She was relieved the woman was gone, but she also experienced a niggle of regret. Could she have handled that better? She supposed that, at a minimum, she could have handled it differently. Melanie Doerr wasn't a common or garden-variety oddball; the woman clearly knew a thing or two about art. Hopefully, she wouldn't transpire to be somebody of note, someone Nessa ought to have known and recognised.

She flopped wearily into her chair. Something Doerr had said needled her. It wasn't the fabulous – in the original meaning of the word – claim that she had helped Locke with the sculpture. Locke had always preferred to work on his pieces alone. And the woman's claim of ownership was risible: the Chalk Sculpture had been peacefully in residence with the Lockes for decades, time spent in the cowshed excepted. Neither was Nessa perturbed by the claim that Locke had programmed the Chalk Sculpture for destruction – in the course of her research, she'd listened to a raft of unfounded theories about that sculpture, many from paid professionals, who'd suggested everything from Locke being unable to finish it because of a stroke, to Locke being under the influence of LSD or a book he'd read on alien life-forms. Admittedly, the suggestion that she was herself self-destructive had stung. But what upset her most of all was how Doerr had tried to claim her as a kindred spirit. Would she have presumed this if it was the director she was speaking to? No, she would not. Henchy was never mistaken for a likely ally of the demented, whereas Nessa seemed to offer herself up as a candidate without even trying. On the floor by her feet was one of the strips of paper Doerr had used as a bookmark, the one with the toilet paper ad. She picked it up and discovered a different picture on the reverse. She thought that she recognised the image. It was almost certainly a detail from an Impressionist painting, a field of poppies in the fields of Grez-sur-Loing.

Later, when she knew Melanie better, Nessa would learn that her accent had not originated in Flanders. She wasn't born in Belgium, never lived there at all, though she did pass through it once as a young woman, travelling alone. She was born in Rijeka in Croatia, not far from Rabac, the port she hitched to one August afternoon at the age of twenty to catch a ferry to Venice. From there she travelled farther west across Europe, as far as Northern Ireland. Her father was a boatbuilder. Her rolling gait was not acquired on hillsides, but came from an injury climbing a flagpole as a child. The ensuing limp became a matter of habit as much as anything else, as is the way with so many things that damage or shape people. Of her mother, few details were available, though there was a suggestion of a long-standing alcohol problem, one that dated back to her mother's girlhood, and which might account for Melanie's unusual facial features.

8

The counsellor had suggested that they take walks, not separately but together, and that evening they put Bailey on his lead and headed down Sunday's Well Road. They paused on the pedestrian bridge on North Mall, where evening was settling on the water, bobbing ducks dipping and splashing. Bailey squatted to relieve himself beside the rusty railings, and she plucked a bag from the bone-shaped dispenser attached to his lead.

'Allow me,' Philip said, taking the bag from her.

'Who says romance is dead,' she said as he stooped to clean up after the dog.

He laughed, and they crossed the bridge, walked upriver to the Lee Maltings.

Bailey, as he always liked to do, snuffled at the quay walls and the flowers blooming in their crevices. They looped down Liberty Street and onto Patrick Street. Philip stopped outside the Moderne clothing store. 'Didn't you have a yellow jumper like that?' he said, pointing to a mannequin in the window. Nessa looked. The jumper wasn't remotely like the one she used to own, apart from the fact that it had sleeves and a hole for the head and was yellow. She felt the familiar dread rising all the same. 'I always liked that jumper on you,' he said. 'How come you never wear it anymore?'

Nessa tugged at Bailey's lead. 'Come along, Bailey,' she said.

The day she'd found out about Cora Wilson and Philip, she was wearing a yellow Ted Baker jumper, with pink trim at the cuffs, and a pair of black trousers. She'd bundled the jumper in a ball the next day and put it in the bin. She'd known she'd never wear it again, although in fact she missed that jumper. The black trousers went in the bin too, but at least they'd been from Penneys. She'd never replaced the jumper, not even with a cheaper model. But after she threw it out, every time she opened the wardrobe door and saw the empty hanger she was reminded of Cora Wilson. She threw the hanger in the bin too.

But then the empty space reminded her of Cora, and when she pushed other things along the rail to fill it, every item that swung into that space seemed to take up a chant, *Cora, Cora, Cora*, until she knew she had to move them back to where they'd come from, or they would all be tainted by Cora Wilson, and she'd have nothing left.

One evening, she'd pulled the door off that wardrobe, wrenched it off with a pliers in such a way that the body of the wardrobe cracked, and there was nothing for it but to throw the whole thing out. Philip carried it outside and chopped it up and put it in the bin. Now as she walked ahead of him down Patrick Street, Bailey straining at the leash, registering her need to be away, she thought that she couldn't recall Philip remarking on the wardrobe. But then, a lot of things got broken around that time. For a while she'd resisted getting a new wardrobe, because the only space for it was in the space vacated by the old one. Even now she used the new one sparingly and without lingering, pulling a shirt quickly off the rail and shutting the door again. She felt despair settle on her. Every place and everything was steeped in reminders; how could a counsellor fix that? How could she ever move on?

'Steady on.' Philip had caught up with them. 'I didn't know it was a race.'

'It's Bailey,' Nessa said, 'I think he's had enough.'

In the kitchen, they encountered an open Nutella jar and a scattering of bread crusts. Jennifer, foraging for food while they were out. Music, too loud, was coming from upstairs. Their next-door neighbour, Mrs Moriarty, would be round. 'Jennifer,' Nessa said, banging on the door of her daughter's bedroom, 'turn that down. And come give me a hand with the bins.'

Grumbling, Jennifer followed her mother downstairs. 'I have *so* much studying to do. Why don't we have a house cleaner anymore? Everyone else at school has a cleaner.'

'She went back to her own country.'

'Don't say that!'

'What?'

'"Back to her own country." It's racist.'

'I didn't tell her to go back to her own country, she just went. The bottom line is, she's not here anymore.'

'Why don't we get another one?'

'Because it costs money,' Philip said. 'And because we don't need one. We have three people living in this house who are all perfectly capable of cleaning.' He took the newspaper from the countertop and settled in an armchair.

'We'll do the recyclables first,' Nessa said. She didn't miss the cleaner. The woman had never cleaned particularly well. It was more like having a poltergeist: coming home to find things moved around.

The recycling bin was piled high, cans balanced on empty milk cartons balanced on cardboard boxes. It could pass for contemporary sculpture, Nessa thought. She packed it down and gathered up the overflow scattered around it. Jennifer grudgingly sorted the glass. 'My friends' parents never have this many empties,' she said, tossing in another wine bottle. Nessa resisted the urge to inquire who these abstemious new acquaintances might be; Cora Wilson had certainly known how to put it away. She wheeled the bins out to the gate. Jennifer, walking behind her mother, picked up a sheet of newsprint that blew off the top. 'There,' she said, magnanimously, with the long exhale of someone who'd spent a day milling oats by hand.

9

On the following Monday, a letter arrived for Nessa at the gallery. It came in a recycled envelope – not one made from recycled paper, but an envelope with someone else's name scratched out, and Nessa's name and the address of the gallery written above it. It was sealed with three strips of packing tape. The letter itself was handwritten, the vowels dispropor- tionately fat, giving the words a bloated appearance.

'Dear Ms McCormack,' it said, 'I am presuming that it is "Ms" although I know that you are married and have a husband and daughter. My salutations to both!' There fol- lowed a long, rambling paragraph about the weather in Ireland compared to the dry season in New Guinea, then a shorter, more concise paragraph enquiring about Nessa's general well-being and a recommendation for a tablespoon of manuka honey every morning. She'd noticed, the letter said, a hint of hoarseness when they'd spoken that day.

Nessa read on. Melanie Doerr wrote that she'd called at the gallery in a spirit of sisterhood, of collegiality. She had not expected the Spanish Inquisition. She had expected that Nessa, as a scholar with a particular interest in Mr Locke's work, would have welcomed her intervention. Instead she'd detected a suggestion of hostility and the ambience was such that she hadn't been able to give a proper account of herself. Robert had promised that her role would be acknowledged; he had left careful records of her contribution – *as you well know*, the letter said. She was writing now, she said, to offer Nessa a second chance. It would after all be embarrassing when the true story of the Chalk Sculpture came out, as come out it would. That last sentence was underlined several times.

There followed a couple of disjointed paragraphs about the correlation between economic conditions in Europe during the 1970s and the emergence of certain art movements.

Doerr went on to say that when she was a young woman in 1972 she'd taken a job cleaning and cooking at an artists' colony in Inishowen. In return for bed and board, she was allowed to mingle with visiting artists, and this was where she'd met Robert Locke. Locke, she said, had allowed her to watch him work, and to use the studio space allocated him for some of her own artistic efforts. He'd pronounced her to have promise, and had invited her to come to West Cork as his student after he returned home. She'd been unable to take up the offer immediately – she had to go live with a sick friend in Provence – but they'd kept in touch by letter, and in the spring of 1973 she travelled again to Ireland, south this time, taking up residence with the Lockes on terms similar to what she'd had in Inishowen: a roster of daily chores in return for board and tuition. *Nineteen seventy-three*, Nessa thought – *the year Locke made the Chalk Sculpture*. 'I worked on it with him,' Doerr wrote. 'I worked on it more than he did, and when he worked on it, I sat for him. And at the end of the summer, when the time came for me to depart, he told me it was mine. If you've read his notebooks, this will come as no surprise to you. He was never without a notebook that summer; it was his practice to always carry one, plain blue with wide ruled lines, like a schoolchild's. Neither he nor I were in a position to arrange for the statue's transport, and so it rested, pending further arrangements, at the Lockes' premises – on loan, if you like. It is mine, to do with as I wish,

64

and what I wish – no, what I insist upon – is that the public record be amended. If my name is placed alongside that of Robert Locke, then this will be sufficient. If this is done, this one small thing, then you will hear no more from me, and I will make no further claims regarding the Chalk Sculpture.'

The letter was signed 'Melanie Doerr'. Nessa put it down on her desk. There couldn't possibly be an ounce of truth in it, she thought. Still, it was unsettling in the way that a drunk shouting obscenities on a street corner was unsettling. Locke had indeed been in the habit of carrying notebooks, but it seemed that carrying them was all he did. She had read them and discovered little of interest, academic or otherwise. Shopping lists, the jotted notes of telephone conversations, the occasional doodle. What few existed were black with leather covers, most unlike a child's notebook. She placed the letter in her in-tray, upside down so that she wouldn't have to look at it while she worked through the rest of her mail. Then she opened the file where she kept her research notes and con-sulted her list of Robert Locke's private students and mentees. She didn't find the name Doerr there, but then she hadn't expected to. This was her territory. She knew the list prac-tically by heart – it did not include a Melanie Doerr. From a shelf, she took down the only published biography of Locke – a hagiography, it had to be said – and consulted the index of names. No Melanie Doerr there either. She took out her phone and rang Loretta Locke.

'*What* did you say her name was?' Loretta said.

'Melanie Doerr.'

'No, I don't recall my father referring to anyone of that name. Why?' It sounded as if she'd got Loretta at a bad time.

'Oh, just someone mentioned that they used to be a stu-dent of your father.'

'I gave you a list of those. Didn't you check it? Goodness knows, you asked us about it often enough.'

'Yes, thank you, Loretta, I'm aware of the list, it's very useful. I've checked it already, thank you. There's nobody by the name of Doerr.'

'Well then,' Loretta said. 'There you go.'

'Do you remember any notebooks?'

'Yes, there were three black notebooks. You have them already.'

'Are you sure there weren't any blue ones?'

'I know my colours,' Loretta said. 'There were three black notebooks, I gave them all to you, I have no more.'

There was little to be gained when Loretta was in this mood. 'Perhaps when I call on Wednesday . . .' Nessa said, but Loretta had already hung up.

Nessa opened a new document on her computer. 'Dear Ms Doerr,' she typed. 'Thank you for your interest in our recent exhibition featuring work by Mr Robert Locke. Regarding your claim to have studied under Mr Locke, I have checked with the Locke family, and there is no record of a student of your name. Neither is there any record to substantiate your other claims in relation to the sculpture. Allow me to say how much I appreciated the opportunity to speak with you, and I hope that you will continue to find enjoyment in the work on display in our gallery.' She licked the envelope and put the address – care of a B & B in St Luke's – on the front, before taking it to the post room.

On Wednesday, as she drove to the Lockes' house, the ditches were sodden and thick with fuchsia. Grasses reached in from the sides of the road, and she thought the giant rhubarb plants that bloomed by the front path had grown larger since her last visit. Loretta, unusually, was waiting on the porch. 'Did you hear any more from that woman claiming to be a student of Daddy's?' she asked as she took Nessa's coat.

'No,' Nessa said.

'Good. If you do hear from anyone like that again, be sure to come to me, not my mother.'

'Of course,' Nessa said.

Loretta ushered her inside. 'There was a time when she was younger when she'd have handled a thing like that as easily as drawing breath, but these days, well . . . you know how she is.' She paused outside the door of the little back room. 'She's been having trouble with her varicose veins; you may find her mood somewhat dampened.'

Eleanor was in tetchy humour that afternoon. She'd barely settled to addressing Nessa's first query – a question about an early piece of soapstone that had turned up in a box containing some of Locke's later work – when she suddenly needed to use the bathroom. She rarely asked to use the bathroom during interviews, perhaps viewing it as a show of weakness. 'Loretta,' she said, and her cheeks grew red. In seconds, Loretta crossed the space between alcove and table and guided her mother by the elbow to the downstairs bathroom off the hall.

Nessa sat by herself, waiting for them to come back. She could hear Loretta saying something, Eleanor replying crossly, 'Yes, yes,' and then a door closing. Now she could hear Loretta moving around in the hall.

She was rarely alone in this room and she took the opportunity to go to the window to get a better look at the back garden. A bank of storm-flattened grass fringed with nettles; a rotting timber bunker that might have been for keeping turf; the rusting frame of a camper. Farther up the yard she could see Loretta's Land Rover, a Defender in gunmetal green with running boards at the sides and bull bars at the front. She'd hankered after one herself for a while; they were briefly in vogue in Sunday's Well. Loretta's was an old model.

She sat back down and examined the carpet – an old-fashioned pattern, but it must have been of good quality because the tufts had held up well. And still there was no sign of the women returning. It felt wrong to be alone and silent at the table, knowing that Loretta was alone and silent just a few feet away.

She got up and went out to the hall. The moment she saw Loretta's face, she knew she'd made a mistake. Rustling noises were coming from the bathroom. She wanted to ask if everything was all right, but it seemed indelicate in the circumstances. She smiled at Loretta, who grimaced in response. What to do now? She could hardly turn on her heel and slink back to the table, and anyway, would it kill Loretta to be a small bit civil? Thinking to allow Eleanor some privacy, she positioned herself in a recess where there were hooks for coats. She hadn't noticed them before because on the days she brought a coat, Loretta would take it from her on arrival and return it when she was leaving. Now she also noticed something else. Above the hooks was a photograph of Robert Locke standing by a pier with his arm around the shoulders of a man she didn't recognise. And there, in the background, was a familiar brown and white dog.

A photograph of Robert Locke with a brown and white terrier had appeared in a calendar of Scottish artists in the early seventies. In it, Robert had the dog scooped up in his arms, man and animal cheek to jowl. It was one of those calendars that attempted to make artists more palatable by adding animals, and Nessa had presumed the dog was a prop. Sam Black was photographed with a lamb; Mark

Boyle with a basset hound; Wyllie and Bellany were both holding rabbits.

'You really had a dog?' she said.

'Yes.' Loretta's voice was so low she was practically whispering.

'What was its name?'

'Its *name?*' Loretta said, as if the question were ludicrous. And then, reluctantly: 'Its name was Pirate. We had it for only a short while. It was a gift from a friend of my father's, someone who didn't know him very well.'

'Did it die?' Nessa immediately felt foolish, because even if the dog hadn't died back then, it must surely have died since.

Loretta frowned. 'No, it was given away.' She seemed to think that this was the end of the matter.

Nessa tried to imagine giving away Bailey, what Jennifer might have to say about it if she did. 'How old were you then?' she asked.

Loretta beckoned her over, and Nessa crossed the hall to stand beside her.

'I was fourteen,' Loretta said, in a low voice, 'I wasn't a child. We had no need of a pet. It wasn't practical.'

'All the same,' Nessa said, 'it must have been hard. Why was he given away?'

'My father was away so often, it made sense. And the dog seemed to impact him in a negative way, it made him bad tempered. I remember him taking off on one of his "disappearances" shortly after it arrived. A woman, an artist, who came to visit wanted the dog. I remember she was very taken with Pirate, and he with her. I think she was lonely.'

And you weren't lonely, Loretta? Nessa barely stopped herself saying. *You weren't lonely at all, here in this house? I bet you could have done with the company of Pirate.* Still, she wasn't

69

surprised; she'd never thought of Robert Locke as a man cuddly with animals. She'd often wondered if the person who asked him to grace that calendar was conversant with his *Hills and Dales* series, done in the late sixties, *Badger 1, 2 & 3, Toad, Adder, Sand-Lizard*, small marble sculptures that were at once both immensely suggestive of the animals represented and nothing like the animals at all – misshapen heads and the beginnings of torsos trailing away into a twist of snuffed-out end.

'I think it was very wrong of your father,' she said. 'Speaking as a parent, it's not something I would ever have done, to take a dog from a child like that.' It was perhaps the only time she'd been disloyal to Robert Locke since she'd started coming to the house.

Then something remarkable and shocking happened: Loretta Locke pinched her on the soft skin of the underside of her arm. Nessa yelped, and gaped at Loretta in disbelief, but Loretta merely inclined her head to the bathroom door. And Nessa understood immediately that it was Eleanor who had given away the dog.

When she got home to Sunday's Well, she made a pot of coffee and drank it sitting by the patio doors that led to the garden. She had an urge to ring her sister in Canberra but remembered the time difference. She gazed instead at the mess of foliage that ran down to the river. It was not exactly the stuff of *Homes & Gardens:* the rusting fence, a shrub that had once been yellow-flowering but was now a mulch of brown leaves. There was a dark green weed creeping over the fence that would have given the Lockes' wild rhubarb plants a run for their money. From where she sat, she could see the muddy patch where Bailey liked to bury bones, or root for no good reason in the dirt, pretending he was a puppy again. As if her thoughts had summoned him, he came meandering up the lawn, stopping to snuffle at something in the grass on his way. He loped up to the door and stood with his tail banging against the glass. She let him in and he lay down, rolled over to have his belly tickled. As he dozed by her feet, every so often one of his paws would shoot out, scrabbling at the floor, as if he'd been about to slip deeper into sleep but had been called back. When Nessa reached down to soothe him, she noticed the imprint of Loretta Locke's nails on the inside of her arm, a row of purpling crescent moons.

She thought she heard the front door opening, but it was only a flyer being shoved through the letter box. Earlier, when she got in, she'd called Jennifer's name but there had been no answer. Upstairs her daughter's bedroom looked as if it had been burgled, with eye shadow palettes, aerosol canisters, and discarded clothes scattered across the floor. Jennifer couldn't be at hockey – she had resolutely refused to return to the team. When Nessa asked if it was because of Mandy Wilson, she'd scowled and said no, it was because hockey made her thighs fat.

After a while Bailey got up and ambled off. She knew he would have gone to stand beside his food bowl, trusting her to follow, and she went into the kitchen and shook some dog food into his bowl, topped up his water. She spotted a note on the whiteboard: *extra choir practice today*. Jennifer crossed her *t*'s with such vigour that they ran almost the full length of the word, forming a canopy above the more squat letters.

Relieved, she heated up some soup, then got out her laptop and replied to emails.

Jennifer didn't come home until after 7 p.m.

'Hey, sweetheart,' Nessa said. 'I was beginning to worry. Do you know the time?'

Jennifer frowned. 'I left you a note.'

'Yes, I know, but the after-school stuff doesn't usually run this late, does it?'

'Choir does.' Jennifer dumped a folder of sheet music on the kitchen island. 'Did you feed Bailey?'

'Yes, the dog's fed. How about you? Shall I make some pasta?'

Jennifer shook her head. 'I grabbed a sandwich on the way home.' She took a yoghurt from the fridge, began to eat it standing beside the sink. 'Where's Dad?'

'He had a meeting with clients.' *Like you had choir practice.* The thought, which she knew was unfair, popped, unbidden, into her head. She was disappointed in herself.

'Will he be home soon?' Jennifer asked.

'I expect so.'

Jennifer didn't look entirely satisfied with this answer, but she must have decided it would do, because she went upstairs and a few minutes later Nessa heard through the ceiling the murmur of her daughter talking on her phone.

She opened the cupboard beneath the stairs and got out the old photo albums. Since bumping into Katherine Ferriter, she found that her mind kept wandering back to their college days, and to the years in London, but mostly back to Amy. There was one photo in particular that she was looking for. It had arrived by post many years ago, without a letter or even a note, just Amy's signature scrawled on the back. She thumbed through the first album without finding it, and started on the next. She was beginning to wonder if memory was playing tricks on her, when there it was: a colour photo of a small child straddling a plump pony: Amy's son, Luke, when he was about two and a half. It was incongruous, to think that she would soon be meeting this child as a grown man. And there was Amy: even more beautiful than Nessa remembered, proud, glowing. It was the kind of shot one saw in *Grazia* of film stars in the blaze of youth, all dazzling promise and fierceness, and Amy too was like a goddess, the fields of Tipperary stretching out behind her, as magnificent as any Hollywood backdrop. You could search that photo for an eternity, Nessa thought, and it would yield no hint of how their lives would go, this beautiful woman and her beautiful child. Amy would have returned to London a few days after that photo was taken. *Gallop away now*, Nessa wanted to say, *gallop to the farthest corner of the most distant field, child and mother, go! Live among the plants and the small wild animals, eat beetles and grass if you have to, don't ever come back.*

Philip wasn't home yet and so she took *Flight of the Doves* from its shelf and went upstairs to bed, though it was still light outside. She closed the curtains and climbed under the covers. After reading a chapter, she fell asleep, to dream of a battalion of dogs cresting a hill, one small pony galloping after them, and even though the hills were not the coastal cliffs around the Lockes' house, but the green valleys of Tipperary, there, bringing up the rear, was Loretta Locke. Philip slipped into bed later, his movements as quiet and ghostly as the dogs in her dream.

Katherine Ferriter, good to her word, had got in touch, and on the Friday of the following week they were all to go to Lough Hyne for supper at the cabin. Katherine's husband was driving down from Dublin, and would collect Luke at his great-aunt Gretta's in Tipperary on the way. Amy Corrigan, Luke's mother, had been born into a farming family in southeast Tipperary in a parish that oscillated between sleepy and watchful. The soundtrack to her childhood was the hum of milking machines, the bawling of calves, as well as the more widely referenced rural sounds of birdsong and chapel bells.

On the Friday morning, Nessa was in a café two doors down from the gallery getting a coffee. 'To go,' she told the barista. As she waited, she noticed Henchy, the gallery director, in a booth in the corner. He was looking straight at her, so she couldn't pretend not to have seen him. She waved, then immediately took out her purse, pretended to be engaged counting change. He got up and came over. 'A word, before you leave,' he said, and then he scurried back to the booth, where she now saw his friend, the poet HK, was with him.

She paid for her coffee and went over. A local free newspaper was open on the table to a photo of Melanie Doerr. The headline said: 'Woman Pleads with Gallery for Truth.' The byline was no one she'd ever heard of. The photo was captioned: 'I ask them only for this one thing'. Nessa picked up the paper, scanned through the article. The 'one thing' requested by Doerr was that the gallery acknowledge that she collaborated on the Chalk Sculpture, and that they add her name beside Robert Locke's. Doerr had also repeated her claim that Robert Locke had gifted her the sculpture. There was only a fleeting mention of the concept of impermanence, but then, that newspaper wasn't noted for its arts coverage.

Doerr was one of those people who look better in photos than in real life. Someone had persuaded her to part with the canvas bag while the photograph was being taken, and the blue of the mohair coat had been enhanced. 'Interesting,' Nessa said. 'I hadn't seen this. I don't usually read that paper.'

'We had the electrician in yesterday,' HK said, 'he left it behind. If you want my opinion, I don't think you should worry too much about it.'

'I'm not worried,' she said.

'I think we should have a strategy,' Henchy said.

'I'll send her in to you if she comes back,' Nessa said, 'how about that? You might be able to talk sense to her. Goodness knows I tried my best.'

'*Back?*' Henchy said. 'What do you mean "back"? I wasn't aware she'd graced us with her presence.'

'She was at the lecture on the Cambridgeshire pieces,' Nessa said. 'And she came to my office after.'

'And you didn't think to tell me?'

'I was able to handle her myself.'

'I wonder,' HK said, 'if this might be classed as an instance of appropriation? Immigrant's contribution to body of work subsumed by affluent Western man? Just throwing it out there. Devil's advocate, if you like.'

'I did check with Loretta Locke,' Nessa said. 'She compiled a list of all her father's students. There's nobody called

Doerr on there. And Robert Locke made no reference to her in any of the papers he left behind, despite Doerr's claims that he promised to acknowledge her. I'm sad to say the woman seems a bit delusional.'

'What's the word we use for that now?' Henchy said. 'Do we say she's "not well"? What do we say?'

'We say nothing,' Nessa said. 'We don't lend it any credence. It's an article in a free newspaper by someone who isn't a journalist.'

Henchy ran a hand several times over the top of his thinning hair. 'Maybe you could send me a note for my file,' he said. 'I should probably notify the board, and you're the person dealing with her. And with the Lockes.'

As she walked back to work, she'd squeezed the takeout cup so hard that a little volcano of milky coffee erupted through the hole in the top, though she didn't realise this until it ran down the sides and burned her fingers.

Lough Hyne was an hour and a half southwest of the city, a ten-minute drive beyond the Lockes' house. Four millennia ago it had been freshwater, but the sea had forced its way inland, up through a narrow channel known locally as the Rapids, to create something of an ecological miracle: a warm seawater lake with woods, cliffs, and a salt marsh. It was tiny, little over half a square mile, with a stony beach and sections of the seawall built as relief works during the Famine. In the fields surrounding it were a couple of farmhouses and, on the brow of a hill, one larger manse house owned by an Irish American family who returned every summer. And there were the cabins, twelve of them, constructed on concrete stilts on land reclaimed from the marshy foreshore.

They left the city shortly after half past six, Nessa driving, Philip in the passenger seat, his laptop on his knees, and Jennifer in the back. They took the coast road and caught the last of the evening sun on the water. She thought how the Irish landscape was often described as green but rarely as 'slow', when really, *slow* was a more fitting word. It was a steady, plodding sort of landscape, all the mountains, all the mists, like the one now blowing in off the sea, preventing her doing anything above forty miles per hour. The earth here was static to its core, generation after generation of slow-living people dying and being laid down, layer upon layer, their slow bones compacted into the limestone landscape.

'That used to be the changing huts,' Jennifer said as they passed Grainger's Fine Food Store, a wooden structure with its back to the sea, its entrance facing the main Skibbereen road. Nessa remembered wrestling a preschool Jennifer into a swimsuit in those huts – the splintered benches, the rough concrete floor. 'You made me pee behind it once,' Jennifer said, 'because you said it was too far to walk to the toilets.'

'I did not,' Nessa said, although as she spoke she was aware of a memory stirring in the far recesses of her brain.

She had intended to rehearse some anecdotes for Luke – things that were funny, but also safe and touching. Because what on earth could she usefully tell the boy? How his mother, in her teens, used to drive a tractor around the back lanes like it was a Ferrari; that she'd been taught how to put her arm into a cow, find a grip on a calf and pull? How much interest would these things be to a twenty-one-year-old from Manchester? She felt the stirrings of queasiness and let down the car window to get a little air.

She'd spent a while deciding what to wear. She'd settled on a green dress with a repeating pattern of tiny birds that looked at first glance like herons but which, if one looked closer, were dodoes. It had a green Victorian-style velvet ribbon that tied, in what she judged an ironic fashion, at the neck, and another length of ribbon by way of a belt that flattered her waist. She hoped it was formal enough to convey to Katherine that she'd made an effort, and at the same time wasn't so formal that it made her look fussy and middle-aged. She wanted to present as a plausible one-time friend for this boy's beautiful dead mother. What would he be like? When he was a baby, he'd been very like his mother, and what came to mind now was a dark-haired Goth with kohl eyes, a boy who looked like Amy in drag. *Keep your hands off him*, she heard Amy say, *I know what you're like.* 'That's not fair . . .' Nessa began to protest in her head, before pulling herself up, forcing her attention back to the road with its treacherous bends.

Usually when she drove that road it was to see the Lockes, and now every few miles, her brain, unsolicited, suggested a new question for Eleanor or a fact to be checked with Loretta. She'd arranged to visit them again the following Wednesday. Eleanor would only ever meet on a Wednesday, and only in the afternoon. If she was unable to meet on any particular Wednesday, Nessa would have to wait until the following week – there was no question of meeting on a Monday or Tuesday – though what other commitments Eleanor or Loretta might have she couldn't imagine. 'These interviews,' Loretta had said on the phone, 'will there be many more of them?' and Nessa had been hurt, because wasn't she the one who'd been tormented, Wednesday after Wednesday, with the minutiae of Eleanor Locke's reminiscences? And anyway, were the Lockes not being paid?

Philip, in the passenger seat, glanced up from his laptop. 'What's Katherine's husband called again?'

'William,' Nessa said. 'William, Katherine, Luke.'

'Don't forget Amy,' Jennifer volunteered from the back. 'Amy was his mom's name.'

'I don't need reminding about Amy,' he said, patting Nessa's knee, and she gave him a grateful smile.

He snapped shut the laptop and put it away. 'What's the story with Luke's father?'

'He's still alive, if that's what you mean,' Nessa said.

'What's he called?' Jennifer asked.

'Stuart.'

'William, Katherine, Luke, Amy, Stuart,' Jennifer chanted. 'This is like one of those games we used to play in primary school, where you had to keep adding stuff on and remembering. *I went to the moon and I took a rabbit, a box of Cheerios, a parrot, a lolly, a microwave, a horse . . .'*

'You don't need to remember Stuart,' Nessa said. 'He won't be there.' She switched on the radio, began fiddling with the dials.

Jennifer sank back in her seat and looked out of the window. As they drove along the coast, evening sun warmed the fields and the surface of the water. Perhaps as a form of minor protest, Jennifer was wearing what Nessa considered to be her most unsuitable outfit, a denim jumpsuit. Earlier, she'd come into her parents' bedroom when Nessa was getting ready. She'd watched her mother straightening her hair. 'Have you met this guy before?' she asked. 'Luke?'

'I met him when he was a kid. Just a baby, really. I haven't seen him since.'

'And his mother was your friend?'

'She was my best friend.'

'The one who killed herself?'

Nessa put down the tongs. 'You know you have to be careful how you say things tonight, Jennifer.'

Her daughter rolled her eyes. 'His mom died, like, a million years ago. I thought he was coming to talk about her. I thought that was the whole point.'

'Yes, but we need to be careful *how* we talk about her.'

'So I have to be all, like . . .' She affected a sarcastic tone: '. . . *thoughts and prayers?*'

'You have to be appropriate, that's all.'

'I'm going to pretend there's something wrong with me,' Jennifer said. 'I'm going to pretend I'm nonverbal.'

Nessa raised a finger in warning. Jennifer just laughed and walked to the door. She looked like she was about to leave, but then she said, 'Why did she do it?'

Nessa sucked in her breath. But perhaps better now than at Katherine's supper table. 'There was a row,' she said slowly. 'We were away for a weekend, a group of us. There was a naming ceremony for a friend's baby. I didn't even know Amy was coming. We hadn't been . . .' She swallowed. 'We'd lost touch. Amy showed up with her hair cropped tight to her head; she could get away with it, of course. She had the bone structure. But she was so terribly thin. And she argued with everyone. She even argued with the mother of the baby. And that night . . .' Nessa stopped. Dear God. She had forgotten how difficult this was. It was years since she'd had to recount it to anyone. 'That night Amy took her own life.' She barely made it to the end of the sentence.

'OMG, Mom. You were *there*?' Jennifer's hand flew to her mouth.

'I was the one who found her,' Nessa said quietly. 'Most of the others had gone home the next morning, and . . .' She trailed off. 'You know what, Jen?' She ran a hand through her hair, forgetting that she had just straightened it. 'I don't think we need to go into this. Not the details. It won't help anyone. Amy was troubled. She was ill. Luke was being cared for by her in-laws, her relationship with Luke's father had broken down . . .' She stuttered to a halt.

Jennifer came over and put her arms around her mother, laid her head on her shoulder. 'Poor Mom,' she said. It was so rarely that her daughter hugged her these days. Nessa held her close and was reminded of a day a couple of years ago when she'd been sorting clean laundry in the spare bedroom and the freshly laundered towels were so fragrant and soft, and she was so tired, that she'd lain down in the middle of them on the bed. Philip, passing the door, came to see if she was okay, and without being asked, lay down beside her. She could remember, as if it were yesterday, lying there, looking up at the ceiling, and not minding at all the stains where a pipe had burst two winters ago. Jennifer had put her head around the door, seen them, and wrinkled her forehead. They'd begun to laugh and slowly, cautiously, she'd made her way over and lain down beside them, the three of them arms around each other like they hadn't been since she was a little girl.

'Don't worry,' Jennifer said. 'I'll be the perfect daughter tonight. I'll be so well behaved you'll think I'm a change-ling.' Philip put his head around the door. 'Are you sure you need me there?' he said. 'This is your time with Katherine. I'd only be in the way.'

'Nice try,' Nessa said, 'but this is not "my time with Katherine". That's not what this is at all. I'm only going to meet the boy. I figure I owe Amy that much.'

Philip had sighed. 'I'd better go iron a shirt then.'

'If we had a cleaner, you wouldn't have to do that,' Jennifer said. 'A cleaner would iron your shirts.'

Five miles beyond Skibbereen, there was a signpost for the cabins, and an auctioneer's For Sale sign, faded and weather-beaten. They turned off the main road and down a muddy lane fringed with trees – ash, beech, sycamore, a patch of interloper pines planted for Christmas. Fragments of water flashed silver through the branches until, rounding a bend, they were faced with a breathtaking view of the lake. She had read on the internet that only two of the twelve cabins had sold. It was clear immediately which one was the Ferriters' because there was a Volvo parked beside it. The remainder of the cabins looked to be boarded up. Farther away, on the opposite bank, two children chased after a dog in the front yard of a farmhouse.

To the side of the cabin were a number of raised vegetable beds containing what might have been parsley or carrots. She parked and they climbed the four steps to the deck. A glass door was set into a glass wall overlooking the lake. The view was spectacular, and in that moment, while Katherine made her way toward them on the other side of the glass, she was struck by how very beautiful it was, how immensely peaceful.

'Nessa!' Katherine said, and she kissed her on the cheek. 'I'm so pleased you could make it. It will mean so much to Luke.' She turned to Philip. 'Where does the time go?' she said. 'I don't even want to think how long it's been since we last met,' and she kissed him too.

'This is Jennifer,' Nessa said, gently pushing her daughter forward.

'Look at you!' Katherine said. 'You're as gorgeous as your mother.' She glanced quickly at Philip. 'And tall like your dad, of course. You can't beat good genes.'

They were in a large open-plan room with Klimt prints on the walls. To the front, close to the glass, a table was set for dinner. A staircase rose in a spiral to a mezzanine level, where Nessa saw there were more Klimts. She noticed Philip giving the place the once-over with his architect's eye – light, angles, space. 'Come on through to the kitchen,' Katherine said. They followed her into a smaller room that looked out on the woods, and the vegetable patch to the side. Katherine went to the stove and lifted the lid of a casserole. 'I panicked when I heard the car,' she said, peering into the dish. 'I was glad when I saw that it was you, not William and the men. I'm behind with supper.'

'Men?' Nessa said. 'It's just Luke, isn't it?'

'Guess who invited himself along at the last minute?' Katherine said. She put the lid back on the casserole. 'Stuart.' When Nessa said nothing, she added, 'Luke's dad.'

'Yes,' Nessa said, 'I know.' She walked to the other side of the room and pressed her face to the window, pretending to be absorbed in peering out. Her cheek felt hot against the glass. 'I don't know if you remember Stuart?' she could hear Katherine saying to Philip.

'I met him at the funeral,' Philip said. 'That's about it.'

'Even at the funeral he behaved quite badly, I thought,' Katherine said.

Nessa turned around. 'We were all so young then,' she said. 'I don't think Stuart knew whether he was coming or going that day. I think he worried that people blamed him. For Amy's suicide.'

'I think I *did* blame him,' Katherine said. 'Maybe I still do. Not that it makes any difference. Poor Amy. God, I shouldn't even be talking like this.' She glanced in Jennifer's direction. 'Sorry.'

'When did you find out he was coming?' Nessa asked.

'Luke texted last night, asked if it was all right. What could I say?'

'I hate when parents do that,' Jennifer said. 'I bet Luke's raging.'

Katherine smiled. 'Actually, he sounded pleased. He seems a sweet boy.'

She pulled out stools at a breakfast bar and gestured to her guests to sit down. 'Look at you,' she said again, opening a bottle of Diet Coke for Jennifer. 'You're the image of your mother when she was your age. Or at least when she was young – I didn't know her when she was your age exactly. We were . . .' She looked at Nessa. 'What was it, Nessa? Eighteen?'

Nessa nodded.

'Eighteen when we met,' Katherine said. 'Did your mother tell you how we lived together in London for a year – your mother, Amy, and me. All girls together, like *Little House on the Prairie*.'

Nessa made a face. '*Little House on the Prairie*? I don't think so, Katherine.'

Philip cocked his head to one side. 'I can see you in farm-girl pinafore and braids. It's a rather fetching image, if I may say so.'

'Dad!' Jennifer said. 'You're so embarrassing.'

'All right,' Katherine said, 'maybe it wasn't exactly like it, but it was the nearest I got to having sisters.' She took a bottle of Prosecco from the fridge and poured three glasses. 'It's good to have you here, Ness,' she said, touching her glass to each of theirs in turn. 'It's like old times. Except for Amy, of course.'

Nessa looked at the Aga stove, at the granite countertops, at her dodo-print dress, which even in the sale had cost two hundred euros. It was nothing like old times.

From outside, there was the crunch of tyres. Katherine went to the door, slid open the glass, and a gust of air rushed in from the lake.

Nessa got down off the bar stool and went to stand in the space between kitchen and living room, leaning against the doorjamb. She realised she had a fistful of her dress bunched against her thigh and every muscle in her body felt like a coiled spring. Slowly and deliberately, she exhaled, unwound, trying to remember the breathing exercises the counsellor had given her.

'You okay, love?' Philip came to stand beside her. 'This must bring it all back.'

'Yes,' she said, distractedly, because she could see Katherine going to the railing now, leaning over, speaking to someone. Katherine laughed – a bit forced – and a moment later Stuart Harkin came up the steps.

He was indisputably middle-aged but he wasn't bald and he wasn't paunchy. At St Martin's he'd studied photography. Nessa had googled him once or twice in the intervening years: at one stage he'd headed up a health food cooperative in Bristol, and for a while he ran a crafts fair that did the rounds of market towns in the southeast of England. Katherine grudgingly accepted his hug. He'd acquired a beard, Nessa noted, which suited him, and his hair was shorter, almost respectable, and he was wearing a sports jacket.

He released Katherine and stepped into the cabin. 'Nessa!' he exclaimed, though he must have known that she was coming. 'I can't believe it!' She couldn't decide whether to go to him or not, and while she was making up her mind, he strode across the room. 'How are you, Ness?' he said.

'Fine, Stuart, fine. You?'

He grinned. 'Still above ground.' He glanced at Katherine, then back at Nessa. 'Look at us,' he said, 'all grown up,' and he laughed and threw his hands in the air in mock disbelief.

Closer up, Nessa saw that his jeans were faded, and he'd paired them with shoes that looked like they belonged to someone else, the kind of shoes a stockbroker might wear to the office. His jacket was baggy at the elbows and shoulders, as if the material had lost some of its substance, and she thought, *He hasn't done so well; Eleanor Locke would have something to say about that jacket.*

'This is my husband, Philip,' Nessa said. 'And,' she added, inclining her head toward the breakfast bar, 'our daughter, Jennifer.'

The men shook hands. Jennifer got down off her stool and came over. 'It's nice to meet you, Mr Harkin.'

'Please,' he said, 'call me Stuart. Otherwise, I'll start feeling old.'

William came puffing up the steps and into the cabin. His face was pink and shiny and he was carrying a suitcase.

'Here,' Stuart said, 'let me take that. Where's that son of mine got to?'

William seemed glad to be relieved of the case. 'He's gone to look at the water,' he said, 'and who could blame him? I never tire of looking at it myself.' When he embraced Nessa, his bulk radiated heat. He'd doubled in girth since she'd last seen him, and all his hair was gone, apart from a patch of soft blond fuzz above each ear.

A splash from the direction of the lake caused them to turn. Luke, because it could only be him, was skimming stones. He stooped and picked up another, sent it spinning across the surface of the lake, which erupted into a series of splashes. He dropped to his haunches and, with the camera that was slung around his neck, began to photograph the ruffled water. He was well built, Nessa saw, like his father. And peculiar like his mother, because there was Katherine, standing on the deck waiting to greet him, and still he continued to take photographs.

'Luke!' his father shouted. A parcel of crows rose out of the trees and flew noisily inland. 'Come on in, son.'

Luke raised a hand in greeting. He bounded across the narrow patch of grass between the cabin and the shoreline and came up the steps. He was wearing a raincoat buttoned to the neck that wouldn't have been out of place in a 1950s detective comic, and a pair of Converse sneakers. He held out a hand to Katherine in a curiously formal gesture and smiled. 'You have a very beautiful place,' he said.

'Thank you,' Katherine said. She ushered him inside and brought him directly over to where Nessa stood beside Stuart and William. 'This is Nessa,' Katherine said, proudly, as if presenting a prize. 'She's so looking forward to talking to you.'

Behind round-rimmed glasses, Luke's eyes were dark, so dark that they looked almost black, but Nessa knew that if she were to move closer they would be navy, just like his mother's, navy with irises so large they'd made Amy look like she might be on drugs, even when she wasn't. He also had his mother's clear complexion. There was the slightest wave to his dark hair. He was, despite a slight awkwardness, very beautiful. It was Amy come to her again, reincarnated on this evening in late April in the Ferriters' kitchen. *Haven't you girls done well for yourselves?* Nessa could almost hear her saying, teasingly. *Isn't this all very cosy?*

Katherine introduced Philip and Jennifer. 'Nice camera,' Philip said, nodding approvingly to Luke's Nikon. Nessa saw that it was the kind of camera Stuart had liked to use – perhaps it was even Stuart's camera; it was an old model.

'Thanks,' Luke said, smiling. He unslung the camera from around his neck and placed it carefully on a side table. 'I like to shoot in thirty-five millimetre. A mate in Manchester has a darkroom; he does the developing for me.' His looks, Nessa thought, had not gone unnoticed by Jennifer, who'd been shy on shaking his hand, and had even blushed a little.

'You guys probably want to freshen up,' Katherine said. 'William – will you show Luke and Stuart where the room is? And the switch for the hot water.'

When the three men had gone upstairs, she turned to Nessa. 'Well,' she said, 'what do you think?'

Nessa's right leg had begun to tremble, a nervous tic from childhood that surfaced occasionally. 'Those eyes,' she said. 'Did you notice?'

Katherine nodded. 'He seems a little shy, but better that than being like his father.' She made a face. 'He's got old-looking, hasn't he? Stuart.'

'Yes,' Nessa said, 'I thought the same.'

William came clattering back downstairs. He went to the fridge for the bottle of Prosecco, topped up their glasses, and poured one for himself. 'Katherine tells me you're doing great things with the Chalk Sculpture,' he said. 'My sister went to see it, years ago. It didn't do her any good, they adopted in the end. But I believe it's a very fine statue.'

Nessa smiled. 'It's pretty special.'

'How much would something like that cost?' He seemed genuinely interested. She half expected him to say that he knew a consortium that would cut her a slice – they'd buy on the rise, flip it in six months, invest the profits in real estate in Detroit. 'It depends,' she said, 'it's not like there's a market index. The gallery put a funding proposal to the European

Cultural Institute. It's being acquired from the Lockes as part of a larger body of work.'

'My wife is very modest,' Philip said. 'She says "the gallery", but really, this is her brainchild.'

Nessa shrugged. 'What can I say?' she said lightly. 'I wanted a job, so I made one up.'

'I'd say the Locke family is glad of the money,' William said. 'I hear Robert didn't leave them particularly well provided for.'

'I really don't know.'

'Bet you could have done without that Czech woman sticking her oar in.'

Out of the corner of her eye, she saw Katherine, too late, making warning faces at William. 'Croatian,' Nessa said. 'She claims to be Croatian.' That newspaper must have a wider circulation than she'd credited it with.

'Nessa hasn't come to talk shop,' Katherine said. 'I'm sure she'd rather leave all that behind in the office.'

Fat chance, Nessa thought. Several times on the journey down she'd caught herself ruminating on the article about Melanie Doerr. And then there was the note she'd had to prepare for Henchy, which had proved tricky.

'Of course,' William said. 'My apologies.' He turned to Philip, who was sitting on a sofa beside Jennifer. 'How's the architecture business these days?'

II

When, during supper, Stuart asked her to pass the bread basket, she set it down in front of him without looking at him, dropping it as if it were hot. It wasn't easy to sit beside a man you'd once slept with, no matter how long ago it had happened. Did Katherine suspect anything? Nessa doubted it. Katherine was not the sort to place her, literally, in such an uncomfortable position. No, Katherine, happily dishing out carrot tagliatelle tossed in thyme butter, was oblivious. Katherine didn't know, because nobody knew. Apart from Stuart, who didn't seem the least bit discomfited.

The lake was a sheet of silver tinged with pink as the sun began to set. It was glorious, but the scale of its grandeur made her feel small and insignificant, like an insect in a jam jar. She wondered how Katherine spent nights here alone – if at 3 a.m. she woke to find an unfamiliar face pressed to the window, who could she usefully call?

Stuart was telling Philip about his job with a telecom company, a marketing role, apparently, that could be done from anywhere on a laptop. As a sideline, he and a friend tended garden allotments for people who only thought they wanted an allotment, who didn't have the time to weed or water or spray. Luke, in contrast to his father, was quiet. It couldn't be easy for the boy, Nessa thought; he would not be choosing to spend his Friday night with them were it not for his mother. She was attempting to think of some way of drawing him out of himself when Jennifer surprised her by asking, 'What are you doing at college?'

'I dropped out,' he said.

Oh dear, Nessa thought, *that didn't go well,* but Jennifer, unfazed, said, 'What did you drop out of?'

'Digital media.'

'He's taking a year out,' Stuart said, putting down his fork. 'He can go back any time he wants.'

Luke looked at his father. It was a difficult look to interpret, Nessa thought. 'I'm not going back,' he said. He looked away, out to the water, and to no one in particular said, 'I need to get a job. Earn some money. I need to figure out what I want to do with my life. Maybe it's not shuffling stock photos around a computer screen.'

'You can't go wrong with computers,' William said. 'Anything in the computer line will stand you in good stead.'

'Street photography is what I like to do now,' Luke said. 'When I go back to Manchester I'm starting this project called 2.17, where I take a photograph from the same angle on the same street corner at the same time every day, no matter what the weather or the light is like. No matter what shit is going on in my life. Every single day, 2.17.'

'That is so cool,' Jennifer said. 'So it'll be, like, photos of ordinary people going down the street? At exactly 2.17?'

'That's the idea,' Luke said.

'Ordinary people are the new celebrities,' Stuart said. There was a hint of mockery in his tone.

'Imagine if somebody really famous came along,' Jennifer said, 'at just the wrong time. Imagine if Taylor Swift came down the street and you were like, "No, please, get out of the way, Taylor."'

Luke laughed good-naturedly. 'I'd have to let her be in the photo, wouldn't I?' he said. 'It would kill me, but that's what I'd have to do. If it was 2.17.'

'How many days do you plan to shoot it for?' Philip said.

'One hundred,' Luke said. 'I was going to do it for a year, but a few of my mates are going backpacking in Vietnam and I'm thinking of going with them.'

'OMG,' Jennifer said, round-eyed. 'That is the coolest thing ever.'

Nessa hoped her daughter meant the photography project and not the backpacking. It occurred to her that a psychotherapist would have a field day with Luke's proposal: a young man whose mother had died tragically, purposefully getting stuck in a moment, not allowing himself to move on. As if he had channelled Nessa's thoughts, Luke turned to her abruptly and said, 'Did you know my mother well? I know you shared a flat, but did you talk about stuff?'

'We had some very nice times in that flat,' Katherine said. 'We were good friends, the three of us.'

Nice, Nessa thought. How useless a word was that? She could almost hear Amy whispering in her ear: *Boring. She's still so very boring.*

'I went there once,' Luke said. 'Dad' – he inclined his head toward his father – 'took me when I was younger. There was a family living in it by then, so we only got to see it from the outside. It's not in flats anymore.'

'We did ring the bell,' Stuart said, 'but no one answered. I probably wouldn't have answered either. It's not the most salubrious part of town.'

'I heard it was all gentrified now,' Katherine said.

'The bars are gone from the windows,' Stuart said, 'if that's what you mean.'

'Remember the woman in the basement who used to grow ivy in biscuit tins?' Nessa said.

'Oh God, yes!' Katherine said. 'And she had a Child of Prague statue that the head kept falling off of.'

'Amy had a theory that she ritually beheaded it,' Nessa said.

'What was she like?' Luke said. 'My mother.'

'Well . . .' Katherine said.

They were being tested, Nessa thought, like Andie Mac-Dowell in *Green Card*, but with the process made more complex by the fact that there were more than two of them.

'She – I mean your mother – was a very special person,' Katherine said, 'a sensitive person. And she was a very talented artist.'

Stuart became suddenly busy with the salad bowl. How many times over the years must he have been asked that question? *What was she like?* Nessa looked at Luke. What would Amy want him to know? He had come all this way. What a waste if he were to go home with nothing more than Katherine's banalities, Katherine who – for all that she'd thrust herself into the middle of this – had never really known Amy at all. She took a deep breath. 'I first met your mother when I was five and she was six,' she said. 'Your Granny Corrigan and my mother were in the same Legion of Mary praesidium. I remember playing Matchbox cars with your mother on the floor of our sitting room. I was so jealous of your mother's toys. She had a SodaStream and a Space Hopper and a Girl's World Styling Head that Santa brought even though she hadn't asked for it. I think our mothers must have had a falling-out, because I didn't see Amy again until I was fifteen, when we went to visit the farm in Tipperary. By then she was back-combing her hair, and taping posters of the Cure to her bedroom wall.'

'I remember visiting the farm when I was little,' Luke said. 'And when I saw it again, last week, it was just like I remembered.'

'You couldn't remember it from back then,' Stuart said, 'you were too young.'

'I do,' Luke said. 'I remembered all the tools hanging in the outbuildings – they're still there. And I remember being on a pony in a field round the back.'

'Your grandparents wouldn't have tolerated anything as sentimental as a pony,' his father said. 'If it didn't earn its keep, old Pa Corrigan wouldn't have kept it.'

'It was a small black pony,' Luke said. 'I clearly remember someone carrying me into a field, and there was this pony. Aunt Gretta remembers it too.'

'Maybe it was a pig?' Stuart said. 'You were practically a baby. You wouldn't have known any different.'

'I have a photo of you on that pony,' Nessa said. 'With Amy holding the reins.' She hurried on before Stuart could object. 'She was Goth, your mother. Black dresses and torn fishnet stockings. Doc Martens and white makeup. I was so impressed! Leg warmers were the most radical thing allowed in our house. She took me for a walk up the fields behind the farmhouse once. We brought a bottle of Fanta and a packet of biscuits and we dug up a rabbit she'd buried the week before.'

A little 'ugh' sound escaped Katherine. 'Dare I ask where the adults were when this was happening?' she said.

'Praying, I expect,' Stuart said. 'Mrs Corrigan did a lot of praying.'

'Amy gave her plenty of cause,' Nessa said. It was out before she could stop it, but when she glanced at Luke, he was smiling.

'We used to have a painting of two women on a boat by Westminster Bridge,' Luke said. 'I think you gave it to my mother.'

'Oh!' she said, because she'd forgotten about that painting. 'Yes, that was the first original painting I ever bought. I gave it to Amy for her twentieth birthday.'

'I wish we still had it,' Luke said.

'We do still have it,' Stuart said. 'It's in storage at Eddie's place.'

Luke looked as if he was about to say something, but instead he gave the slightest shake of his head. For a second or two there was silence and everybody looked down at their plates.

'Tell me, Nessa,' William said, 'what are you going to do about this Czech woman?'

'Now, William . . .' Katherine said.

'It's fine,' Nessa said. She turned to William. 'I don't expect I'll have to do anything about her. These things usually fizzle out.'

'Is this the woman objecting about the statue?' Luke said. 'I read about that.'

'Where?' Nessa said, dismayed. The free newspaper had hardly made its way to Tipperary.

'On Facebook. I saw your name mentioned and so I read it.'

'What's this?' Stuart leaned closer and now his jacket was brushing the bare skin of her lower arm.

'It's nothing,' she said. 'A storm in a teacup. There's a statue called the Chalk Sculpture that's quite famous locally.'

'Notorious, more like,' Philip said.

'And,' she continued, 'this rather odd woman . . .'

'Czech,' William said.

'. . . is claiming to have had a hand in making it.'

'What I find most interesting,' Luke said, 'is what she says about the sculpture not being intended to last.'

Trust a twenty-one-year-old to find that the most interesting part, Nessa thought. The chairman of the gallery's board had found Doerr's claim of ownership to be the most interesting. He'd told Nessa so in an email that had pinged into her inbox just as she was about to leave the office. 'There's no evidence to suggest that Locke ever intended that to be the case,' she said now. 'And in any event, it's no longer his call. His time for having a say in anything is over.' *Life trumps death*, she might have added if she wasn't sitting across from a boy whose mother had killed herself. Rock Paper Scissors. Life Death Art. If Amy were here, she could tell him this.

'The way I see it,' William said, 'if Mr Locke didn't intend it to be permanent, then he should have smashed it up while he was still alive.'

'Purposeful impermanence,' Luke said. 'We did it in college. Not that I'm saying this is necessarily an instance of it.' He smiled uncertainly at Nessa. 'But it's interesting, that's all.'

Nervousness flickered behind his dark lashes. She saw that he was unsure of himself. She had come here wanting him to like her, and now she realised that her need for approval was reciprocated.

'Have I got this right?' William said. 'She wants to be credited with making something she says should be left to disintegrate?'

'In a nutshell, yes,' Nessa said.

William shook his head. 'I've never understood art,' he said.

'You should photograph it,' Jennifer said to Luke. 'Especially if it's going to be part of a big controversy. That'd be so cool.'

Great, Nessa thought, *just bloody great*. She looked to Katherine to save her, but Katherine was beaming. 'Now, there's a brilliant idea,' she said. 'Luke – do you think you'd like to do that? I don't know much about these things, but I bet it would be marvellous in your portfolio. If Nessa doesn't mind, of course.'

'I'd quite like to shoot it,' he said, looking at Nessa. 'If that would be all right? It interests me: the idea of capturing the act of disintegration. If you don't mind . . .'

'Well,' Nessa said doubtfully, 'I suppose I could ask the Lockes.'

'Wonderful!' Katherine said, clapping her hands.

The cabin gave a little quiver. 'Only the wind,' William said. 'Nothing to worry about. Ergonomically designed.'

Nessa looked out to the lake and saw that the surface of the water was rippled, as if someone had found a loose thread in a piece of silk and tugged. She couldn't imagine Loretta Locke being exactly thrilled with the suggestion. She should have said that capturing the act of disintegration would have been an affront to Robert Locke's wishes, would have defeated the temporality of the work. But it was too late now. Jennifer was asking Luke how much flights to Vietnam cost, and everybody had moved on.

12

After dessert, she excused herself and went outside for a cigarette. She lit up on the deck. Katherine came out with a shawl, and Nessa allowed her to drape it over her shoulders, though it looked expensive and she knew it would end up smelling of smoke. When they'd arrived at the Ferriters', it had still been bright. Now she could just about pick out the shapes of the other cabins along the shore. The spaces beneath them – 'space for a kayak or a small boat,' according to the auctioneer's website – looked in the dusk like the voids of open mouths. When she descended the steps, the perimeter lights came on. *Caught*, she thought, as she crossed the small square of grass between cabin and shore. She walked by the water's edge, smoking as she went, shivering and glad, after all, of the shawl. The shorefront wasn't sandy like a beach, but a darker, peatier silt embedded with small glistening stones.

She sat on a low rock to finish the cigarette. After a few moments, she heard footsteps and saw an outline approaching along the shore. Katherine, she thought, come to fetch her. But no, it was taller than Katherine. One of the men, then. It wasn't wide enough to be William. As the figure drew closer, she saw that it was Stuart. 'Are you the search party?' she said, shuffling over on the rock to make room.

'You're my only option for a cigarette,' he said. 'I lost mine somewhere between the airport and this place.'

She took a cigarette from the pack, handed it to him.

'What happened here?' he said, sweeping his arm in a wide arc.

Did he mean the cabins? And was it the blight on the shoreline that bothered him, or the fact that they were empty?

As if he'd guessed what she was thinking, he said, 'I can think of a few people who'd give an arm and a leg to live here. Surely somebody must want them?'

She shrugged. 'Builder went bust, developer went bust. They'll probably rot on their ergonomically designed stilts.'

'Katherine and William must be pretty pissed off.'

'I suppose so.'

Neither of them said anything for a while. She was grateful that it was dark, that if he looked at her now he couldn't see her properly, and this made her braver. She turned, intending to ask about Manchester, and discovered him staring at her. 'You must be cold in that dress,' he said, beginning to take off his jacket.

'It's fine,' she said, 'I don't need it, I have the shawl,' but he helped her into the jacket anyway.

'Thank you,' she said. They listened to the shuffle of the water, advancing and retreating.

'I came to Ireland once after Amy's funeral,' he said. 'Her family wanted to maintain links with Luke, and I wanted that too, I felt it was only right. But let's just say there were tensions.'

'Like what?'

'Well,' he said slowly, 'old Pa Corrigan told me that his daughter would still be alive if she hadn't met me.'

'Ouch. What did you say to that?'

'What could I say? I wasn't exactly Husband of the Year.'

This was impossible to contradict. 'Is he still alive? Amy's father?' she asked.

He seemed surprised by this. Perhaps he'd presumed that she'd kept in touch. 'No,' he said, 'he's dead, her mother too. I'm sorry, on Luke's account, that, in a way, this is all happening too late. But he tells me he's got on great with Aunt Gretta this past week. And now he's met Katherine. And you. I appreciate your taking the time to talk to him.'

'It's no trouble.'

'You know, Nessa, you've not changed as much as I expected. I thought you might be different. You know – architect's wife, suburban mom . . .'

'Oh, I've changed all right,' she said as lightly as she could. She kept her eyes fixed on the lake.

'Are you happy, Ness?' he said abruptly. 'I've wondered that off and on over the years.'

'We should go back,' she said. She stubbed out her cigarette on the side of the rock and buried the butt in the silt.

He tossed his cigarette on the ground and stood up. 'Come on,' he said, holding out his hand. She hesitated a moment before taking it, and he pulled her to her feet. With her free hand she brushed down her dress, which felt clammy after the damp rock. She waited for him to let go of her other hand, but he didn't and they started back toward the cabin like that, side by side, hand in hand. She told herself that he was being friendly and she should relax. She allowed herself to enjoy walking in that beautiful place, the feel of her hand in his. Then she told herself that it wasn't friendly at all, that it was something else entirely, but she didn't take away her hand, and they walked on together like that, saying nothing. He let go when they drew level with the cabin. Silently, she handed back the jacket. They didn't go inside immediately, but stood for a while on the patch of floodlit grass. 'We should meet up before I head back to Manchester,' he said. 'Grab a coffee and catch up properly.'

'Sure,' she said.

He took out his phone. 'What's your number?'

She'd no sooner called out the digits than she experienced a rush of panic and wished she could take them back. She had an urge to hurry inside, to tell Philip immediately that she'd agreed to have coffee with Stuart Harkin, so as to neutralise it, but she only had one foot on the bottom step when the others came out. Jennifer was dressed in water sports gear that made her look enormous. She was talking excitedly to Luke and William, who were similarly dressed. The men began pulling kayaks from the space underneath the cabin. 'Is it safe to go out on the water at this hour?' Nessa asked.

Katherine smiled. 'Now is the very best time,' she said. 'They'll get to see the phosphorescence.' Jennifer was already dragging her kayak down to a little jetty. 'Don't worry,' Katherine said. 'William's very dependable, and Jennifer tells me she can swim.' They sat on the wall beside the jetty – Philip, Nessa, Katherine, and Stuart – and watched the kayaks disappear across the lake. When Katherine got up and went inside to make coffee, Nessa sat between her husband and Stuart Harkin, looking out to the lake, where only the lights of the kayakers' headlamps remained visible, little pinpricks of light far out on the water. Katherine returned with a pot of coffee and little almond biscuits on a tray. Overhead, the moon shone down. They drank their coffee, then walked the shore again, the four of them this time, and as Nessa walked, everything felt heightened, every pebble making its presence felt beneath her boot, every brush of Stuart's arm against hers registering with disproportionate effect. A plop in the water caused her to jump: a fish surfacing for flies.

When the men pulled ahead, Katherine linked her arm. 'He's no more in a marketing role than I am,' she said, nodding toward Stuart. 'I expect he's selling choc ices out of the back of a van.' It was the only disagreeable thing she'd ever heard Katherine say about anybody.

When the others returned, and pulled their kayaks to dry land, Luke went inside and fetched his camera. Nessa watched him take a photograph of her daughter.

Jennifer shook out her hair, which had got slightly wet, and posed for the camera. 'How about one of Jennifer with her mom and dad?' Katherine said, and Luke, suddenly flustered, said, 'Of course,' and they went and stood beside Jennifer with their arms around her shoulders.

Later, as they left, the trees formed a dark umbrella along the lane, and bats swooped low across the path of their car. The soles of Nessa's boots were caked with dirt and had dislodged pieces of mud onto the floor of the car. They were curiously shaped mud casts, and gingerly she picked a couple of them up and balanced them in her palm. She thought they were the sort of thing Jennifer might like to see, but Jennifer, on a high after the kayaking, was chattering at such a rate it was impossible to get her attention. Once or twice her phone buzzed. 'Who's that at this hour?' Nessa said.

'Oh, that's just Luke,' Jennifer said. 'We're following each other on Instagram now.'

'Isn't he a bit old for you to be following?' Philip said worriedly.

Jennifer snorted. 'It's Instagram, Daddy. Not the dark web.'

Nessa smiled to herself in the darkness. Amy's child and her child – friends. She thought it was rather lovely.

13

During Nessa's first year at St Martin's, Locke had travelled over from Ireland to deliver a lecture. He was then a man in his fifties, handsome, in a dark blue shirt and light brown cords. Nessa remembered that he was wearing boots. Men back home didn't wear boots in those days, unless they were Wellingtons or hobnail boots. The lecture was called 'Dark Bogs: The Impact of Geography on the Works of Edwin Miles' or something approximating that. It was a public-access lecture and most of the people in the room weren't students, but older people. She and Amy took chairs near the back.

Locke began his lecture. Nessa glanced round at the rest of the audience. They appeared rapt, composed, good-humoured. Locke said that the landscape that surrounded Edwin Miles in Roscommon was responsible for Miles's work being dark, bleak, and demanding. 'Ridiculous,' Amy said, out loud, and her hand shot up. What about Beth Kimmerling, who'd lived all her life in a village three miles east of Edwin Miles, and whose work was all blues and yellows and light? Everywhere light, light, light. Amy began to speak faster, the words spilling out: Yes, they'd worked some thirty years apart, but geology didn't move that fast. The physical landscape was the same for both of them; neither of them had lived through a war. She ended by suggesting that perhaps it was Miles him-self who was dark and bleak and demanding.

It wasn't audience question time, and nobody had responded to the raising of her hand by inviting her to speak.

Locke talked over her for a while, before realising that he had a challenger and slowly petering to a halt. Most people only heard the last bit of what Amy said, the bit where she called Miles dark and bleak and demanding, which made her sound like a heckler. There was a silence, during which most of the room turned to stare at them. Then Locke smiled, nodded almost imperceptibly at Amy, and began to speak again as if nothing had happened. One of the college's administrative staff came down from the front and positioned herself in the aisle a few feet from where Amy and Nessa sat and remained there for the rest of the lecture.

She remembered Locke's eyes from that visit, sharp and blue, and the curl of dark hair where his shirt was open. There was a question time at the end, an official one. The moderator, a professor at the college, asked Locke about his influences and he listed seven or eight men whose names meant nothing to Nessa. He was asked how he would describe the process of sculpting, and he said the block of stone was like the birth canal, and the sculptor's chisel set the contractions in motion. He was asked about how his art impacted on his loved ones and he said artists bore a great responsibility not to hurt those closest to them, to be careful what they used. He was asked about the influence of Ireland and he said he suspected there were people in the audience better qualified to talk about Ireland than he was. Everyone laughed.

Afterwards, before the crowd had cleared and when they were putting on their coats, Nessa saw Locke and the professor coming down the hall toward them. She thought that they were about to be reprimanded. The professor looked as if he would indeed like to do that. Locke, though, was smiling. He invited them to go for a drink, and they went to a wine bar around the corner from the college.

Nessa was starstruck, tongue-tied, but Amy told Locke immediately that she disagreed with what he'd said. Nessa thought she was going to do the whole Edwin Miles thing again, but instead Amy told Locke that he was wrong to say that there were things an artist shouldn't use. 'There's nothing that doesn't get used,' she said.

'Nothing?' Locke said. 'No matter who gets hurt?' He raised an eyebrow, but his expression was more amused than angry.

'It's not like we have a choice, is it?' Amy said. 'It's not the use we make of it, it's the use it makes of us.'

Locke looked like he was about to say more, but the professor took him off to dinner then, and the girls were not invited along. Years later, in the course of her research for the Locke acquisition, Nessa would find herself reading one of Robert Locke's final interviews. 'There's nothing I wouldn't use in my art,' Locke told the interviewer. 'It's not the use I make of it, it's the use it makes of me.'

14

The director called a meeting on Monday morning to discuss what he termed 'the Doerr situation'. The meeting room at the gallery used to be a storage room for paintings not currently on display before Henchy had fitted it out with a table and chairs and called it the boardroom. In the corridor outside were the components of a dismantled installation that had been in the foyer the previous week – lengths of PVC piping, copper tubing, drain rods. It looked like the plumber had been and not tidied up after. The room was too small: eight feet square, with a round table in the middle that Nessa had to suck her tummy in to squeeze around. The walls, though, were magnificent: a series of gouache mountain scenes; a portrait of a woman in her late teens standing before a fireplace, believed to be by Sarah Purser; a watercolour of dogs on a beach. A dozen or so religious icons had been lobbed into the mix, the slapdash nature of their arrangement oddly pleasing.

'There's no doubt that it's not the sort of media coverage we aspire to,' Nessa said, 'but I don't think it's of any material import.'

The table was so small that it was possible to make out everything Henchy wrote in his notebook, even though she was reading it upside down. Now she watched him note down 'material import', underscoring the words several times.

'So,' he said, 'the question is, what do we do about the situation?'

'Nothing,' Nessa said. 'It's not a situation.' She picked a spot on the wall – the watercolour of the dogs – and observed how the sand kicked up by the child running in their wake was a darker mirror of the spray of foam at the water's edge.

'I've been talking to the publicist,' Henchy said, as if she hadn't spoken. 'He thinks something short and to the point is the way to go. Something to nip it in the bud. Something that conveys, in a nice way, that the unfortunate woman concerned is completely wrong, both legally and morally, and that also conveys how we wish her well and hope that she gets the help she needs.' He paused. 'I thought that you might draft something up, and the publicist will okay it and issue it this afternoon.'

'We issue nothing,' Nessa said. 'We don't give this thing oxygen.'

'The publicist was very clear in his advice,' Henchy said. 'I never like to depart from professional advice.'

Nessa returned to her desk, in bad humour, to find an email from Katherine saying how much Luke was looking forward to photographing the Chalk Sculpture, and when would be a convenient time?

'I have a bone to pick with you,' Loretta Locke said, when Nessa rang to tell her that a young photographer, a friend, would be coming with her on Wednesday.

'What's that?'

'I've just spent the past half hour calming my mother down. A friend of ours in the city cut out that newspaper article and mailed it to her.'

'Friends,' Nessa said. 'Where would we be without them?'

'I wish you'd told me. If I'd had advance notice, I might have been able to intercept it.'

'I didn't want to trouble you. It isn't even a proper news-paper. Nobody will take any notice.'

'My mother, I can assure you, has taken notice.'

Nessa sighed. 'I'm sorry, Loretta. You're right, I should have told you. I only learned about it myself on Friday and I had a lot on my plate. But please tell your mother not to worry. We get these . . . um . . . *characters* . . . in the arts sec-tor all the time.' As she said it, it struck her that she'd never encountered anyone quite like Melanie Doerr.

'I have a passing familiarity with the arts sector, thank you, Nessa. And I'd like you to try telling my mother not to worry, and see how you fare.'

'Okay,' Nessa said, 'fine. I get it. But why is she taking this so much to heart? My teenage daughter would call her triggered. Are you sure you haven't heard of Doerr?'

'I'm positive. Are you going to issue a denial?'

'We're going to issue a press release,' Nessa said. 'I'm working on it as we speak.' She glanced at the document open on her computer; she had typed precisely five words. 'I'll send it to you later this afternoon for your approval.'

'All right,' Loretta said grudgingly. 'And next time maybe you could remember to keep me in the loop. Who did you say is coming with you on Wednesday?'

'A photographer,' Nessa said. She saw no reason to expand any further.

'Another one?' Loretta sighed. 'The sooner this business is done and dusted, the better.'

Nessa was about to retort that she felt exactly the same, but she bit back the words. 'I'll see you on Wednesday, Loretta.'

15

On Wednesday, Nessa arranged to collect Luke from the Ferriters' cabin. It was his last day staying at the lake before heading back to Aunt Gretta in Tipperary. This time she was expecting the lake vista, but it was no less breathtaking: blue at that hour, the trees fringing it, moss and ferns tumbling over the remains of the old walls that had been built during the Famine. Everything lush and plentiful now, no sense of the want that had stalked the place once, apart from the boarded-up cabins. Katherine was coming down the steps toward her before she'd even switched off the engine. Nessa let down the window.

'It's so good of you,' Katherine said. 'He's been looking forward to this since the weekend.'

'It's no trouble,' Nessa said.

'You two will get on great,' Katherine was saying, 'I know you will. You got on like a house on fire over supper. But ring me if there's a problem, okay? Anything at all, just ring.' She spoke in much the same way Nessa might if she were waving Jennifer off for a day out. In other words, with a certain degree of trepidation.

Luke appeared then, his camera bag slung over his shoulder. 'Hey,' he said, opening the passenger door and getting in. 'It's very cool of you to do this. Thank you.'

'It's no trouble,' Nessa said again, and turned the key in the ignition. She was relieved that there was no sign of Stuart. He was most likely still in bed; he always had liked to sleep late. It had rained overnight and the wheels spun in the mud as she drove away. In the rearview mirror she saw Katherine still standing beside the cabin, waving.

A mile or so passed without either of them saying anything.

'When are you heading back to Manchester?' Nessa asked in an attempt to break the silence.

'Gretta says I can stay with her in Tipperary as long as I like. Provided Dad isn't with me.' He laughed awkwardly.

'Oh?' Nessa glanced at him.

'Yeah. Aunt Gretta isn't like Katherine. She's not keen on Dad staying. I'm guessing he rubbed her the wrong way once or twice in the past. So Dad's going home next week. Katherine has offered to suffer him in the meantime.' He turned to Nessa. 'But I'm in no rush to get back. I need to sort out a place to live in Manchester first.'

'I thought you were living with your father?'

'Dad's couch-surfing again. He's currently staying with friends in Luton. I'm not sure how they'd feel about me showing up on their doorstep.'

She felt that she should offer him some advice, but what exactly she wasn't sure. It wasn't as if she were *in loco parentis*. What would Amy say? She listened for Amy's voice in her head, but this time, when she needed it, nothing came.

When they arrived at the Lockes' house, Loretta looked Luke up and down on the doorstep before standing aside to let him in. 'This is Luke Harkin,' Nessa said, 'the photographer I mentioned.' To her surprise, Loretta granted Luke a smile. He was looking particularly boyish that day, in a brightly checked yellow and blue shirt, and a wave of hair was falling onto his forehead. Loretta ushered him with some ceremony into the studio and then went to the kitchen to fetch him a coffee. Nessa watched Luke getting his bearings in the room, setting up the tripod. Over the years, Nessa had attempted to banish the memory of the small child in the ridiculously formal black jacket sobbing in his father's arms at Amy's funeral. It wasn't as if the boy hadn't impinged upon her consciousness from time to time; he had, mostly on family occasions – birthday parties or Christmas morning – when she would look at her daughter and think, *Amy should have had this too.* Now she looked at Luke standing beside the Chalk Sculpture, both of them tall and alabaster skinned and beautiful, and thought, *What a shot that would make.* She went over, placed a hand on the sculpture's rump. She always thought of it as a rump instead of buttocks, as if something bovine had infused the stone during its years in the cowshed. It invited hands, this sculpture, and she wondered if Locke had realised that he was doing that, if he'd deliberately sculpted something into it that made people need to reach out and touch. When she took her hand away, there was a film of white powder across her palm, and she wiped it, reverently, on her sweater. She looked down into a crevice between floorboards, and thought how there must be particles of stone down there that were last touched by the hands of Robert Locke. When the floorboards would be taken up and moved to the city, the next person to touch those particles might very well be her.

Loretta came back, set a small tray with a cup and saucer, sugar bowl, and milk jug on a table in the corner.

Luke glanced up from adjusting a lens and smiled. 'Thanks,' he said.

Loretta beckoned to Nessa. 'I need to speak with you in private,' she said.

'Is Eleanor all right?' Nessa said.

'She's fine.' Loretta went down the hall, Nessa following behind, but today, instead of turning left into the little back room, Loretta turned right.

The kitchen was small and sparse, almost as if it belonged to a different family. 'Excuse the mess,' Loretta said, even though the only things that could have been out of place were the saucepan and mug sitting on the otherwise empty draining board. 'Have a seat.' She gestured to a chair at the kitchen table. 'Mother thinks we're having a discussion about financial matters, which in a way we are.'

She went over to the dresser and, crouching, pulled a brown envelope from underneath. She brought it back to the table. 'We've got mail,' she said grimly. The envelope was fresh and crisp and bore no stamps.

'This was hand-delivered?' Nessa said.

Loretta nodded. 'Yes,' she said, 'overnight.' She grimaced. 'The thought of someone prowling around here while we slept makes me nervous. I haven't told Mother, it would upset her too much. She still hasn't got over the shock of that newspaper article.'

Nessa shook the contents out onto the table. There was a poor-quality copy of a photograph and one sheet of blue-lined writing paper. She glanced at the signature at the end and sighed. Melanie Doerr.

'It's trespassing, of course,' Loretta said. 'And in the middle of the night too. I trust this is the same woman who contacted you?'

Nessa nodded, suddenly queasy. Doerr had certainly ramped things up a notch – this was akin to stalking. The photograph accompanying the letter was one she hadn't seen before. It was of Robert Locke in middle age standing in front of a block of white stone, which rose several feet above him and was wide enough for the two young women pictured on either side to stand in front of it without fully concealing it.

'I know I told you I hadn't heard of her before,' Loretta said, 'but Daddy had so many callers it was impossible to remember them all. And I'm positive I never heard the name Doerr.'

The older of the women in the photograph was very tall. There were the unmistakable wide-set eyes. And what a magnificent head of hair Doerr had back then, dark and rippling past her shoulders. But could that girl beside her possibly be Loretta? She was no more than fifteen or sixteen, in a billowing tunic that she wore uncomfortably, her shoulders hunched, as if someone else had dressed her. Nessa turned the photo over, but there was nothing on the back, no date. She glanced at Loretta, who had taken to studying her fingernails and didn't look up.

Nessa took up the sheet of notepaper. 'Dear Lotty,' the letter began, 'I am sorry to hear that you have apparently forgotten me. I would rather that we were renewing our acquaintance in more agreeable circumstances, but such is life. How have you been? I was sorry when I discovered that you were still there. At Tragumna, I mean. At the house. All those afternoons when we plotted how you would run away! I can see now, in retrospect, that our plots lacked precision. But perhaps you are all the happier for staying put, who am I to say. How is Eleanor? I expect she is the same as ever, which is why I'm addressing this letter to you. I cannot stand by, Lotty, and watch her lay claim to what is mine, and you will know what I mean by that. For years I thought that it didn't matter to me, and now I realise that it does. And if I delay any longer, it will soon be too late to speak up at all, possession being nine parts etc. The lawyers will work their black arts, the world will move on, and I will become nothing more than an old woman shouting at clouds. Perhaps that is what I am already. One thing I have learned, Lotty – and I would have told you this back then, if I knew – is that a little shouting does no harm at all. I'm writing this as a plea to your conscience. I must trust that you will do the right thing.'

There was a neat signature and a phone number.

'*Lotty?*' Nessa said.

Loretta grimaced. 'He had students who visited and stayed from time to time. There were so many, coming and going always, it was impossible to keep track. I'd come down for breakfast and there would be someone in the kitchen who hadn't been there the night before.'

'Did you really plan to run away?' It was impossible to think of Loretta doing anything of the sort.

Loretta flushed. 'Of course not. But they were like that, the artists. Self-obsessed, always presuming that we were as interested in their imaginary problems as they were. There were days when my mother and I would go out into the garden, and we'd lock the door, and the side entrance gate, and just sit there, to get away from them.' Her voice trembled. 'It was why we never minded so much when people started visiting the Chalk Sculpture. We were used to it, people tramping all over our home. I remember a woman in the town asking one day how we could stand it. But it's how we'd always lived, when my father was alive.'

And the money, Nessa thought, thinking of the donation box. She cleared her throat. 'I expect Doerr saw the statement issued by the gallery,' she said. 'The publicist placed it with a couple of media outlets. So we find ourselves in a slightly awkward position. I mean, we've put out a statement saying the family had no record of her, and now Doerr produces this photo . . .'

Loretta tutted. 'You were the one who issued the statement,' she said. 'Not me. In retrospect, perhaps it was a bad call.'

'But, Loretta,' Nessa protested, 'I rang you. We had a conversation. I sent you a draft for approval.'

'Yes, you did, that's true,' Loretta admitted. 'You did send a draft. But you're the expert; I was depending on you for guidance.'

'I was depending on your memory, Loretta. I asked you if you knew her.'

'We're going back more than thirty years,' Loretta said. 'And I'm still quite sure I never heard of a student called Doerr. Am I expected to remember every visitor, every . . . *stray*, that came through the door? People visited Daddy all the time. We were public property. It's just the way it was.'

Nessa held up the photo. 'Do you recognise her?'

Loretta shrugged, shook her head. 'I was never good with faces.'

Nessa glanced again at the photo; she thought that she'd know those eyes anywhere. Neither woman said anything for a moment. Nessa sighed. 'We are where we are,' she said. 'I suggest that you don't ring her.'

'I hadn't the slightest intention.'

'If she comes round again at night, even if she comes round in daytime, you could call the police.'

Loretta shook her head. 'That's not my mother's way of doing things. We haven't had reason to have dealings with the police since we moved here; I don't want to start now.'

'Well then, if she turns up, at least don't answer the door. Don't speak to her if she rings.'

Loretta cleared her throat, and when she spoke again she didn't meet Nessa's eye. 'I hate the thought of it, and to think of someone gaining from this kind of behaviour makes me feel ill.'

Nessa was puzzled. 'She hasn't gained anything.'

'What I meant . . .' Loretta grappled for words. 'What I was going to say was, perhaps we could offer her something to go away?'

'You mean pay her off?'

'If you must put it that way, yes.' Loretta sounded defensive.

Nessa was taken aback. 'Why would you want to do that?'

'My mother is eighty-four years of age. She already took a bit of a turn after reading that clipping. She hasn't been herself since. It means so much to her – my father and his work being properly honoured at last. And to come so close, and now have some grubby swindler take all the good out of it . . .' She got up, took a tissue from a box on the dresser and dabbed at the corner of her eyes. 'It sickens me,' she said, sitting back down, 'to reward a grasping fraud, but I'm not sure how much more my mother's health can withstand.'

'It's unethical,' Nessa said. 'And say we were to pay her off: where would this money come from?'

'I thought the gallery might pay it.'

Nessa shook her head. 'The gallery isn't going to get involved in anything like that. Even the suggestion that someone else might have a legal interest in a piece of art would have the lawyers frothing at the mouth, even if there turns out to be no truth in it . . .'

'Of course there's no truth in it,' Loretta snapped. 'I'm trying to be pragmatic.'

Nessa raised her hands in defeat. 'I'm sorry, Loretta. The money's restricted by funding guidelines. There isn't any extra.'

She hadn't intended to speak harshly, but Loretta appeared chastened. Her eyes clouded over. 'My mother is my life,' she said quietly. 'All we have is each other. I promised her she would see Daddy's work properly lauded during her life-time, given that it didn't happen during his. And now time is running out.'

Before Nessa could reply, there was the sound of a door opening upstairs.

'She's out of bed,' Loretta said. 'I told her to stay in bed.' She stood up and her words came faster. 'You don't have to live here,' she said, 'miles from a police station or a doctor, no one to run to if someone breaks in except an arthritic sheep farmer five fields away. I don't want to pick up a newspaper and see that woman staring out at me, spouting her lies and her nonsense, and wonder what she's going to say next, wonder if she'll come prowling round in the dark. I want her to go away.' She wiped away a tear. She seemed embarrassed. 'If I had the money myself, I'd pay it, but I don't.'

'I'm sorry,' Nessa said softly, 'but it can't be done.' She preferred Loretta when she was stern and patronising; at least then she knew what she was dealing with.

'Anyway, I've met Melanie Doerr and I don't think it would work. It's not about money with her, it's a fixation.' *One that's getting worse*, she thought but didn't say.

'You've met her?' Loretta had started toward the door, but now she halted in the middle of the kitchen floor.

'Yes. She's been to the gallery. Twice. She came to my lecture on the Cambridgeshire pieces.'

117

'Dear God,' Loretta said. 'Imagine if my mother had been there. She'd never have recovered.' From overhead there came a creak of floorboards. 'She's going to do the stairs,' Loretta said. 'How many times do I have to tell her that she mustn't do the stairs? Not on her own.' She ran out of the kitchen, and a moment later there was a sharp exchange of voices, then silence.

Nessa remained sitting at the table. She wondered how Luke was getting on with his photo shoot, but she didn't want to look like she was checking up on him.

Overhead, she heard the slow progress of two sets of steps. Loretta had left the kitchen door ajar when she ran out, and after a few moments Nessa glimpsed her with Eleanor on her arm in the doorway of the poky room where they held their meetings.

Nessa waved. 'Hello, Eleanor.'

'Don't think I don't know about money,' Eleanor said. 'I managed the finances of this house for years. When Robert was wandering around like a vagrant, I was the one who talked to the milkman and the butcher, and kept bread on the table for my child.'

'Don't go upsetting yourself,' Loretta said. She put a hand on her mother's back as if to steer her into the room, but Eleanor didn't budge.

'I had a little job before I met Robert, you know. I used to be a wages clerk. I worked in a mill for two years and I paid the men their wages every Friday.' She turned to her daughter. 'I hope she hasn't been trying to bargain you down.'

'It's nothing like that,' Loretta said. 'We were just going through the paperwork.' She had her mother by the arm and was coaxing her along, settling her finally at the small circular table. Nessa left the kitchen and joined them. Eleanor placed her fingers at the edge of the table as if readying them above an imaginary typewriter. Then the expression on her face changed, not a darkening exactly, but a flicker of frailty. She sat straighter on her chair. 'Who have we here?' she said.

Nessa turned and saw Luke in the doorway, his camera bag over his shoulder.

'This is the photographer I told you about,' Loretta said. 'His name is Luke. He's very interested in Daddy's work.'

Luke stepped forward hesitantly and shook Eleanor's hand. 'The Chalk Sculpture is a magnificent piece of art,' he said. 'It's easy to see why the people around here are so fond of it.'

'The people around here had their own reasons for coming to see it,' Eleanor said. 'Reasons that had nothing to do with great art. The people around here are not very well up on great art.' She gave a little shrug. 'But who is to say, who is to say?' She smiled magnanimously. 'Perhaps they found some solace in their own fashion.'

Nessa distinctly remembered Eleanor referring to those who came to petition the Chalk Sculpture as fools. Not that that had ever stopped her accepting their donations.

'Thank you for permitting me to take the photographs,' Luke said. 'I can send you some prints, if you like?'

'Will there be a charge?' Loretta asked.

'No charge,' he said quickly. 'I'd be honoured to send them.' He turned to Eleanor. 'Actually, I was wondering if you'd allow me to take your photograph?'

'Later, perhaps,' Loretta interjected. 'We can do that later, Mother, if you're not too tired by then.'

'Of course,' Luke said. 'I'm sorry. I didn't think.'

'How could I be tired?' Eleanor said. 'I spend most of my day in bed. And it's not every day I have a young man come calling on me.'

Luke smiled, and Nessa thought he even blushed a little.

119

'Maybe you'd like to go outside and take some photos of the gardens while you're waiting?' Loretta said. 'There are some very fine views of the sea to be captured from here. There was a photographer who used to come when Daddy was alive and he liked to take pictures over by the fuchsia hedge, looking toward the dunes.' She led Luke through the kitchen to the back door. Nessa realised that she felt irrationally proud that Luke had made such a good impression.

Was she imagining it or did Loretta, when she returned from the garden, position her chair a little closer that afternoon? She had a book as usual, but it spent most of its time upside down in her lap. Nessa had a list of what she wanted to cover. The director had an idea – a bad one, in Nessa's opinion – that Eleanor might be persuaded to make a speech at the opening. But what Nessa most wanted to do was fetch the photo that had been delivered overnight and say, *Do you remember this photo, Eleanor? Did you perhaps even take it? And could you sense it even then – pulsing out of the stone – the Chalk Sculpture?*

'The rain is with us again today,' she said. A drizzle had started, and was spitting half-heartedly against the window-pane.

'Why must you always talk about rain?' Eleanor said. 'Does it never rain in the city?' Now that Luke had gone outside, she had reverted to her usual self. She made a clicking noise with her tongue, and almost without drawing breath said, 'I don't know if there's much point in us continuing, if people are going to make a mockery of my husband's life, and his work. Make a mockery of me.'

'Now, now, Mother,' Loretta said soothingly.

'It's not people,' Nessa said. 'It's just one person.'

Loretta threw Nessa a warning look. 'It's just a newspaper clipping,' she said.

Eleanor rested her weight, such as it was, on the table. 'It's not that woman's statue,' she said, 'it's mine.' She appeared frailer that afternoon, smaller. Nessa looked at the well-cut navy jacket, the high-necked blouse with its broderie anglaise, the turquoise scarf. If the superstructure of clothes was taken away, Eleanor just might disintegrate.

'Yes,' she said gently, 'I know it's yours.'

'Well, why did you let her say those things to the press? That woman invented a cock-and-bull story. Am I expected to tolerate that?'

'You mustn't pay her any heed,' Nessa said. 'She's an unfortunate distraction from our work, but that's all she is.' She was no longer entirely sure that this was true, but there was no point in upsetting Eleanor.

'Where I come from,' Eleanor said, 'she'd be locked up.'

Nessa rummaged in her briefcase for her Dictaphone. 'I thought we could go back over some of our Cambridgeshire notes,' she said. Those years in Cambridgeshire were Eleanor's comfort blanket; she never tired of talking about them. She would let Eleanor talk a while about Cambridgeshire and then she would see if she could put some questions to her on the subject of the essay she was hoping to finish. She planned to ask whether Locke had been in the habit of seeking his wife's opinion on his works in progress. As she switched on the machine, Eleanor said sullenly, 'It's the only thing he did of me.'

In the forty-odd years that Robert Locke had been a sculptor, the Chalk Sculpture was the only piece he'd done of his wife. And if there was only this one piece of Eleanor, there was none for Loretta. Had there been nothing else in the marriage in the years before or afterwards that Locke had considered worthy of marking? Nothing in fatherhood that had struck him as a suitable subject of his art? Even Philip had designed her a kitchen extension, Nessa thought. 'The Chalk Sculpture is yours,' she said. 'Robert made it for you, and it's yours.'

'You'd better make sure they all know it, young lady. And why are you always asking me about Cambridgeshire? I'm tired of talking about it.'

She turned to the window overlooking the back garden, where Luke was on his haunches photographing the wild rhubarb plants. 'It's nice to have youth around this place,' she said.

Some twenty minutes later, Luke came back in holding a thick, furred stalk that wouldn't have been out of place in the fairy tales Nessa used to read Jennifer when she was small. 'Wild rhubarb,' Loretta said, getting up. 'They've colonised the place. I remember my father used take a scythe to them every spring. I keep meaning to cut them back.'

Eleanor struggled up from her chair. 'You may take my photograph now,' she said to Luke. 'Where would you like me to stand?'

Luke thrust the plant cutting at Nessa. 'Would you mind holding this?' he said. He took Eleanor by the elbow and guided her outside to the hall. Nessa held the plant stalks out from her body as if they were noxious. The broad leaves were heavy with rain and drops were falling onto the carpet.

'They'll ruin your clothes,' Loretta said. 'The green will stain. You should wrap them in plastic. You'll find some bags on a hook by the back door. I need to keep an eye on my mother.' She turned and went out to the hall.

Nessa went through the kitchen, into an old-fashioned scullery. It was dusty, crammed with boxes of nails and rusty hinges and what looked like twenty years' worth of empty jam jars. As she took a plastic bag from a cache by the door, something on a shelf caught her eye. It was an old margarine tub, containing what looked like pieces of discoloured silver, tiny pieces the size of snail shells. She put the plant stalks on top of a clothes dryer and, careful not to knock anything over, lifted down the tub. The pieces, all animals, reminded her of a series Locke did in marble in larger format in the mid-seventies, though she'd never heard of him experimenting with metalwork. Mixed in with her excitement was a twinge of irritation. Why had Loretta not shown her these earlier? She took out a miniature bird in tarnished antique silver. It was very like a marble one carved by Locke, only smaller, its neck tilted skyward, beak open, roots for feet. When she closed her hand around it, it fit snugly inside her fist.

Loretta put her head around the door. Nessa jumped.

'I'll take those,' Loretta said, nodding at the tub and frowning.

'I'd like to take a look at them, if that's all right.'

'No,' Loretta said, shaking her head. She took the tub from Nessa. 'They're not Daddy's. That's family silver, I took it out for cleaning.' She paused. 'Why don't you go back out to our photographer friend? I think he's ready to leave.'

Cheeks burning, Nessa left the scullery. Loretta remained behind and there came the sound of cupboards opening and closing, the tub presumably being moved to a place of safety.

In the studio, Eleanor was sitting on a chair, watching Luke, with his back to her, unscrew the lens and stow away the tripod. All the fire of earlier had gone out of her and now she looked every bit of her eighty-four years. She tutted in exasperation. 'Where has that girl got to? Loretta!'

Loretta came hurrying down the hall. 'Mother,' she said, 'I think it's time for your nap.' Turning to Luke she handed him a plastic bag – the wild rhubarb stalks. 'Don't forget these,' she said. It was then that Nessa realised she still had the tiny silver bird curled tightly inside her fist, but Loretta was already shepherding her toward the door.

Nessa drove down the lane, Luke quiet in the passenger seat beside her. The tiny silver bird she'd surreptitiously dropped into the ashtray in the dashboard. She'd been unable to think of a good way to hand it back to Loretta on the doorstep; Nessa wouldn't put it past Loretta to accuse her of attempting to steal it. She would have to find a way of returning it, quietly, the next time she called to the house.

After they'd reached the main road, Luke said, 'I know this will probably be difficult for you, but I'd like to ask you about the weekend my mother died.'

'Sure,' she said. 'Go ahead. Anything at all.' She gripped the wheel tighter, steeled herself.

'That weekend . . .' He cleared his throat. 'How did it all . . . I mean . . . how did it play out?'

Nessa hesitated. 'Has your father told you much about it?'

'A little. But I could never get him to discuss it properly. He always got so cut up about it that I stopped asking. He did say that my mother had lost the plot.'

Nessa took a deep breath. 'Your mother wasn't well,' she said. 'That's the first thing to remember.'

Luke nodded.

'We were at a christening for a friend's baby,' she continued. 'It was a weekend away; a mini-break we used to call it then.' She smiled wanly. 'I didn't know that Amy was going to be there. I didn't even know she was back in Ireland.' She glanced at Luke, worried that he might judge her. 'We'd lost touch.'

'I understand,' he said.

She felt the familiar guilt returning, but hurried on. 'It turned out that your mother had been staying at home in

Tipperary, at the farm, for some weeks. You were living with your Granny Harkin by then.'

'Yes. Dad told me about that.'

'It was all wrong from the beginning, that weekend. When your mother arrived, we saw that she'd shorn her hair right off. She was still beautiful, of course. Amy was always beautiful. But she'd gotten so thin. On the Friday evening, we went to an exhibition of watercolours by a woman who Lizzy – the baby's mother – knew from college. Amy became difficult. A bit obnoxious, if I'm honest. She criticised the paintings, all of them, said the work was cowardly, derivative. Lizzy got mad on her friend's behalf, told Amy not to bother coming to the ceremony. I took your mother off to calm down. She kept saying she was going to pack and go home, and I kept having to talk her out of it. She began to get paranoid, unreasonable, started asking me to promise things I couldn't possibly agree to.'

Nessa's hands were shaking on the wheel. She would have liked to pull over, except she knew she wouldn't be able to look at Luke while saying all this. At least while she was driving she had an excuse to keep her eyes fixed on the road.

'I'm sorry to put you through this,' he said. 'But I need to know.'

'Of course,' she said. 'It's why you've come here.'

'What kind of things was she asking?'

Nessa swallowed. It occurred to her that she'd gone further than she'd intended. 'All kinds of things,' she said. 'She wasn't making any sense. The next morning . . . Well, the next morning, I found her in the bathroom.'

Luke was silent for a moment. Then he said, 'I went to see the Corrigan family solicitor with Aunt Gretta last week. He let me see the note they found that morning among my mother's things. He'd had it on file since the inquest.' He paused. 'Have you seen it?'

'No, but I heard it read out at the coroner's court. I remember how it said her friends had let her down. Lizzy was inconsolable. On account of her and Amy having had that row the evening before. No matter what anyone said, Lizzy couldn't be persuaded that it wasn't her fault.'

'I hope you don't feel like that,' he said.

'No,' she said sharply. 'Why should I?'

'I don't like to think of you blaming yourself, that's all. On account of you being the last person to see her. You did what you could, I'm sure.'

Instinctively, her foot exerted a fraction more pressure on the accelerator. Ditches and trees and telegraph poles blurred by. 'Sometimes I think I could have done more,' she said.

'No,' he said. 'You mustn't think that. I can tell that you're a good person. I'm glad you were with my mother that weekend. It's a comfort to me. To my dad too, I expect.'

At Lough Hyne, she parked outside the Ferriters' cabin. 'Thank you for taking me to see the Chalk Sculpture,' Luke said. 'I got some really good shots. I'll send them to you.' He was hooking his camera over his shoulder, preparing to get out of the car.

Katherine came down the steps of the cabin. 'I have dinner ready, Nessa,' she said. 'Maybe you'd like to stay and eat with us?'

Nessa could see the outline of Stuart Harkin, standing by the kitchen window, looking out. He raised a hand in greeting. 'Thanks,' she said quickly, 'I wish I could, but we're having dinner with one of Philip's clients.' *Coward*, she heard Amy's voice in her head. *Can't face meeting lover boy?*

Nessa had never liked the idea of the dead being privy to the minds of the living – it was unlikely to do her any favours. *Actually, Amy*, she thought, *we really are having dinner with a client*. It happened to be true, but she knew she would have lied if she had to.

16

Nessa first had sex with Stuart Harkin on an April night some two decades previously in a shed in the yard behind a warren of flats in Shepherd's Bush. To make room for dancing, the furniture from the ground floor flats had been dragged into the yard. It was Nessa's second year at college and she and Amy were no longer sharing with Katherine, who had moved into nurses' quarters near the hospital.

Amy had met Stuart Harkin during her first year at St Martins and it was Nessa who'd introduced them. Nessa had invited Stuart back to the flat one afternoon and was filling the kettle to make tea when Amy came home. It was raining, and Amy's hair had sprung into waves the way it always did when it got wet. Her cheeks were flushed pink after the walk from the bus stop and drops of rain lay on her cheeks and eyelashes. That term, she'd been engaged on a project of her own devising which involved travelling the city with a bag of wooden picture frames, old-fashioned frames that she'd sourced in charity shops with the glass removed. She would glue or nail these frames around graffiti at bus shelters, or on hoardings where lichen had colonised the remnants of a poster. Beside each one she stuck a red dot and a laminated card with a title. That afternoon, she'd thrown a bundle of frames onto the living room floor, pulled off her coat and scarf and tossed them on the sofa beside Stuart. She stood in front of him, shaking out her magnificent wet hair the way a dog might shake itself after coming out of the sea. As Nessa set a tea pot and three cups on the flat's Formica table, she'd understood, with a twinge of loss, that Stuart Harkin was now Amy's.

Amy had been at the party in Shepherd's Bush also that April night, but there'd been a fight quite early on between her and Stuart, a jealous row perhaps: Nessa had heard Amy shouting obscenities at another girl as she left. Possibly she'd expected Nessa to leave with her, but Nessa stayed. She hadn't seen Stuart in a while; he'd taken to skipping college, and now that Amy stayed most nights at his place, he rarely had reason to call at the bedsit.

Years later a therapist would suggest to Nessa that what began that night in the tenement yard might have had something to do with the fact that she no longer spent any meaningful time with Amy, or Stuart either; that she was attempting, subconsciously, to insert herself back into their lives.

He'd brought a bottle of whisky and they passed it back and forth between them as they sat outside on the grass. A girl sauntered over. She took the bottle from Nessa, put it to her lips and drank. Nessa saw how the girl was eyeing Stuart, as if he was there for the taking, as if her own presence was of no consequence. Nessa leaned a little closer into him, mostly for the girl's benefit, but he put his mouth on hers and began to kiss her. The girl went back indoors.

There was a dilapidated shed in the corner of the yard and inside on the floor was an old mattress. As she lifted her dress over her head, Stuart paused in his own undressing to stare at her, and she could tell he liked what he saw. Kneeling beside her, he placed his hands flat on either side of her head, holding her in a gentle vice, while he kissed her eyelids, nose, chin.

The mattress was narrow, more suited to a camper bunk than a bed, and she was pressed tight against the wall, the timber chafing her skin. As he pushed into her, her hip connected with a joist and, with every thrust, ground repeatedly against it, so that the next day she would be left with a patch of red, grazed skin. After he collapsed onto her, they lay for a while, hearts pounding. For a few minutes neither of them spoke. The particulars of her surroundings, which had momentarily retreated, began to come slowly back into focus, the way images gradually develop on a Polaroid. The tangle of wires dangling from the ceiling overhead; a mildewed shirt on a nail; the scatter of empty beer cans.

'I need to get out of here,' she said. 'I need to get dressed.'

'Not in that order,' he said, rolling off her. He handed her her bra, watched while she fastened it. She found her knickers and pulled them on.

'They'll wonder where we are,' she said.

He shrugged. 'I doubt it. Everybody's too drunk for wondering. If they think about us at all, they'll presume I behaved badly and you decided you'd had enough of me and went home.'

In the weeks that followed, they began a haphazard affair. When Nessa went home that summer, she swore to herself that it was over, but a week into the new term in September she slept with Stuart again.

A Monday in mid-October, Amy approached her in the corridor at college. They were seeing less of each other this year; Amy had moved in with Stuart, and Nessa was sharing a house with two textile students. 'I need to talk to you,' Amy said. Nessa felt her stomach lurch. Her first impulse was to say no, but she'd never been good at saying no to Amy. 'Will we go to the canteen?' she suggested nervously. If Amy was planning on bawling her out of it, possibly the presence of onlookers might inhibit her anger. Or possibly not. Amy shook her head. 'Not here,' she said. She suggested a café a couple of streets away. On the way there, she was subdued, and Nessa found herself compensating with anxious chatter. They took a table in the corner of the café. There was only one other customer, a young woman with a buggy.

Nessa ordered a toasted sandwich, but Amy said she wasn't hungry, and wanted only a coffee. When the waiter had gone back to the kitchen, Amy said, 'I'm pregnant.'

Nessa stared at her.

'Yes,' Amy said, 'it happened over the summer. I haven't told Stuart yet.'

Slowly, Nessa processed the news. She opened her mouth, closed it again. She knew from the expression on Amy's face that congratulations weren't appropriate.

'What am I going to do?' Amy said.

Nessa didn't look at her. She looked away, across the café, to where the baby in the buggy was drooling spit onto the floor.

'What do you want to do?' she said, still not looking at her friend.

'I don't know,' Amy said. 'I don't know if I should have a baby with Stuart. It wasn't exactly part of the plan, you know?' She paused. 'Do you think he'd make a good father?'

The mother at the table in the corner was looking in their direction, as if she'd intuited the urgency of their conversation. She didn't bother to look away when Nessa caught her staring. She had what Nessa in later years would come to recognise as that 'shoot me now' look so often worn by new mothers. The baby started to fret and the woman took it out of the buggy, bounced it up and down on her knee, in a way that wasn't particularly gentle, saying, 'Now, now, now, now, now.' Stuart Harkin would make an extremely bad father, Nessa thought, if his behaviour as a boyfriend was anything to go by.

'He's very young, isn't he?' Nessa said. 'You both are.'

'So you think I should get rid of it?'

'No,' Nessa said, alarmed. 'I mean, I don't know.' She was sideswiped by the enormity of the question. People didn't talk about this back home. It felt like a question for a much older person, a grown-up, someone who was not sleeping with Stuart Harkin.

A waiter set a salad down in front of the woman in the corner. She took up her fork, the baby clamped to her chest with one hand, the other struggling to bring food to her mouth, dropping bits of lettuce on the child's head while it wriggled.

'Do you think I'd make a good mother?' Amy asked.

'You'd make a great mother.'

'How do you know?' Amy's coffee had arrived and sat untouched in front of her.

'I just know,' Nessa said. 'Why wouldn't you be a good mother?'

Amy sighed. 'I don't know,' she said. 'How does anybody know?'

In the corner, the woman with the baby put her fork down and pushed her plate across the table. She put the baby into its buggy, strapped it in. It stopped crying, and she just sat there, staring at the far wall of the café, which Nessa guessed might have been her way of giving them some privacy.

Nessa reached out and squeezed her friend's hand. She still couldn't bring herself to look at her.

'I love Stuart,' Amy said. 'And he loves me. So I suppose there's no reason why we shouldn't give it a shot.'

Nessa's throat felt dry. She swallowed a couple of times before she answered. 'It'll be fine,' she said.

The woman with the baby put some money on the table. She stood up and, giving a curt nod in their direction, wheeled the buggy out the door.

At the insistence of Amy's mother, Amy and Stuart married in a small, private ceremony just before Christmas.

17

After dropping Luke off at the Ferriters' cabin, Nessa drove home to Sunday's Well. She showered and changed and went with Philip to a dinner party hosted by a banking lawyer called Dennis Fogarty and his wife, Olga. The Fogartys lived in Elgin Woods, a gated development of detached five-bedroom houses on the city side of Blackrock. The 'wood' comprised four oak trees that had grown for several hundred years in the grounds of an adjoining manor house recently converted into apartments. There were twenty houses in Elgin Woods, each with large gardens in the back and smaller gardens with circular driveways out front. They all had the same miscellany of shrubbery, tended to, Nessa suspected, by the same gardener. All the topiary was shorn that little bit too tight, and the roots of all the black bamboos were causing tiny undulations in the otherwise neat lawns.

Olga was from Carlow, her father a beef farmer, her mother a primary school teacher who had encountered the name Olga in a romance novel. Olga talked a good deal, almost exclusively about books. She'd had some short stories published and occasionally wrote reviews for newspapers. That night in the Fogartys' dining room, Nessa was seated beside her. There were three Louis le Brocquy prints and an original Gottfried Helnwein on the dining room walls. The Fogartys had caterers looking after everything, so there was no respite, no lull when Olga might otherwise have got up to check on vegetables. Nessa listened politely, a smile fixed to her face. Halfway through the starter, Nessa thought that she'd rather chew off both her own arms than listen to Olga for another minute. The particular book she was talking about that night involved a man attempting to generate a new life-form in the hull of a beached schooner in Patagonia. Olga had been speaking about it for a while and all that had happened, as far as Nessa could make out, was that the man had broken a cup. It was all about the very particular way in which he'd broken it – Olga was careful to explain this – and how the broken cup was a metaphor for a fractured world.

After a while Nessa allowed her gaze to wander and caught a man directly across the table staring. Immediately he looked away. He wasn't by any stretch of the imagination an attractive man, but all the same Nessa felt flattered. She turned her attention back to Olga, who'd moved on from the cup to some new occurrence. When a moment later she glanced back at the man, he was staring again, this time in a more intense manner that made her uncomfortable. 'Excuse me,' she said, interrupting Olga mid-sentence, 'I'll be right back.'

She wove through the bustle of catering staff in the Fogartys' kitchen and let herself out into their garden. In a different age, the Fogartys' butler might have come after her and escorted her back inside, or perhaps fetched a warm wrap. But the caterers couldn't have cared less, and she pulled the door shut, walked a little distance down the path. The city glittered like a circuit board, the grids and boxes of lights, the rows of streetlamps. How magnificent, by night and from a distance, the homes of Cork. She stood there, breathing deeply, and tried not to think of anything at all.

Behind her, she heard the kitchen door opening. When she turned, she saw the man from across the table, and she realised she wasn't surprised. He was approaching through the grass, in long strides. When he was within a few feet of her, he stopped. She wondered if he'd said something very quietly and she hadn't heard. He had his hands in his pockets, and was rocking back and forth on the heels of his shoes.

She said, 'It's a nice house, isn't it?'

'Only the best for Dennis and Olga.'

He was very drunk, she realised. He must have been getting quietly and inconspicuously drunk indoors, and now the cold air had hit him.

'If my wife could see me now,' he said, 'out here with you.' He took a step closer. 'What would your husband make of it, I wonder?'

'He'd make nothing whatsoever of it,' she said lightly. What was it about men, that they always presumed a woman was about to jump on them?

'Trust each other, do you?'

'As a matter of fact, yes.'

He laughed. 'Oh dear,' he said. 'Oh dear.' He shook his head. 'You don't know who I am, do you?' He held out a hand. 'Richard Wilson.'

It took a second to register. Richard Wilson. Cora's husband. She had never seen him before. He wasn't one of the small number of fathers who graced the school gates. She didn't take his hand and after a moment he withdrew it. 'He's some man, your husband,' he said. 'He fucks my wife; he, presumably, fucks his own wife. Maybe he's got a harem going up there in Sunday's Well?' The Wilsons lived in Hollyhill, though not in one of the estates. Nessa went to step around him to go back to the house, but he caught her by the elbow.

'Let me go,' she said. She glanced up at the Fogartys' kitchen and was relieved to see the outlines of the catering staff. She could shout, if it came to that.

He brought his face close to hers. 'What do you think?' he said. 'Maybe you and I should give it a go. That'd show them.'

She shrugged off his hand and walked to the house, trying not to show how panicked she was. The caterers paid her no notice; they were in the middle of a different sort of crisis – a sinkhole of soufflé sat on the countertop. In the dining room, Philip was in conversation with a woman she knew to be a project engineer. Nessa went up, tapped him on the shoulder. 'A word,' she said.

They went down the hall and outside to the front steps. 'Did you even notice I was missing?' she said, when she'd pulled the door shut behind them.

'I presumed you'd gone to the bathroom.'

'I went outside, because I was stuck with Olga, who has the social skills of a small slug.'

'I thought you liked Olga.'

'I hate Olga. I can't stand her. Olga and her books. Do you know who I met just now?'

He shook his head.

'Take a guess.'

He looked away.

'Richard Wilson,' she said. 'He followed me out to the garden. I thought he was going to make a pass at me.'

'But he didn't.'

'He suggested he and I should get together.'

'He's drunk.'

'I was frightened, Philip. And I should not have to put up with being at the same party as Richard Wilson. I have been humiliated enough.'

'I don't see where the humiliation is.' An edge had entered his voice. 'Richard was the junior barrister on a big case that just concluded. That's why he's here. Dennis sends a bit of work his way. So what? It's not up to us to tell Dennis and Olga who they can have to their home. And he's here on his own. It's not like . . .' He trailed off.

'Go on,' she said. 'Say it.'

When he looked at the ground, she said, 'It's not like *Cora's* here. Is that what you were going to say? What if she *had* come? What a sideshow that would've been. Your wife and your mistress at the same dinner table. They could've sold tickets.'

'Can you stop shouting, please?' he said.

She wasn't aware that she'd become loud. She looked to see if there was anyone who might have heard, but there wasn't a soul out in Elgin Woods, apart from Richard Wilson, who might still be in the garden. The curtains of the house across the way remained closed. If this were happening at their house in Sunday's Well, Mrs Moriarty would be at her window by now. 'But what if Cora had come?' she repeated. 'You must have known they'd be invited, and you didn't warn me. You were prepared to let me be shamed.'

'Stop it, Nessa,' he said. He ran a hand through his hair, and swore. She had a flashback to a night outside Supermacs in Eyre Square when they were in their twenties, screaming at one another, and Philip making the exact same facial expression he was making now. They were back in that place again, but this time without the optimism of youth to carry them forward. 'I knew Cora wasn't going to turn up,' he said. 'I wouldn't have done that to you.'

'How did you know?'

He looked away. 'Let's not do this here,' he said, 'let's not spoil the night for Dennis. Come back in and have dessert.'

'You're still in contact with her, aren't you?'

'She texted to ask if I thought she should come. I texted her back to say that I thought it might be better if she didn't. That was all.'

'You promised me,' Nessa said. 'You promised you'd have nothing more to do with her.'

'I told her to stay away. That's hardly having something to do with her.'

At some point she'd begun to cry. She wiped a finger underneath her eyes, hoping to stop her mascara from running. 'She still does your bidding,' she sobbed. 'Cooperative Cora.'

'I really don't want to have to leave,' he said. 'I don't want to upset the Fogartys.'

'God forbid. Whatever else happens, let's keep the Fogartys happy.'

He reached out and pulled her close, held her so tightly that it felt more like restraint than love. 'You're here,' he said, 'Cora isn't. Isn't that enough?'

She allowed herself to relax into his chest. She thought that she should stop speaking about Cora. 'Richard Wilson hates you,' she said.

'I wasn't expecting him to give me a medal.'

'You need to keep an eye on him,' she said. 'He's a nasty human. He'll sell you down the river first chance he gets.'

'Richard Wilson couldn't sell water in the desert. Dennis only briefs him on account of Cora and Olga being cousins.'

Cora and Olga were related? That was news to her. And still Cora had had to stay home. A game had been played tonight, the rules of which were hazy to her, but it seemed that she had won and Cora had lost.

Philip stroked her hair as she rested her head against his shoulder. 'Come back inside,' he said.

'You go on,' she said, 'and I'll follow.'

After he'd gone in, she sat awhile on the steps. If anyone asked what she was doing, she would say that she was looking at the stars. But there were no stars, not with all the lights, or the light pollution, as Jennifer might say.

Was she this angry about everything when she was her daughter's age? She remembered her own teenage anger as being more domestic in nature, more circumscribed.

She wondered if Richard Wilson had gone back to sit at the table, if he was right now staring across at her empty chair. Her life – their life – had been recalibrated in the aftermath of Philip's affair; deals had been struck, and tonight was one of them. Dennis, Richard, Philip. Rock Paper Scissors. Cora Wilson had been removed from the board, but her absence impacted the relationship of all the pieces remaining. It occurred to her then that perhaps Olga, being Cora's cousin, had known before she did about the affair. Perhaps that was why she'd always spoken to her so urgently about books, to guard against accidentally speaking about anything else.

18

On Thursday morning, Nessa was at her desk in the gallery, still fragile after the dinner party the night before, when the phone rang. 'There's a Stuart Harkin on the line for you,' the reception-ist said. With the phone in her hand, Nessa swivelled her chair over to the window. The flat roof of an adjoining building was crusted with rubbish – empty crisp bags, soggy flyers, twigs so pale in colour they mightn't have been twigs at all. She watched the ragged fluttering of a plastic bag that had snagged on a nail. 'Do you want to take the call or not?' the receptionist said.

'Okay.' She pressed the flashing light on the desk set but didn't say anything for a moment.

'Hello?' Stuart said. 'Nessa?'

'Oh, hi, Stuart,' she said. 'How are you?'

'I'm fine,' he said. 'I'm still at Katherine's place. You might have heard.'

'Luke mentioned something about it.'

'Yeah. Well, you'll know the story then. But the good news is that Aunt Gretta and Luke are getting on like a house on fire. She's rounded up some cousins for him to meet.'

He didn't sound particularly happy.

'I think that's sweet,' she said. 'I think Amy would like him to meet his cousins.'

'The cousins aren't the problem. It's Gretta who's causing me grief.'

'Maybe she just doesn't have the extra room.'

'It's not that. I don't care about her not letting me stay, though it's typical bloody Gretta. But she's gone and given

Luke a box of Amy's things. At first I thought, "Fine," you know, "probably some photos, old Valentine cards, that sort of thing".' He whistled. 'You wouldn't believe the shit that's in that box. Stuff I didn't know Amy had kept. Stuff I didn't even know she *had*. Pretty much any letter she ever got from anybody. She must have taken them all home to Tipperary before . . . well, before.'

She sensed that he was leading up to something, and so she said nothing.

'I'm not sure I should even be mentioning this,' he said, 'but there are letters in that box that you wrote her.'

'Oh.'

'Yes, and I'll put it this way. You don't exactly come out of them sounding like Mother Teresa.'

'Darn,' she said. 'And you always thought I was Mother Teresa before.'

His laugh broke the tension. 'Fair enough,' he said, 'but you're pretty critical of Katherine in some of them. And you don't pull any punches about Amy's family either.'

It was a fact that she'd sometimes bitched about Katherine to Amy. In the way that some triangular friendships are not equilateral, but isosceles, so it had been with them. She forced herself to ask the question: 'Are they very bad?'

'Bad enough.'

'We were practically children back then,' she said. 'We'd no idea what we were doing. Or saying.'

'You were quite clear about what you were saying. Anyhow, I've told Luke not to show them to Katherine.'

It hadn't even occurred to her that Luke might consider doing that. Surely he would know better? She set the receiver down on a pile of papers on her desk. *Damn you, Gretta*, she thought. And had Gretta read those letters before handing them over? Of course she had. If the situation were reversed, Nessa would have read them, though she liked to think that she might have done so with an eye to Luke's best interests. She heard Stuart's voice leaking out onto the desk. 'Hello,' he was saying. 'Hello? You still there, Ness?'

She picked up the phone again. 'Sorry,' she said. 'Don't know what happened there.'

'I thought I should tell you,' he said, 'in case Katherine was in touch. Forewarned being forearmed and all that.'

'Thanks.'

'I hope I haven't worried you.'

'No, not at all.'

'I'm angry at Gretta, as you can imagine. Lobbing emotional grenades at the boy like that. There was other stuff as well that he could have done without reading. But I don't want to put a spanner in the works. She's family, at the end of the day.'

Nessa was about to say that Gretta was trouble, but she reminded herself that she shouldn't get involved. 'When are you leaving?' she asked.

'Luke's going to stay on in Tipperary for a couple of weeks. I'm heading back next Thursday, presuming Katherine can suffer me until then.'

'I hope you didn't write any nasty letters about her. You might be out on your ear.'

'I think I'm in the clear,' he said, 'although it's not as if I was high in Katherine's estimation to start with, so it would hardly make much difference.' He paused. 'She's very forgiving, Katherine.'

They were both silent for a moment.

'Safe travels,' she said eventually.

'We must have that coffee before I go back,' he said, 'it's a shame to be over here and hardly speak with you. Are you around on Tuesday? William could drop me in the city on his way to the train station.'

She hesitated. 'Sure,' she said finally. 'Where will we go?'

'You choose,' he said. 'Surprise me.'

19

Ten years after graduating college, Nessa had received an email about a party in London billed as a reunion of 'All the Old Gang'. Her initial reaction was that she wouldn't go. She was a stay-at-home mom to six-year-old Jennifer by then, and didn't want to hear how everyone else was curating at the Guggenheim. But then, the woman organising the reunion seemed to be sending emails in between her shifts at Starbucks. 'We'll go!' Philip had said, all enthusiasm. 'We'll get a babysitter, make a weekend of it. I'll book us a decent hotel. I might give a couple of the lads a shout while I'm there. There's a building in Chelsea I wouldn't mind taking a look at.'

On the morning of the reunion, Philip came out of Jennifer's bedroom waving a thermometer. 'She has a fever,' he said. He handed Nessa the thermometer.

She checked the reading and frowned. 'Typical,' she said, 'but it's not much of a fever, is it? Give her a spoon of Calpol. I'll pick up another bottle at the pharmacy before we go. I don't want it to run out while the babysitter's here.'

'We can't ask the babysitter to administer meds. It's too much of a responsibility.'

'It's Calpol, Philip. It's not like we're asking her to perform a tracheotomy.'

'I don't think we should go when Jennifer's sick. I don't think it's right to leave her.'

'What are you saying, Philip? That we should stay at home? She has a cold.'

'I'll stay,' he said. 'You go. I don't want you to miss it.'

And now she knew what was happening. 'Has your site meeting fallen through?' she said.

'I can't believe this,' he said. 'I'm worried about our daughter. Who is sick.' He grabbed back the thermometer, waved it in her face.

'Yes or no,' she said. 'Has your London deal fallen through?'

He didn't meet her eye. 'There was never any deal. It was something I thought I might fit in while we were over there. As it happens, there was a problem with the legal title.'

'I knew it,' she said. 'You don't want to go, and you're using Jennifer to try and get out of it.'

'Listen to yourself,' he said. 'Or maybe just go in there' – he pointed to their daughter's bedroom – 'and put your hand on her forehead.'

'Do not tell me how to look after my child,' she said. 'I look after our child seven days a week, while you are out meeting people.'

'It's called work.'

'And what I do here isn't work?'

'I didn't say that.'

'You didn't have to. I haven't had a holiday in ages, Philip, and now you want to cancel because your business plans have fallen through and suddenly it isn't worth your while any-more. It's only a weekend with your wife now.'

'I'm going to stay home with Jennifer,' he said. 'Go, or don't go. Up to you.'

She had a glass of wine before she boarded the plane, and another after she checked into the hotel. The two classmates she'd kept in contact with texted at the last minute to say they had to cancel. 'The old gang' turned out to be quite small in number; most of them she didn't recognise. She didn't think it was that they'd changed; she wondered if she'd ever known these people in the first place. A woman drunkenly called to her in the toilet. 'I know you,' she said. 'You're the Irish girl. Amy, isn't it?'

'That's right,' Nessa said, and left without drying her hands.

And then she was at the bar drinking peach schnapps and Stuart Harkin was at her elbow. 'What's your poison?' he said, nodding to her glass.

'I'm not staying,' she said, 'I'm going after this one. I don't know anybody here. I should have stayed at home.'

He laughed. 'Charming as ever,' he said. 'May I remind you that you know me? Have another drink. It might get better.'

'All right,' she said. 'But just the one.'

They went to sit at a table in the lobby, where it was quiet and they could talk. 'It was brave of you to come,' she said. 'I suppose everyone has been asking about her.'

He shrugged. 'I'm used to it. It's a long time ago now.'

'Yes,' she said. 'Too long. I don't know anyone anymore. I don't know why I came.'

'Well, I'm glad you came,' he said. He touched her lightly on the arm.

'I should go now,' she said. 'I should go back to my hotel.'

'Where are you staying?'

She told him. He raised an eyebrow. 'Nice,' he said.

'It's fine,' she said, embarrassed. 'A hotel is a hotel, isn't it?'

He looked amused. 'I wouldn't know,' he said.

She stood up to go, but he placed a hand on her arm. 'Don't leave right away,' he said. 'Wait until I take some photos of this lot, I promised I would. And then I'll go too.'

It was after midnight when he walked her back to her hotel. He pulled her into a doorway to kiss her. When she asked him to come up, he appeared shy. 'I thought you might have consigned me to history,' he said. Afterwards, she'd wonder if she imagined the shyness, in an attempt to persuade herself that something out of the ordinary was happening. Stuart Harkin wasn't known for his diffidence.

Up in the room, she had walked out onto the balcony. The London Eye, newly built and still a novelty, was set against the city skyline like a still from a film. Stuart came up behind her, pressed himself against her. She pointed to a cathedral lit up in the distance. 'What's that?' she said. 'Is it Westminster, or is Westminster the other direction?' She was conscious that she was babbling. She was wearing a pale blue dress that zipped up the back and he undid it and slipped it down over her shoulders. When it caught on her hips, she tugged it until it fell to the floor. She stepped out of it and kept her back to him as he unhooked her bra. He put his arms around her from behind and cupped her breasts. He slid his hands down to her hips and turned her round to face him and she shivered at the coarse rub of his sweater against her skin. 'Let me look at you,' he said, steering her over to an armchair. She obliged, reclining her head against the chair, stretching out her legs. He led her over to the bed, scattered with three or four cushions, and began to take off his clothes.

When an older Nessa would discover in years to come that her husband had slept with Cora Wilson, she would force herself to contemplate the possibility of sex in midlife with men other than her husband. She wouldn't contemplate men known to her, but generic figures, the men of stock photos, or from the online catalogues of department stores. These men, as she imagined them, would have the advantage of not being partial to Cora Wilsons, but the disadvantage or not knowing how she liked sex. Also, they wouldn't have had the opportunity to adjust over time to the slow gradual ruin of her body. In these imaginings, sometimes exciting but mostly worrying, it would be her thighs that concerned her most, the way they'd lost structure sometime in her late thirties, followed by her décolletage, which sun damage had wrinkled and made ruddy, like the landscape of a wind-ridged desert. But in that turn-of-the-millennium London hotel room, she was still a moderately young woman and had not yet appropriated these concerns as she straddled Stuart Harkin, watching his face as she moved on top of him. They came quickly, then did it again half an hour later, more slowly this time.

The ensuite had a large bath tub. She ran the hot water, poured in two little bottles of scented body wash. Stuart sat on the carpet outside the open bathroom door, watching.

'Do you like what you do?' he said, over the din the water was making as it poured into the tub.

'I like what we've just done.' She tried to keep her voice light. She wanted the bath – the aftereffects of the alcohol had kicked in, and she had a headache. She wasn't ready to start thinking about anything. She had sobered up sufficiently to know that her thoughts were unlikely to be her friends.

'I meant being a mum. Does it make you happy?'

He was going to spoil everything, she thought. She hadn't brought him back to her hotel so they could talk about her child, who was more than likely completely fine and suffering no more than a head cold, regardless of what Philip said. And now she was thinking of Philip. Surely there was an etiquette to these things, an understanding that certain subjects were off limits, and surely Stuart Harkin of all people would know that. She turned off the tap so that she didn't have to raise her voice. 'Sure,' she said. 'It's fun.' This was both true and not true.

'It's just that I've been thinking about how success didn't really happen for either of us. Or for any of the people there tonight. Apart from Donna Clothilde.'

She considered asking him when exactly he'd been thinking about this. She stepped into the bath, lowered herself gingerly into the very hot water. There was a low hiss coming off the foam, millions of tiny bubbles exploding simultaneously. Stuart's eyes were on her breasts, which were just cresting the water.

'It was only the boys who talked like that,' she said, 'wondering who was going to be the next Francis Bacon. Anyway, I majored in art history. I haven't been waiting for anything to "happen".'

Maybe it was the air quotes she put around 'happen', but he left her to her bath then and went to lie on the bed. For a while she heard nothing but the rustle of him turning the pages of the complimentary newspaper, and then even that stopped. She stayed in the bath after the water grew cold. As if the expensive bath salts had leeched the alcohol out of her system, she was feeling suddenly clearheaded. But the thing was, even when viewed through the lens of sobriety, the sex had undeniably been good, even better, she thought, than when she'd slept with him as a younger woman. Perhaps now their sex was computed on a different abacus, an abacus for older, damaged, more desperate people, the beads of higher denomination made heavy by the weight of consequence.

She would ask him to leave, she decided, sitting up in the water. Better that he not stay the night. But when she finally got out of the bath and dried herself, prepared in her head what she would say, she found him under the covers, sleeping. She looked at this man in her bed and tried not to wonder if Jennifer's temperature had worsened, if Philip was awake with her right now. She shook Stuart's shoulder but he didn't stir. She shook him again, but he just grunted and turned over in a belch of alcohol fumes. She couldn't find her pyjamas in the dark but she took a spare eiderdown from the wardrobe and settled herself in the armchair. The air-conditioning was too cold, but no matter how many times she fiddled with the dials she couldn't turn it off. For an hour she tossed and turned until, too cold to remain in the chair any longer, she tiptoed to the bed and carefully peeled back the duvet, making sure not to touch him as she climbed in.

The next morning she woke early and dressed quietly. She raised the blinds a fraction. The view was less spectacular at this hour, without the lights, but there in the distance was the circle of the London Eye, turning slow as a screw, and she thought, *How strange, the things that people will pay money for.*

'Off so soon?' She turned to find Stuart raised on one elbow, watching her.

'I'm going on standby for an earlier flight back.' She paused. 'My daughter's sick and her condition has worsened.' There'd been no contact from Philip, and she didn't have the stomach to text him. But she wanted to get out of that hotel room; she wanted to get home.

As she was brushing her hair in the mirror, Stuart said, 'When's checkout? My head's not the best. I might lie in for a while.'

'The room's booked and paid for for another night,' she said, 'so there's no rush.'

He seemed to consider. 'I might stay then,' he said. 'I'd like to hang around, maybe meet up with the gang later. It would be a shame to waste a room like this.' She remembered thinking how curious that he could use the word 'shame' in that context without the slightest hint of irony. It seemed to her that they'd already done enough to merit shame without factoring in the use, or non-use, of hotel facilities. It wasn't as if what they'd done could be disregarded as long as they got value for money. She wondered if he would offer to share the cost of the room, but he didn't, and she thought that most likely he couldn't afford it.

That evening as she drove the road home from the airport her knuckles were white on the steering wheel. She'd spent the day

151

worrying about what would happen if Stuart charged something to the room after she'd gone, and how she would explain it if Philip noticed it on the credit card statement. Would Jennifer be up when she got home? She hoped not, she didn't want to face anyone right now. In spite of herself, the details of the night before rushed back – the initial surprise of Stuart's mouth on hers, the way she'd lain down for him on the bed, the searing pleasure as he'd entered her – and she had to force her attention back to the road and the headlights of oncoming cars. The lights of the city came into view in a soft fog of orange. She turned down a side road and parked with the hazard lights on. Reaching into the backseat, she unzipped her suitcase and took out the knickers she'd been wearing the night before and had stupidly packed rather than dumping in the hotel bin. She stepped out of the car. The muddy ground sucked at her shoes, and she almost lost her balance. A noise that she failed to classify as either human or animal came from the other side of the ditch. It would not do to be murdered now. The coroner would lay her out on a steel table and would find Stuart in all those places where she'd failed to properly wash him out. She flung the knickers over the ditch. When she got back into the driver's seat, her hands were shaking. In the course of twenty-four hours, she had become a woman who had cheated on her husband, and would always be one of those women, regardless of the level of virtue with which she conducted the rest of her married life, and with no allowances made for the virtue with which she'd conducted it previously. She had never strayed before. Sitting there in the car, she regretted – deeply regretted – all those men over the years that she could have slept with but didn't. Because she might as well have slept with them, if it were all now to be set at nought by this one indiscretion.

She had texted Philip before boarding her flight, saying that she was coming home early, that she hoped Jennifer was okay, that she was sorry. Immediately her phone rang, but she couldn't bring herself to answer it and let it ring out. He texted: 'Don't come home. Stay.' What did that mean? Stay, he never wanted to see her again, or stay and have a good time? She texted back, 'Am coming home ♥,' then switched off her phone and went to stand in line at the departure gate.

What would it feel like to walk through her front door as an adulterer? Much like every other time, as it turned out. When she stepped into the hall, the mess of toys and discarded socks irked her, just like it always did. Philip came out of his studio. 'Hey,' he said. He put his arms around her and hugged her. 'How did it go?'

'It was fine.' She tensed in his arms.

'Only fine?'

'Oh, it was fun, as these things go. The girls send their love.'

He ran a hand through his hair. 'Listen,' he said, 'I feel so bad about ruining your weekend. You should have stayed. I was a jerk.'

The last thing she needed was for him to start apologising. 'I should never have gone,' she said. The truth of it hit her like a bucket of cold water.

'You had every right to go.' He kissed her. 'I'm glad to have you back, even if I don't deserve you.'

'How's Jennifer?' she said.

'She's asleep. You were right. It was just a cold. Her temperature is back down.'

She wanted to go straight upstairs and get in the shower. 'I think I might go lie down,' she said.

He stroked her cheek. 'My poor darling's all partied out,' he said. 'Remember when we used to push through till dawn and then do it all again the next night? You go on up and I'll bring you some toast.'

'I'm not hungry,' she said quickly.

'A mug of tea then.'

She stayed in the shower until her skin turned pink and patchy. Drying herself with the towel, she remembered what the scratch of Stuart's sweater against her bare skin had felt like the night before and was mortified to experience a jolt of desire. She climbed into bed and wondered what she would do if Philip wanted to have sex. She would have to plead tiredness; it would swell the proportions of the betrayal to something too gigantic if she allowed sex to happen with traces of Stuart still inside her. As it was, Philip brought the tea and went back downstairs. She would be a model wife from now on, she thought. Thus far she hadn't been a particularly notable one, but she hadn't been a terrible one either, leaving aside the thing that had just happened. It would never happen again, she decided; that was ten years ago and it hadn't.

20

At home in Sunday's Well on Thursday evening, Jennifer was in the kitchen when Nessa began getting out the pots and pans, but she didn't glance up from her phone. Schoolbooks were spread out in front of her on the kitchen table. 'How's school?' Nessa said.

'Super.'

'Is the Sullivan girl better yet?'

'What?' Jennifer kept her eyes on the screen.

'Deirdre Sullivan. Is she feeling better now?'

Jennifer sighed. 'Yes,' she said. 'It was just a sore throat.' She stood up and walked to the back door, still not taking her eyes from her phone, circumventing a footstool and the dog's bowl with the deftness of a blind person. She slid open the door and went around the corner of the house to a patio area with a cast-iron bench.

Bailey slipped inside when the door was opened, and now he sat at Nessa's feet as she browned minced beef on the stove. 'Be glad you're not a mother, Bailey,' she said. 'You're damned if you do and damned if you don't.' The dog yawned and stretched, lay down with its head on its paws.

'Something smells good,' Philip said. She hadn't heard him come in. He settled himself on a high stool at the kitchen island and unfolded a set of plans. He took a pencil from his pocket. Bailey got up, licked her elbow, and when she still didn't offer him any scraps, he switched allegiance and wandered over to Philip.

'Where's Jennifer?' Philip said.

'Outside.' She inclined her head toward the back garden.

'How are things going at school?'

'Okay, as far as I can tell. Not that she's volunteering much.'

On cue, Jennifer came in. She hugged her father, then took a bag of crisps from the cupboard. The tidings on her phone must have been good, because she was more cheerful than earlier. 'You haven't forgotten it's Bring and Buy evening tonight, have you?' she said.

Nessa had forgotten. Bring and Buys, as far as she was concerned, were opportunities for unscrupulous people to clear out their houses. Every year when she saw the tables of junk lined up in the school hall, she imagined stretching out an arm and sweeping the whole lot into a giant refuse bag. The Fundraising Committee, on the other hand, swore by it. A shelf in Jennifer's bedroom was heaving with the spoils of previous years: a teddy bear in plain and purl knit, the stitches so loose that you could see its yellow stuffing; a set of Russian dolls, with three of the dolls missing, so that it was hardly worthwhile to stack the remaining two away; a kitten made from cheap orange glass.

Cora Wilson would be there. Cora was always there.

'I was thinking of giving it a miss,' she said.

Jennifer stared at her mother as if Nessa had suggested selling one of her daughter's kidneys on eBay. 'Everybody else's parents are going,' she said. 'All the mothers will be there.'

'They won't all be there,' Nessa said. 'When have you ever seen Maisie Green there? And Laura Stevens never goes. I have never once seen her there.'

'Maisie Green has a disability,' Jennifer said.

'She has a limp,' Nessa said. 'It doesn't stop her going to the cake sale, I notice.'

Jennifer turned pleadingly to her father. 'Tell her she has to come.'

Philip looked uncomfortable. 'That's not how it works,' he said. 'I don't tell your mother what to do. But aren't you helping out at the tea and coffee station, Nessa?'

'That's the first I've heard of it.'

'I put your name down,' Jennifer said. 'You're on the rota.'

It was unthinkable. Pouring tea for Cora Wilson, asking her if she took sugar. 'I can't do it,' Nessa said, 'I have too much work to catch up on. You'll have to do it instead, Philip. Anyway, you always have more to say to the mothers than I do.'

'None of the fathers do the tea and coffee station,' Jennifer said. 'This is going to be so weird.' She walked out of the kitchen.

Philip looked at Nessa. 'That was a cheap dig.'

'What?'

'Me having more to say to the mothers.'

'God, no. I wasn't even thinking that, Philip.'

'I was looking forward to us going to this together,' he said.

'You mean like a date?' she said. 'The last of the true romantics.'

He sighed. 'I'm trying here, Nessa. I'm really trying.' He put down his pencil and followed his daughter out of the kitchen.

In the end, she went to the Bring and Buy. As she had feared, Cora Wilson was there. She used to think that if she lost in love, it would be – on a scale of one to ten – to an eight or a nine. Cora Wilson she would put as a four. Sometimes when Cora was going through a phase of working out, she might edge up to a five. But never more than that. Cora was short, five foot two inches or thereabouts. She did not look like a stereotypical mistress. Cora Wilson did not look like beautiful Ms Johnson, who was currently going around selling raffle tickets. Cora looked like a wife. She brought to mind beef stew with dumplings, lavender-scented sachets in the linen closet. Cora Wilson wore a blanket across her knees when she drove to her aqua-aerobics class.

It was said that Cora's grandfather, and his ancestors before him, had owned a country pile in the Midlands, a stud farm and a herd of prizewinning cattle that didn't exist for any purpose other than to grace the fields and be admired. At coffee mornings, Cora was given to telling stories about chasing calves, complete with lots of posh swearing at the horrors of it all. In every word she uttered, Nessa heard 'money'. She could only conclude that Philip had compensated for not marrying up by cheating up. Whoever inherited the country pile, it wasn't Cora, whose circumstances were now firmly middle class. But Cora still carried herself like someone who could trace her ancestry back to a medieval court. And she had always looked at Nessa like she should be on her knees scrubbing flagstones in a scullery.

Mandy Wilson was helping Ms Johnson sell the raffle tickets. She was careful not to come anywhere near Nessa, concentrating her efforts on the other side of the hall. She spoke only to adults, the mothers mostly, and didn't hang out with any of the girls. Nessa's heart went out to her. Had they, the adults, done this to her? Jennifer was with a clutch of girls in a corner, shrieking over the contents of a box of old Christmas annuals. Nessa recognised these girls; they were in her daughter's year at school, but they weren't any of the girls who used to come to their house.

Cora ladled out fruit punch in plummy tones. Nessa went to the bathroom, splashed cold water on her face, dabbed calming lavender oil on her pulse. A transaction of some sort was going on in one of the cubicles; the door was open, and she spotted Jennifer holding a worn-looking teddy bear, as if they didn't have enough rubbish. But no, Jennifer was furtively transferring the bear into the bag of a girl whose mother presumably had insisted on donating it. It was a teary reunion she had stumbled upon; in many ways they were still babies. Nessa busied herself with washing her hands and pretended not to notice. She was proud of her daughter, watching out for a friend like that. She dried her hands and went back out to the hall, where she bought twenty euros' worth of raffle tickets from Ms Johnson. Even if she didn't win, it might at least put her in better standing.

21

They were no sooner home from the Bring and Buy than the doorbell rang. 'That'll be Rachel,' Jennifer said, racing to get it.

'You only saw Rachel ten minutes ago,' Nessa called from the couch in the living room. 'What could you possibly have to say to each other?'

She heard the front door opening and muffled exchanges in the hall. Jennifer put her head around the door. 'Someone to see you,' she said.

Nessa put down the book she was reading. 'Who?'

'Melanie something. Dur, Dar . . .'

'Damn it,' Nessa said. 'Don't let her in, whatever you do.'

Jennifer made a face. 'I already have,' she said. 'I put her in Dad's den, because that's tidy.'

Nessa was on her feet now. 'What were you thinking, Jennifer?'

'You're always telling me not to leave people standing on the doorstep. You're always saying it's rude.'

Philip came into the room. 'Why is there someone in my studio?' he said.

'It's that extremely strange woman who's been contacting the newspapers about the Chalk Sculpture. The one who delivered a letter to the Lockes' house in the middle of the night. I told you about her, Philip. And now Jennifer's let her in.'

'She looked normal,' Jennifer said. 'She just looked like an old person. How was I to know?'

'I could tell her that you're taking a bath,' Philip said, 'and that she'll have to come back another time.'

'I don't want her coming back at all,' Nessa said. 'What does she think she's doing, turning up at my house like this? At our home! How does she even know where I live? Send her away, Philip. Get rid of her. Tell her to email me at the gallery, if she must.' And then, behind him in the doorway, she saw Melanie Doerr.

'I wonder if I might trouble you for a glass of water?' Doerr said, tapping Philip on the shoulder. 'I'm feeling faint.'

'Of course,' he said, glancing apologetically at Nessa. 'Sit down, please.' He led her over to an armchair. 'Let me open a window.'

'Thank you,' Doerr said. She took off her coat and loosened the top buttons of her blouse. She fanned her face with one hand, and smiled. Nessa retreated to the couch, settled herself at the farthest end. Doerr had a bag slung over her arm and now she plonked it on the floor beside her. Too large to be a handbag, it was like a tote but with several smaller purses tied to it with orange string. Philip had gone to the kitchen to fetch the water. Doerr looked completely and utterly well. Nessa had never seen anybody look less faint.

'You can't turn up like this, at my home, without an appointment,' she said. 'It's completely inappropriate.'

'It's so warm,' Melanie Doerr said. 'Aren't you warm? I fell and hit my head once, it was in the Ramblas in Barcelona. When I woke up I thought I was in the engine room of a ship, there were so many pipes, and the noise! Oh my goodness, the noise. Turned out I'd been rescued by a woman who worked in the laundry room of a hotel and she'd got the doorman to carry me in off the street. There was a mattress where the man who serviced the air-conditioning system slept sometimes when he was in the city, but he wasn't there that night. He was a great-grandson of Isaac Babel. The door-man, that is. Imagine.'

Philip was back with a beaker of water. 'Thank you so much,' Melanie Doerr said. She turned to Nessa. 'I felt that we should talk before things went any further. You got my letter.'

Nessa nodded. 'You're quite fond of letter writing, aren't you?' she said.

Doerr didn't rise to the bait. 'And I presume you read my article in the newspaper?' she said.

'I read it,' Nessa said. 'I'm surprised that they published it.' Actually, she wasn't surprised in the least. That particular paper had once published an article on how to make your own suncream from buttermilk.

Philip, who'd been hovering uncertainly, must have cat-egorised their visitor as harmless, because he backed slowly out of the room. Melanie Doerr drew herself up on the edge of the armchair. A flush rose on her cheeks. 'May I ask what part of the article you had difficulty with?' she said.

'All of it,' Nessa said. 'I had "difficulty" with all of it. The same way that I have difficulty with you turning up at my home.'

'This is the problem with life nowadays,' Doerr said. 'Nobody wants to listen. Nobody wants to open their minds to the possibility of other truths. Everybody wants to keep to the set knowledge. There's a test they use in London called that – the Knowledge. The taxi drivers have to take it. Have you heard of it?'

'I've heard of it,' Nessa said, 'I just don't know why we're talking about it. I don't like to be rude, but I'd rather you left. You can contact me at my office during office hours.'

She got up and took a few steps toward the door, hoping it might encourage her visitor to do the same. What would she do if the woman refused to leave? There would be no point in calling Philip. He'd be polite. It was one of the fault lines in their marriage: her husband being too nice to other women.

Melanie Doerr bent and began to fiddle with the straps of her bag. 'I've been thinking,' she said, 'thinking and recalibrating my convictions, something the advance of years has taught me to do.' The zip on the bag was broken and she had it pinned together with an oversized safety pin, the kind that might grace a Scotsman's kilt. 'When I visited you at the gallery,' Doerr said, 'I presumed you would know who I was. I couldn't believe that you hadn't heard of me, especially when Robert had filled all those notebooks with an account of our collaboration.' She had the bag open now, and began to take things out. There was a long, tasselled length of material that might have been a scarf. This was followed by several towels. Doerr laid them down on the floor, with the quiet absorption of someone engaged in a private activity in their own bedroom. 'What are you doing?' Nessa said.

Doerr glanced up. 'Some things technology is no use for,' she said. 'Where was I? Oh, yes, Robert's notebooks. Well, I began to consider it possible that Eleanor – or Loretta, take your pick – may have destroyed them. It's a hellish thing for anyone to do to an artist's papers, but those two, of course, had their motives.'

There was another towel, then a pair of thick knitted socks. 'You should ask Loretta about me,' she said. 'Loretta knows. Eleanor knows too, but Eleanor would tell you that black was white when it suited her. I never knew anybody to lie as well as Eleanor Locke. Her family were never friendly with the Swindons, you know; that's a fabrication.'

'I *did* ask Loretta,' Nessa said. 'Several times.'

All the time Doerr was taking things from the bag: a compass, a half-eaten Twix bar, a hat with medals pinned to it. She paused briefly. 'I went there once in disguise,' she said. 'I figured they wouldn't let me in if they recognised me, so I got myself a wig and sunglasses and some pan stick makeup.'

'Where was this?' Nessa said.

'At the house in Tragumna. Ten years ago, or thereabouts, I had a yearning to see the Chalk Sculpture. It was on the anniversary of Robert's death, and I'd been ill. I thought I mightn't have long left and I wanted to see it one last time. Of course, here I am still, but my point is, I got in past the door, I got to see it, I got to touch it. But Loretta recognised me. I know that she did, even though she pretended not to. She knew it was me, even after all these years, even with the wig and the makeup and me talking funny, she knew. Poor Loretta. But she left me on my own with it for a while that day, I was grateful to her for that.'

Doerr took what looked like a knotted pillowcase from the bag. She stood up while she opened it. 'You wanted evidence,' she said. 'Well, what do you make of these?' As Nessa watched, she upended the pillowcase and a dozen or so lumps of stone tumbled out onto the living room floor, an avalanche of dusty white rocks. They were deformed half-things but Nessa saw immediately that they resembled miniature Chalk Sculptures, cousins rather than offspring, because there was something inchoate about them, something crude and strange that reminded her of the raw fury of the sheela na gigs, ancient fertility symbols carved in stone. She stooped to get a better look. One of them had broken in two, whether just then or on some previous occasion, it was hard to tell. Others had lost chips and left small belches of powder on her floor. Doerr looked triumphant. 'There,' she said, 'now you see why I had to come. I could hardly send these by email.'

Nessa picked up one of the pieces, turned it over in her hands. Maquettes, she thought at first, preliminary models that sculptors sometimes worked with. Yet these differed from each other in small but fundamental ways. She looked at Doerr. 'Are these by Robert Locke?' she said.

Doerr gave a tight-lipped smile. 'You're the expert,' she said. 'You tell me.'

Nessa tried to keep her voice steady. 'Are they his or not?' she said. She'd never heard of Locke working with maquettes. Some of them if placed next to the Chalk Sculpture would have looked like poor facsimiles, but others had something that was remarkably similar to Locke's, the way the stone turned as if it were a body of moving water.

'Some of them are his,' Doerr said. 'Some of them aren't.'

Nessa picked up a fragment and examined it. 'Why would you treat them like this,' she said, 'if they're really his?'

Doerr shrugged. 'Because these weren't intended to last either. Robert was going to toss them into a ditch behind the house, but I rescued them, smuggled them out.' She laughed. 'I exaggerate,' she said. 'It wasn't smuggling, exactly. He helped me pack them into my suitcase.' A look of sadness came over her face. 'The important thing is, they're now mine to do as I like with.'

'The way you think the Chalk Sculpture is yours?' Nessa said. She noticed how some of the white chalk had got under her nails. Some of the pieces were undeniably from the same school as Locke's work. There was something in the turn of their hips; and the way the clavicle bone of one rose out of the stone had been Locke's signature from that period, a fetish of his. She looked at Melanie Doerr. 'These are very interesting,' she said. 'Can you leave them with me for a couple of days? I'd like to study them. And it would give me a better insight into what you say about the Chalk Sculpture.'

'By "study" you mean keep,' Doerr said.

'No,' Nessa said, 'I'd like to have them on loan. I'll take good care of them. I'd like to authenticate them as Locke's work.'

'I've told you already. Only some of them are his.' She reached out and took the piece that Nessa was holding, put it back in the pillowcase. Then she began to gather up the others, tossing them in higgledy-piggledy.

Nessa flinched. She could hear them cracking one against another as they were dropped into the pillowcase. 'Here,' she said, 'let me help you with that,' but Doerr shook her head.

'See?' she said, though they were all put away again now. 'See?' She shoved the towels back in on top, then the scarves and the rest of the paraphernalia. She slung the bag over her shoulder and strode out to the hall.

'Hang on,' Nessa said, but the older woman had already pulled open the front door and was going down the path.

In bed that night Nessa found herself on edge, her mind full of thoughts of Locke's maquettes, if that's what they were, that Doerr had tumbled so flippantly onto her living room floor. She would have to see them again, she thought, as she pulled on a nightdress; she would ask Doerr to bring them to the gallery for assessment. The evening's avalanche of events had unnerved her: Cora Wilson at the school hall, and poor Mandy, so clearly miserable, Jennifer awkward too, both of them caught up in a mess of their parents' making, and then Doerr arriving on the doorstep. Nessa had a need for intimacy with someone she could trust, someone who would not lie to her. Her husband was no longer that person, but he was all she had and she wanted Philip to come to bed.

The walking that the counsellor had advocated so strongly did not appear to be working. And how much walking could a marriage take, or need? It was half an hour before he followed her upstairs, and then he brought a book that he proceeded to open. She edged closer, rubbed her foot against his. He turned his head and smiled, then went back to the book. She laid her head on his chest and still he continued to turn the pages, but when she ran a hand slowly down his stomach he stopped and let the book fall to the floor. He kissed her and she thought what a long time it had been since she'd had a kiss like that. She closed her eyes and, not for the first time and in spite of herself, Robert Locke's face materialised. She froze, opened her eyes again.

'You okay?' Philip said. He'd been stroking her breast, but now he paused.

'Yes, yes,' she said, 'I'm fine.'

But when she shut her eyes again, Locke returned, his white-grained hands moving over her body, as if in tandem with Philip's, as if there were two sets of fingers touching her, so that everything that night felt more intense. It was not wrong, she thought; it was nothing more than a different way of thinking about art, a sweetly neutered necrophilia. It wasn't cheating when it was with a dead person.

22

The next day, Nessa suspected everyone coming toward her on the pavement of being Melanie Doerr. She was relieved when people came into view and were revealed to be neighbours or deliverymen, or perfect strangers. But when the weekend came and went and Doerr didn't reappear, she relaxed a bit. She mentioned Doerr's unorthodox visit to Henchy when she bumped into him in the lunchroom. He didn't even break his stride on his way to the scones. 'Daft as a brush,' he said, piling jam onto his plate, 'make a note on the file.' She hadn't got around to mentioning the maquettes before he was gone in search of cream.

In any event, in the cold light of day, she thought that perhaps there was nothing of Locke in the maquettes at all, that it was sheer gullibility on her part to ever think there could have been. She would consider them again when preparing her end-of-month briefing, time enough to decide what to say then. She'd yet to prepare a memo about Doerr's late-night delivery of the envelope and photograph to the Lockes' house, and Loretta's panicked suggestion of paying her to go away. It was difficult to know how best to approach this. Anything that even hinted at an overrun in spending sent the director scuttling to the gallery's accountant. Once, when the accountant thought Nessa wasn't listening, she had heard him refer to the bonus provision in her contract as his 'contingency fund'.

At her desk Monday afternoon, she read over again all the interviews she'd conducted with Eleanor Locke. She went through the inventory of Locke's work and all the catalogues of his exhibitions over the years. Nowhere was there a sign of those creatures Doerr had tumbled onto her living room floor.

By the time Tuesday came around, she'd managed to put Doerr sufficiently out of her mind to allow her to wonder instead why she'd agreed to meet Stuart Harkin. She'd chosen a slightly formal bistro on Emmet Place with table service, and now, as she watched his leisurely approach across the bridge, a sweater knotted round his waist, she wondered if he would tease her about her taste. But most of his conversation, for the first five minutes, was about Katherine: how good she'd been to him this past week, and how, according to him, she'd always been there for Amy, until Nessa thought he might suggest that Katherine should be canonised. 'Saint Katherine,' she said. 'Maybe we should get her to say Mass?'

He laughed, but not as much as she'd have liked. 'Do you ever think about how we treated her when we were younger?' he said.

'Who?' she said. 'Katherine?'

'Yes. We weren't terribly kind.'

'She wasn't terribly interesting. And she only hung out with us really for that one year. She drifted away after that.'

'Who could blame her?' he said. 'But she always kept in touch with Amy, right until the end. The only thing that ever came between them was when she lent Amy money. And it wasn't Katherine who got awkward then, it was Amy. Amy wanted me to pay it back, and I couldn't. I wasn't in a position to at the time, and I think Amy was embarrassed. She stopped calling Katherine then; they didn't talk as much as before.'

It was news to Nessa that Amy had called Katherine at all. She knew it was ridiculous, but she couldn't help feeling as if they'd gone behind her back. But then, Amy used to call Nessa too, in the years after Luke was born, and it wasn't Amy's fault that those calls had stopped. Nessa was the one who had kept her distance.

In an effort to move the conversation to safer ground, she said, 'Are you in contact with any of the old gang?'

'Do you remember Joey Blue?' he said.

She had to think. The name didn't mean anything at first, but like many things from her St Martin's days, it hadn't fully gone away either. Joey: a big guy, that was the first thing that came to mind. The second was him peeing in the closet of a girl from the textiles class who'd invited him home one night. 'Didn't he use to do those apocalyptic streetscapes?' she said.

'That's him,' Stuart said. 'I spent a couple of months with him in Norfolk last year. He and Lulu – I don't expect you know Lulu, she's his second wife – have two babies now. They're breeding alpacas.'

'The things that look like long-legged sheep? But with smaller heads?'

'If you ever run into Joey, don't call them sheep,' Stuart said. 'Those sheep, as you call them, produce very expensive wool. Three hundred euros per sweater. They're the sweetest-tempered creatures; I'm grateful I just had to shear them, not kill them.'

'You were working for Joey?'

'I was helping out,' he said, 'earning my keep. They gave me a roof over my head for a while, when things were bad. I kept the accounts and sheared alpacas. It was my time in the wilderness. Literally.'

'Did Luke go with you to Joey's?'

'Luke's not an alpaca-shearing kind of guy,' he said. 'He didn't inherit the farming gene. Maybe Aunt Gretta will convert him.'

'Maybe she'll leave him the farm,' Nessa said.

She'd meant it as a joke, but Stuart shook his head. 'Nah,' he said. 'Turns out that was tied up in a trust fund years ago. Some grandniece of Pa Corrigan gets the lot when Gretta dies.'

Their food arrived, two bowls of pasta. She found herself absurdly grateful to the waitress for her questions about Parmesan and black pepper. She would have liked to invite the woman to eat with them, would gladly have paid her hourly rate as well as the cost of her food if it would save her from being left alone with Stuart Harkin. She saw something in the way the waitress's eyes flickered over Stuart that suggested she might not have been averse to the idea.

Stuart concentrated on his pasta for a couple of minutes. Then he put down his fork and said, 'There's a problem with Luke.'

'What is it?' she said. 'Is he okay?' It occurred to her that she hadn't heard from him since she'd dropped him off at the Ferriters' that evening. 'I'd love to see how his photos of the Chalk Sculpture turned out.'

'I wouldn't hold your breath,' Stuart said. 'I don't think you'll be getting to see those photos, somehow.'

'What's wrong?' She wondered now if Luke might be sick, and as always when she heard of things befalling other people's children, she thought of Jennifer, wondered if she would be home directly after school or if today was one of the days when she had choir practice.

'I think it can be defused,' Stuart said, 'but we need to go about it the right way.'

'We?' Nessa said, puzzled. She decided Luke must have got into trouble of some sort.

'I won't pretend there weren't problems between Luke and me before we came here,' he said. 'Things weren't exactly idyllic between us, but we'd been getting on better than we had for a long while. That's why I decided to visit. I'm not a total masochist.' He gave a hard little laugh. 'It was after I got here that things got complicated.'

'Complicated how?'

'Aunt Gretta hasn't done me, or you, any favours,' he said. 'She's opened every can of worms imaginable. We're talking cans on a Warhol scale.'

'Is this about the letters?'

He grimaced. 'The letters are the least of our problems. Gretta has given my son bigger fish to fry.'

She waited, saying nothing. She was conscious that her heart had begun to beat faster.

'Gretta in her wisdom – or her vindictiveness, take your pick – when Luke went back to stay with her last week, she gave him his mother's diaries. I didn't even know Amy kept diaries. In all the time we lived together I never once saw her write in one. It threw me, I can tell you. When I think how little privacy we had in that flat, and still she managed to do that without my noticing. She must have shipped them all home with the rest of her stuff that time.' He reached across the table and rested a hand on Nessa's shoulder. She thought about shrugging it off, but didn't. She was thinking of Amy in the years before she died. She didn't like to imagine the darkness of those diaries.

'There's things in there no son should read about his parents,' Stuart said. 'Not that I've seen them all. Luke won't

172

give them to me. He reads me extracts aloud. When he's speaking to me, that is.'

She shifted position slightly so that his hand slid from her shoulder.

'There's no good way of telling you this, Ness,' he said. 'But there's stuff in those diaries about you and me, about what we got up to in our St Martin's days.'

It took a second for her to register what he was saying. 'There couldn't be,' she said.

He nodded. 'I'm afraid so.'

'It's not possible,' she said. 'Amy didn't know. Did she?'

'Yes,' he said tiredly. 'Amy knew.'

'No, Stuart!'

'Ness,' he said. He slid a hand across the table toward her, but she didn't take it. She picked up her napkin, pretended to concentrate on a spatter of sauce on the front of her shirt.

'Amy couldn't have known,' she said, not looking at him. 'There was nobody who would have told her. I've never told another person. Even later on, after I met Philip, I didn't tell him. How . . .'

'Because I told her,' Stuart said.

She stared at him. 'I don't believe you,' she said. 'I don't believe you would do that.'

He sat, mute, looking at his plate.

'Stuart?' she said. 'Look at me. Are you serious? Did you really tell her?'

He nodded.

'You had no right.' It came out as a whisper.

'We need to keep clear heads on this, Nessa.'

'Why did you have to go telling her? It was something stupid we did when we were barely out of our teens. We had left it behind us.'

'She was my wife,' he said. 'I was her husband. It was for us to decide what we told each other. You didn't have an embargo on that.'

'You are a selfish bastard.'

'Maybe I am,' he said. 'In other respects. But what I did back then, I did for her, for us – Amy and me – and for our son. I wanted to put things behind us, all the lying and cheating. It wasn't all on my side, either. Amy was no angel, as you'll be aware.'

They were both silent for a moment. 'When did you tell her?' she asked.

'It would have been when Luke was about to turn three.'

She did a quick mental calculation: about six months, then, before the fateful weekend of the christening. So Amy had known about the affair that weekend and hadn't said anything? It hardly seemed possible.

'We'd decided to start again with a clean sheet,' Stuart was saying. 'Amy said that we should be honest with each other. It was her idea. She confessed things to me that it was hard to listen to – the most detailed descriptions of things that she'd done, and the people she'd done them with, some of them people I'd considered friends. In retrospect, I wonder if half of it even happened, if she even knew all of the people she claimed to have slept with. We'd been taking chips off each other for months, she'd worn me down, and I thought, "All right, maybe this will work, let's get it all out there, and draw a line under it and start over."'

He took a sip of water. 'That night when she was listing her lovers,' he said, 'it was like every time she found a new place to punch me, a softer place than the last. And when it got to my turn, do you know how many I had to confess?'

When she didn't answer, he said, 'One. You. That was all.'

She couldn't look at him. She looked away to a table on her left where two women had stopped eating their lunch to eavesdrop.

'The irony is,' Stuart said, 'if you and I had kept fucking each other, if Amy and I had split up, she might have met a good man who knew how to save her, who got her help. She might have met an accountant who paid for private health care, for a psychiatrist. She might still be alive today.'

'She might still be alive if you hadn't opened your big mouth.' Tears were running down her cheeks. Rooting in her purse, she placed a fifty-euro banknote on the table and stood up.

'Hey,' he said, following her out onto the street, 'don't flatter yourself. Don't even think of going down that road. What Amy did, she did for her own reasons, or lack of reason. She didn't kill herself over you and me.'

'The timing's fairly coincidental, don't you think?' She was crying harder now. 'She finds out about us and a few months later, she's dead.'

He put his arms around her and pulled her against his chest. He rested his chin on her head and rocked her as she wept. Settling into the warmth of him, she felt the old familiar tug inside her. When after a few minutes she raised her head to speak, he kissed her. It was a short kiss, no more than a couple of seconds. Startled, she pulled back.

'No,' she said, shaking her head, 'no. We mustn't.' She took a tissue from her bag and wiped her eyes, horrified at herself. 'Goodbye, Stuart,' she said.

'Hey,' he said as she turned to leave, 'what are we going to do about Luke?' But she kept walking.

23

That weekend of the christening, after Amy had fought with all the others, Nessa had not taken her directly back to their hotel in Crosshaven. She had coaxed her into her car and had persuaded her to go for a drive. A little geographical distance between Amy and the rest of the group would do no harm, she thought. Their relationship no longer had the ease it once had, and conversation was stilted as they headed toward Cork city. Amy sat sullenly in the passenger seat, chewing her fingernails. Since they would not now be joining the others for dinner, Nessa stopped and picked up sandwiches and bottles of water at a petrol station. 'I'm not hungry,' Amy said, when she asked her what she'd like, but Nessa bought the sandwiches anyway.

At the marina, ducks squatted prettily on the bank and swans made sweet ringed circles on the water. Children who reminded her of Peter and Jane from the Ladybird books of her childhood whirred on scooters along leafy pavements. In the car park, Nessa pulled in beside a cabin the council used as a tea hut during summer months.

'We could take a walk, if you like?' Nessa said, indicating the footpath that ran along the waterside. 'We could find a bench to sit and eat.'

Amy shrugged. 'Sure,' she said without much enthusiasm, 'why not?'

They set off in an easterly direction, gulls whirling and crying overhead. It was not particularly warm, and Nessa regretted not bringing a coat. Amy, wearing a light shirt, didn't complain, but she didn't pass any other comment either. It was like marshalling a placid but disinterested child. Finally they reached an unoccupied bench looking out onto the water. 'How about here?' Nessa said. Amy said nothing, but she sat down. They ate their sandwiches in silence for a moment. Amy was troublingly thin. With her pale face, her loose-fitting sweater unravelling at the hem, she looked like a castaway from one of the ships coming up the harbour, albeit a very beautiful castaway, all jutting cheekbones and soulful gaze. This could be something out of a film, Nessa thought, except that she would be played by someone prettier. Amy would play herself.

Nessa took her phone from her bag, checked her messages. There was a curt voicemail from Lizzy, the baby's mother, saying that perhaps it was best for all concerned if Amy didn't join them that evening. They could see how things were in the morning, after everyone had had what she called 'an opportunity to reflect'. Nessa decided against sharing the message with Amy; time enough to face all that.

Amy, without saying anything, put down her half-eaten sandwich and stood up. When she stretched, her prominent ribs put Nessa in mind of a crucifixion sculpture by Michelangelo. 'My mother always wanted me to be more like you,' Amy said.

'Really?' Nessa said. 'My mother wanted me to be more like Katherine.'

Amy smiled. 'Good old Katherine.' She said it without any trace of irony. 'What she had to put up with . . .' She shook her head.

'We weren't that bad, were we?' Nessa said.

Amy grimaced. 'We were bad enough.'

'How's Luke?' Nessa said, to change the subject. 'Is your Aunt Gretta minding him?'

Amy shook her head. 'He's with his Granny Harkin in Sussex. He lives with her now.'

'Oh,' Nessa said, 'I didn't realise.' She paused, attempted to steady her voice. 'Is Stuart there too?'

'Who knows where Stuart is?' Amy said. 'The last I heard, he was planning on spending some time in Berlin. He's been gone a lot.' She looked away toward the mouth of the harbour. 'Things haven't been that good between us lately.'

'I'm sorry,' Nessa said.

Amy shrugged. Then she said, 'Remember you told me once I'd make a good mother? Looks like you got that one wrong.'

'You *are* a good mother,' Nessa said, but she knew she hadn't delivered it with enough conviction.

Amy turned to look at her, raised an eyebrow. 'No lies, please, Nessa. They don't suit you. Granny Harkin says I'm an unfit mother.'

'I'm sorry I didn't return your calls,' Nessa said slowly. 'I was . . . I don't know . . . things were a bit mixed up. I'm sorry we lost touch. But I'd like to help you, Amy. Come and stay with me for a while. We can hang out, it would be like the old days. And you could get some rest.'

Amy shook her head. 'I'm no fit company for anyone these days.'

'This is me you're talking to, Amy.'

Amy said nothing. For a moment, they both sat there, staring out at the water. Then Amy said quietly, 'There is something you could do for me, something that would help.'

'Of course. What is it?'

'Will you be Luke's godmother?'

The question caught her off guard. She played for time. 'Isn't Gretta his godmother?'

'I told her I was planning on asking you instead.'

'I don't think you can do that,' Nessa said. 'I mean, isn't it . . .' She paused, floundering for the right words. 'Isn't it against the rules?'

'Gretta might be upset. So what? It's not like she's exactly done a stellar job to date. Otherwise my son wouldn't be living with Stuart's mother, would he?'

Nessa wanted to say that that was hardly Gretta's fault. Instead she said, 'Mrs Harkin would never relinquish her grandson to me. That's never going to happen. Me being his godmother isn't going to change that one way or the other.'

Amy exhaled loudly. 'Yeah, right,' she said. 'I get it. You don't want the hassle. And who would blame you?'

'That's not it,' Nessa said. There was no way of telling Amy that guilt didn't allow her to say yes. If Amy had even an inkling of what had happened between Stuart and Nessa, she would never have asked. Nessa would be accepting the role under false pretences. But it was impossible to explain this without giving herself away. 'I don't have any experience with children,' she said. 'Luke probably wouldn't even like me.'

'You know,' Amy said, 'I wasn't expecting much from the others this weekend, but I thought you'd be different. But maybe I always had the wrong idea about you, Ness.'

She set off toward the car, Nessa following behind. They drove in silence back to the hotel, where they retreated to their separate rooms.

The next day when Amy didn't appear for breakfast, Nessa went and knocked on her door. Amy didn't answer. When an hour later she still hadn't appeared, Nessa went down to reception, and a porter with a master key accompanied her into Amy's room. When he stepped into the bathroom, he turned ashen-faced to Nessa and said, 'It's better if you don't go in there,' but she pushed past him all the same, and saw her friend on the bathroom floor. Nessa had begun to shake. Her teeth chattered and she couldn't make them stop. Gently, the porter put an arm around her shoulder and steered her across the room to sit on the bed while he rang for an ambulance, although it was already too late for Amy.

24

The day after lunch with Stuart Harkin, she was in her office in the gallery, attempting to keep her mind occupied by going through paperwork. The media interest in the Chalk Sculpture and in Melanie Doerr had provoked a flurry of people writing and emailing, offering what were billed as hitherto unknown facts about Robert Locke. Most of the facts were already in the public domain; many were not facts at all. There was a nice letter from the editor of an arts magazine who'd interviewed Locke shortly before he died. The interview hadn't been published until after Locke's death and the editor had addressed his final queries to Loretta. He sent Nessa a copy of the essay, expressing the hope that it might be of interest. It was a well-known essay, or as well known as these things got. She'd read it previously as part of her research, and when it had arrived in her mail, she'd written and thanked the editor for sending it, but hadn't read it again. Now, as she leafed through it absentmindedly, wondering where to file it, she saw that it was not a final copy, but an early draft, with handwritten notes in the margin. One of these notes was in Loretta Locke's handwriting. *Error*, it said, *please delete*. To remove any doubt, she'd struck a line through the offending piece of text, a passage where her father had referred to one of his students: 'Melanie Petrovic'. Nessa laid the essay down on her desk. *Melanie*. The name was common enough, of course, but it was the first time she'd encountered it among Robert's alumni. She thought of telephoning Loretta again. Then she decided she should speak with Melanie Doerr first. She got out Doerr's letter, dialled the number at the bottom of the sheet of notepaper.

'Yes?' Doerr said, picking up.

Nessa cleared her throat. 'It's Nessa,' she said. 'Nessa McCormack. From the gallery.'

'I know who you are,' Doerr said. 'The question is, do you know who I am?'

Nessa decided not to rise to the bait. 'We seem to have got off on the wrong foot,' she said. 'I was wondering if we could perhaps meet again, start with a clean slate?' She would wait until they met in person, she decided, to ask if she'd ever gone by the name Petrovic.

For a moment, the other woman said nothing. 'Very well,' she said eventually. 'I'll be at your office in half an hour.'

'I have a meeting starting shortly. Are you free next week sometime?'

'Let's say this afternoon, then,' Doerr said. 'At about 4 p.m.?'

'I have to see some students at the art school this afternoon. It might run late.'

'5 p.m. then,' Doerr said briskly. 'We should strike while the iron is hot. We have much to discuss.'

On her end of the line, Nessa raised an eyebrow. '5 p.m. should be okay,' she said. Something else occurred to her. 'Will you bring the maquettes?'

Doerr didn't answer one way or the other. 'I'll speak with you at 5 p.m.,' she said.

At 4.15 p.m. that afternoon, Nessa was in the staff room of the art college, packing her notes into her briefcase, when a young woman put her head around the door. Her eyes were red. 'Can I talk to you for a minute?' she said.

'You're not one of my students, are you?' Nessa said. The girl looked familiar but she couldn't quite place her. She finished putting her things away in her case, fastened the straps.

'No,' the girl said, 'I'm in ceramics.' She hesitated. 'But I'm one of the life models for the visual art students.'

'Oh yes, that's right.'

'Yes,' the girl said. 'I wonder if I could talk to you about something?'

'It's Jerry that's in charge of the life modelling classes,' Nessa said. 'Let me see if I can find his number for you.'

'Jerry's the problem,' the girl blurted out. 'I can't talk to him about it. I need to talk to someone else.'

Nessa felt her heart sink. A problem with the life models was what every lecturer dreaded; the complaints-handling protocol ran to fifteen pages. The staff room was empty apart from her. Nessa set her briefcase down heavily on the floor. She thought of asking the student to come back tomorrow, but the girl was crying now, wiping away tears with her sleeve. Nessa took a box of tissues from a shelf. 'Take your time,' she said, passing the girl a tissue, 'begin when you're ready.' She hoped the girl would begin straightaway. She had precisely ten minutes to spare, otherwise she would be late for Melanie Doerr.

Half an hour later, Nessa paused on the steps of the college to take out her phone. The young woman's complaint had not proved as serious as she'd initially feared. Jerry had stopped booking the model since she'd lost weight, saying that he preferred his students to study the Rubenesque form, not stick insects. 'Can you believe he actually said that to me?' the model said. Nessa could easily believe it; Jerry had said much worse in the past. By the time Nessa had consoled the girl, and promised to speak to the head of the department, it was already

4.45 p.m. She would never make it back in time. Better to postpone Melanie Doerr and arrange a different appointment.

Doerr answered the phone straightaway. 'They tell me you're not here,' she said. 'I told them that couldn't possibly be correct because we had an arrangement.'

'Why are you so early?' Nessa said.

'Why are you not here?'

'It couldn't be helped,' Nessa said. 'Something came up. It's going to take me at least twenty minutes to get back to the gallery. Can we reschedule?'

'You know what else can't be helped?' Doerr said. 'You. You, it seems, are beyond help, because I am trying to help you, trying very hard, but you will not allow me. You think, "Oh, it's just Melanie, the crazy lady. It's not as if she could have anything important to say, it's not as if she matters."'

'I don't think that at all,' Nessa said, but the other woman interrupted her.

'I'm going back to the B & B for my supper,' she said. 'I'm going, and I'm taking my bag of maquettes with me.'

'Wait, Melanie, don't . . . maybe if I call a taxi—' but Doerr had hung up. Nessa sighed, dropped her phone back into her handbag. No point ringing her back now, she thought. She would give her a day or two to calm down and then she would try again.

The next day, Nessa was instructed by the gallery to step down from her dealings with the Lockes until further notice. An email was received by the gallery from a Dublin firm of lawyers, saying, 'We act on behalf of Melanie Doerr . . .' Doerr's lawyers restated her ownership claim, more formally this time, and said that nothing should be done with the Chalk Sculpture without their client's express consent. The matter was referred to the gallery's lawyers, and the texture

'So what do you think?' She would be polite, calm, she decided, regardless of what Luke said. She would behave like an adult.

'I like them,' he said, 'I don't think they're anything like the Chalk Sculpture. None of his other work is. I've been thinking about this and I think that woman – Ms Doerr – is right, I don't think Locke meant it to last, the way he meant these others' – he gestured to the Cambridgeshire pieces – 'to last.' The words tumbled out in a rush, as if he'd practised them, and she realised that this wasn't easy for him either. In his eyes, she was no longer the same person she'd been that night they'd gathered around Katherine's supper table. She had been unmasked. She was about to say that they should talk somewhere else, somewhere more private, when he snapped open the satchel and took out a bundle of yellowed papers.

'Aunt Gretta gave me some correspondence,' he said. 'Including some letters that you wrote to my mother. You weren't exactly complimentary about Katherine in them. You made fun of her a lot.' His hand that held the pages was trembling.

'Letters are private things,' she said. 'I wonder that Gretta gave them to you. And we were young then, we'd probably just had a row.'

'I'm young,' he said, 'but I would never call my friend' – he consulted a page from the top of the pile – '*Redneck. Mother Superior.* You mocked her, bullied her.'

'I did not bully Katherine.'

Keeping the satchel on his lap, he began to read aloud. It was a letter she'd written to Amy all those years ago, one in which she complained at length about Katherine – *Does she have to hang those granny slips on the radiators? . . . If she's that fond of mopping floors, maybe we should hire her out . . . I bet the other nurses take her pulse every day, to check she's actually alive . . .* It was strange to hear her teenage self coming from Luke Harkin's mouth. She cringed at her youthful cruelty. At first he read steadily, but then he became agitated, stumbled over words, until halfway through the third page he stopped. 'Katherine is one of the kindest people I've ever met,' he said. 'She's been unbelievably helpful to me, and to my dad, who, frankly, not everyone has patience for. I don't know how you could speak of her in that way.'

She sighed. 'It was a long time ago. I think Katherine *is* very nice. Would you like to go for a coffee, Luke? We can talk better if we go somewhere else. I'm guessing there's plenty more you want to say to me.' Her heart sank even as she said it.

He shook his head. 'I have to meet Gretta in half an hour. She had a medical appointment in the city.' He pointed to the letters. 'I wonder what Katherine would say if she read these.'

'If you want to use your mother's correspondence to hurt one of your mother's friends, go ahead. It's Katherine you'll be hurting, not me. But I'll tell you this: it's a strange way of honouring your mother's memory.'

'Don't you dare lecture me about my mother's memory,' he said, 'you of all people.' He stuffed the letters back into the satchel and took out a red diary. He opened this to a page marked with a frayed ribbon, and began to read. His voice shook, whether with nerves or anger she couldn't tell. Every so often he stopped and took a deep breath in an effort to steady himself. '"Monday, August eleventh",' he read. '"It isn't the cheating that surprised me, more the scale of it. Bravo, Stuart. Angela Feldman – I'd always known about her. She more or less told me in Sylvester's one night. I told her I'd sent him to her because he was a useless fuck and she was a slag. Maggie Stead – no surprise there either, or Daisy that udderless cow. The girl from the filling station was probably generic. Susan probably wasn't even her name. But Nessa. I thought he was making it up until he said it so many times I knew it was true."'

He let the journal fall closed in his lap. 'Long list, eh?' he said. 'You must have been worried you weren't going to get a mention.'

'Luke,' she said, 'I'm sorry.'

He clutched the diary tight to his chest the way a child might. 'You don't much like to listen, do you?' he said.

'What's that supposed to mean?'

'You only want to hear what suits you. You don't like being told that you're wrong. Like with Ms Doerr. I believe her when she says that it's hers.'

'Listen, Luke, there is no evidence for that. I have read everything there is to read about Robert Locke. I have gone through every newspaper clipping . . .' She stopped. She was wasting her time. The argument they were having had less to do with Doerr and more to do with the fact that having read through the contents of that box, having encountered her disparagement of Katherine, and possibly his relatives also, having learned that she had slept with his father, he was disappointed, enraged at her. She was no longer a suitable friend for his beautiful dead mother.

'Have you heard Ms Doerr talk about Locke?' he said. 'Or about the Chalk Sculpture?'

'Sadly, yes. Have you?'

'She was on the radio yesterday. It got me thinking. She's right. Locke was working with ephemerality, he was

189

specifying the work's temporal limitations in his choice of stone. To disregard that is anti-art.'

So Doerr was on the airwaves now? For a second, Nessa felt like she was standing on a beach, attempting to fight the sea with a bucket.

'If my mother were alive, she'd listen to Ms Doerr,' Luke said. 'She wouldn't stand by and ignore her. She'd ask questions.'

'I know you hate me, Luke,' she said. 'I'm not going to attempt to talk you out of that. I know you have your reasons, and they're pretty valid ones. But I have to get back to work.'

He caught her by the elbow, causing her to jump. 'Tell me what really happened the weekend my mother died.'

She frowned, shook herself free. 'I told you already,' she said. 'That day in the car, coming home from the Lockes' place. We talked, remember?'

'No,' he said, shaking his head. 'You didn't tell me, you fed me a pack of lies. Did you think I'd fall for that? I want you to tell me the truth. Is that too much to ask? If you can't do it for me, can't you at least do it for my mother? Surely you must see that you owe her that much.'

'I've told you how it happened. What else can I do? This isn't going to fix anything, Luke.'

'You fought with her, didn't you? You fought with her that night she took her life.'

'Your mother fought with everyone that night.'

'What did you fight about?'

'It wasn't a fight. Your mother didn't know what she was saying, that was all. She wasn't making sense.' Now, more than ever, Nessa realised the truth of this. She thought of Amy asking her to be Luke's godmother even though Amy had *known* about her affair with Stuart, had known and yet hadn't accused her of it.

Luke looked down at the floor for a moment, and when he looked up again, the expression on his face had changed. 'Does your husband know you slept with my dad?'

She said nothing.

'I thought not,' he said.

'Philip and I weren't together back then. It isn't any of his business who I slept with before I met him.' Her heart had begun to pound harder.

Luke shook his head. He gave a bitter laugh. 'So you think your husband should be spared the truth?' he said. 'Even though my mother wasn't?'

'It wasn't my decision to tell your mother,' she said quietly. 'If it was left to me, she'd never have found out. I believed, until a week ago, that she died not knowing. It was the only solace I had at the time.'

He sneered. 'So you expect me to believe that the subject of you fucking my dad never once came up the weekend she killed herself?'

'I don't expect you to believe anything I say, Luke. Why would you? But it's the truth. I don't know why your mother never accused me of it, but she didn't. If I were her, I'd have torn my eyes out. And I didn't mention it because I thought she didn't know. I didn't want to hurt her.'

'You thought you'd got away with it,' he said.

'Well, I guess I was wrong about that, wasn't I?'

They sat in silence for a moment.

'So are you going to tell me what you fought about?' he said.

She sighed. 'Listen, Luke, I've told you before, your mother wasn't making sense that night.' Nessa hesitated. 'If

191

you must know, she asked me to be your godmother. She had concerns that Aunt Gretta wasn't suitable. I couldn't possibly say yes. I thought that if she knew what your dad and I had done, she'd never have asked me. And now it turns out that she did know, and why on earth she still wanted me to be your godmother I have no idea. But she wasn't being rational that night. She kept asking, and I kept saying no.'

He looked at her. His expression, startled at first, changed to incredulous. 'You're lying,' he said. 'There's no way my mother would have asked you to be my godmother. You're the very last person she'd ask.'

'Why would I make something like that up?'

He shrugged. 'Because you can. Because you think you can get away with it, the way you got away with everything else.'

'I think it's clear by now that none of us got away with anything,' she said. 'Some things it's too late to fix. All we can do is not make them any worse.'

His mother's diary had been resting in his lap and now he put it back in the satchel. He stood up. 'When I think of how you treated my mother . . .' he said. 'When I think of how she must have felt, finding out, it's easy to see how it drove her to kill herself. And there you are, swanning about with your husband and daughter, perfect wife and perfect mother, as if butter wouldn't melt. It's not fair, it's not right.'

'Please, Luke . . .' she said, but he was already walking toward the exit.

She folded her arms across her chest and for a moment she stood very still, as if contemplating the pieces on display, although she was not seeing them at all. Then she went upstairs to her office, locked the door, and burst into tears.

26

Somehow she lasted at the gallery until closing time, not venturing out of her office until 5 p.m., and then she went out the back door that led to a side lane, to avoid bumping into anyone. She knew she looked a mess – she'd caught a glimpse of herself in the mirror – pale, apart from her now-ruddy nose and her eyes puffy from crying. As she walked home to Sunday's Well she put on headphones and kept her eyes fixed on the pavement, in case she met any neighbours. She stopped at the shop at the end of their road. It had once been the club house for a local soccer team. Now it was an emporium of fine food: seaweed crisps, olive tapenades, organic almonds in snack packs of ten. Nessa picked up rye crackers with black pepper, a bag of organic spinach, a tub of ricotta. She made her way up the other aisle, backtracking briefly for fresh egg pasta, a baguette to spread with garlic butter, a half-pint of fresh raspberries. She carried the food like an offering to the till, set it down in front of the cashier. Her life might be spinning out of control, but she could still go through the motions of making dinner.

Walking up the path to their front door, she saw Jennifer curled up listening to music on the sofa. She appeared in that instant more a young woman than a girl, suddenly grown up. The other evening, Jennifer had surprised her by remarking how it must be difficult for Nessa these days, being reminded about Amy, having to talk about all that stuff again. She'd followed this up by bringing her mother a cup of tea. Nessa had waited for her daughter to ask for something: money, or permission to attend some unsuitable event, but Jennifer had simply settled into a beanbag to watch TV. Yes, Nessa thought, as she turned her key in the door, it *was* difficult being reminded about Amy; she was glad that her daughter didn't know precisely how difficult. Imagine if Jennifer knew that her mother had slept with Stuart Harkin. There would be no more cups of tea if Jennifer found that out, no more sympathy either. She didn't like to dwell on her daughter's likely response; it was troubling enough for a teen to grapple with the concept of their mother having sex at all, without adding betrayal and infidelity to the equation, and with a man whom Jennifer had only encountered as middle-aged, unemployed, and in a bad jacket.

She stepped into the hall, the foodstuffs clutched to her chest in a brown paper bag, and was immediately engulfed by the smells of home. She would gladly endure the fate of the prodigal son, she thought – or whatever fate was handed out to prodigal daughters. She would stay on as a servant, she would remain here under any terms, she would wait on them hand and foot without complaint if only this home, this family that in recent months she had felt so equivocal about, would not be snatched from her.

Philip came out of the kitchen and took the bag from her. He looked so pleased to see her that she felt a lump in her throat, even if his pleasure was possibly sparked by the sight of the bread. No matter. She accepted his kiss. 'Let me put these away,' he said.

'Don't put them away,' she said. 'I'm going to cook,' but he'd already hurried into the kitchen and she could hear cupboards opening and closing.

She went into the living room to sit on the sofa next to Jennifer, who, up close, looked a child again. 'I thought

194

I'd make lentil ragu,' Nessa said. This was her daughter's second-favourite meal after tacos.

'Aren't you going out?'

'No,' Nessa said, but then she saw Philip in the doorway with his coat on.

'I think you've got a date,' Jennifer said, beaming.

But Nessa knew there was no date. Philip had a particular expression on his face that she'd come to recognise over the years: anxiety run through with the effort of hiding his anxiety, mouth set halfway between grimace and smile. He was not a man given to surprise dates. Mutely, she stood up. *He knows*, she thought. *Luke has told him about me and Stuart Harkin.* She should have handled the boy more carefully, placated him rather than antagonising him. She should have played for time. She should at least have come directly home and told her husband first, got to him before Luke did. She walked toward Philip the way she supposed people on death row walked to the chair. She glanced back over her shoulder at Jennifer. For a split second, she wondered if her daughter knew also and was playing along, if the two of them had already decided her fate between them. But Jennifer just smiled and said, 'Have fun, you guys.'

Philip put a hand on her shoulder. 'Come on,' he said. His voice was sombre but not unkind, and she climbed into his car with a sense of all she was about to lose settled low and tight in her stomach. She couldn't speak, not even to ask where they were going. She closed her eyes and waited for him to say what he had to say, but he was quiet, frowning at traffic lights as they drove out of the city. How inequitable, she thought, that she was to be undone by an affair that had happened when she was so young, one that hadn't even lasted that long. Philip's affair with Cora Wilson had been conducted by two people in their forties. Nessa had indisputably been the wounded party, or one of them, at any rate, because of course there was Richard Wilson. But it would be harder to wear that mantle from now on, once she was revealed to have done her own share of wounding.

One of the other mothers at the school, a woman who volunteered at an animal shelter, used to tell a story about a road on the north side of the city that was the most popular for abandoning dogs, dogs whose families could no longer afford the vet bills or the microchipping or the dog food. Mummy or Daddy would put the kids to bed, then bundle the dog into the car and drive out to this godforsaken road where they were unlikely to meet any of their neighbours, unless the neighbour was also engaged in an act of dog abandonment. On any given night, the woman said, you would find a wandering dog on this road, a ring of flattened fur around its neck where the collar had been removed. As she sat, miserable, in the passenger seat, Nessa felt like one of those dogs, about to be cut loose.

Philip drummed his fingers on the steering wheel, a thing he did when he was nervous. They turned down a road that led after some miles into the countryside, though it was not the road of lost dogs and they passed no wandering strays. It was a road they used to drive a good deal when they first moved to Sunday's Well. After they went through a crossroads with a thatched pub and a car dealership, she recognised the red gates of a café they used to come to when Jennifer was still in a high chair. They had had the cutest high chairs in that café, wooden ones made to look like the cockpit of a Spitfire. It would be unacceptable nowadays, it wouldn't be allowed, but when she and Philip went inside, there it was still, worn about the edges, the screws faded, the paint chipped, but unmistakably the same high chair she'd once lowered a kicking and screaming Jennifer into. Nessa thought she might begin to bawl. She was careful not to look at Philip.

He put a hand on the small of her back and guided her toward a table by the window. 'I've something to tell you,' he said. 'I thought this might be the place to come, we haven't been here in a while. Do you remember?'

She nodded, confused. His demeanour was not that of a man about to level accusations.

'I've been offered a job,' he said.

'Oh.'

'It's at the University of Cardiff. An assistant lecturer in the Department of Architecture.'

She was attempting to dismantle this news into its various components, but the relief coursing through her was slowing her mental processes. 'That's wonderful,' she said finally. 'You've often talked about doing something like that.'

'I didn't want to say anything until they made me a definite offer,' he said. 'I don't want you to think I was keeping it from you, but I just didn't want to make a big deal out of it and then have it come to nothing.'

'It's okay,' she said, 'I'm pleased, I really am. More than pleased. You deserve it. I'm very happy for you.'

He reached across the table and took her hand. 'For us,' he said. 'This is a chance at happiness for us. For you and me, for Jennifer. It can be our fresh start.'

He couldn't possibly know how much she wanted a fresh start. No more being subjected to Henchy's petty barbs at the gallery; no more being ambushed by sightings of Cora Wilson. 'How would it work?' she said, but already she was mentally calculating the permutations.

'We'd rent out our house here,' he said. 'We won't sell up until we see how we get on. But I think you'd like Wales.'

'I know I would,' she said.

'Cardiff has galleries,' he said, 'and an art school. And it's not like you particularly enjoy working at the gallery here anymore. You seem very down lately. We'd have a steady wage coming in every month, a bit of breathing space.'

'And Jennifer?'

He looked confused. 'She'd come with us, of course.'

'Yes, but how do you think she's going to feel about it?'

'It's not like she's happy here either. You said that your-self.'

Nessa didn't think she'd said exactly that. But salvation was in her sight and she was not about to let it slip away. 'Kids change school all the time,' she said, 'it doesn't do them any harm. They're resilient.'

Philip nodded. 'It might do her the world of good.' His nervousness had dissipated, now that he'd seen she was up for the idea, and the old assured, persuasive Philip was back.

A waitress came to take their order and Nessa could have sworn that she recognised the woman from years before. They ordered two club sandwiches and tea that arrived in a floral china pot. 'I'll be able to declare bankruptcy in Wales,' Philip said. 'It's a shorter process over there. We'll be out of the woods, it'll all be behind us, and we can start again with a clean slate.'

A clean slate. The luxury of it. 'It would be good to get away from here,' she said.

'You don't have to think of it as a permanent thing if you don't want to,' he said. It was as if he'd had all his lines pre-pared and now felt obliged to use them. Perhaps he hadn't expected her to agree so readily. It was the least combative conversation they'd had in weeks. 'Think of it as a trial first,' he said, 'see what you think.' She wondered what he'd have done if she'd said no, if he'd have gone anyway, but she pushed the thought from her mind.

He leaned across the table. 'I take full responsibility, Ness, for the way things have gone between us.'

'You don't have to do that,' she said.

'I do,' he said. 'That business with Cora Wilson . . .'

She flinched, and he reached out, caressed her cheek with his fingertips. 'It was unforgivable,' he said. 'I can't believe how stupid I was. I can't believe you've stuck with me. But I love you, Nessa. I always have. I want you and me and Jennifer to give our life together another shot, far away from all the reminders that keep dragging us down.'

She blinked back tears. 'I want that too,' she said. 'Believe me, there's nothing I want more.'

'I don't deserve you,' he said. 'But I'm going to try harder from now on.'

As they drove home, she was almost overwhelmed by the enormity of her relief. The universe, in its inexplicable generosity, had handed her another chance. She would seize this chance with both hands; it might be their last. One way or another, she would decommission the past that had so rudely intruded; she would find a resolution to the situation she currently found herself in with Luke Harkin. He was just a boy, after all. She could handle him.

27

An evening at the gallery in late May and the sun was slanting through the high windows. The pieces exhibited in the second of the series of talks on Robert Locke were smaller and displayed in glass cases. They were six pieces he'd made during the 1980s. They were half bird, half plant, and there was more joy in them than in his earlier work. They were less on the point of flight, more rooted, even if the birds were gazing heavenward with eyes so startled that it looked as if the roof of their world might be coming off. One of the pieces bore such a startling resemblance to the little silver bird in the ashtray of Nessa's car that her gaze kept sliding back to it.

With the Locke acquisition and the Chalk Sculpture in a limbo of sorts, this event was a smaller, quieter affair. Henchy had floated the idea of cancelling it, but after discussion with the gallery's lawyer, it was decided that it was better to proceed. There was no wine, no photographer, apart from an intern going around with an iPhone. Henchy appeared disgruntled, not just with the quantity of the turnout, but the quality also. 'Look at them,' he said, 'you could tell them anything and they wouldn't know any better.' To which Nessa's brain formulated two diametrically opposed responses: (a) Very likely Henchy was right, the audience couldn't tell the work of Robert Locke from a box of Rice Krispies. Or (b) perhaps they could, or perhaps at least one of them could. And because these days thoughts of Amy were never far from the surface, she remembered her friend challenging Locke about the dark canvases of Edwin Miles. She'd felt bad on

Locke's behalf back then, although in the weeks following the lecture she'd borrowed a book on Miles from the library, and remembered thinking that yes, he did sound like a miserable sort of man, as opposed to a victim of geography.

As she addressed the audience, she was keeping an eye out for Melanie Doerr. She was not, however, expecting Luke Harkin. He must have slipped in at the last minute and was standing at the back, on the edge of the gathering. The sight of him threw her off course. She lost her train of thought, stuttered to a halt mid-sentence, and had to start again. He was wearing the same raincoat he had on that night she first met him at the Ferriters' cabin, now looking a bit worn. He was unshaven, and a lock of hair was curling onto his forehead. Somehow, keeping her eyes on her notes, she got to the end of her speech, and resumed her seat in the front row beside the gallery lawyer, her heart pounding.

Henchy was already on his way to the podium, rubbing his hands together and talking as he went, ready to send the audience on their way. The lawyer was putting his notepad back in his briefcase. Nessa sat staring straight ahead. Luke's voice came from the back of the room: 'I have a question.'

The director looked at him. Frowned. 'Fire away,' he said.

'The question is for Ms McCormack.'

'Oh. I see,' Henchy said. 'Fine. All right.' He beckoned Nessa up.

She got up from her chair and smoothed down her skirt. She walked slowly to the microphone, forced herself to meet Luke's gaze. 'Yes?' she said.

'I've only recently discovered the work of Robert Locke,' Luke began. He paused and cleared his throat. 'I'm a fan.'

Nessa took solace in the fact that however nervous she was feeling about his intervention, he was clearly nervous too.

'I've noticed,' Luke continued, 'how Locke's work shows a marked diversity of approach from one period of his life to the next, often from one piece to the next. If we compare, for example, his sculptures from the late seventies with—'

'Is there a question?' the director said.

Luke coloured. 'I understand,' he said, 'that the gallery is acquiring Robert Locke's studio and with it some of Locke's papers and personal effects . . .'

He had prepared, Nessa realised. He had rehearsed his question, perhaps even borrowed the phrasing from an article somewhere, because since when did a twenty-one-year-old talk about 'personal effects'? It was the sort of thing the gallery's lawyer, currently dozing in his seat, was more likely to say.

'I was in contact recently,' Luke continued, 'with a person, a woman, who also knows a great deal about Mr Locke and his work. She mentioned that he was in the habit of keeping a diary.' He placed just the slightest inflection on the word 'diary'. 'And I'm wondering,' he said, 'if these diaries shed any light on his artistic process?' Several members of the audience grunted their approval at the question, and turned in their seats to look at him.

'No,' Nessa said. It came out blunter than she'd intended. 'The gallery is not in possession of any diaries belonging to Mr Locke.'

'Are you sure?' Luke said.

'Yes,' Nessa said curtly. 'There are a small number of notebooks, but I'm not aware of the existence of any diaries.'

'I could have sworn that my friend said "diaries".'

'Nope,' she said. 'I'm afraid you – or we – are out of luck. I imagine that even if they did exist, they would be regarded by his family as deeply private items and not for public consumption.' She had, in fact, asked Loretta – Eleanor too – whether Locke had kept a diary. He hadn't.

'That's a shame,' Luke said. He seemed less nervous now. 'A diary can provide so many insights into a person.'

'Thank you for the question,' the director said. 'Now if—'

'I'm particularly interested in the Chalk Sculpture,' Luke said. 'I've been reading a lot about it lately, about the inspiration behind it, for example.'

The gallery lawyer started in his chair at the mention of the Chalk Sculpture.

'I'm aware of recent narratives in certain media outlets regarding that particular piece,' Nessa said. 'Having researched Robert Locke's work over many years, I find the accounts provided by the Locke family, and by archived photographic material, to be the more compelling.'

'But there's no photo that directly matches the Chalk Sculpture,' Luke said. This sounded less rehearsed than his earlier contribution.

'As to the significance of photographs generally,' Nessa said slowly, 'the sculptor interprets the photo, the viewer interprets the sculpture, and in that way, the originating image, while an interesting fact, certainly, must no longer be our chief focus. Indeed, it may only serve to detract from the deeper meaning of a work.'

The lawyer was semaphoring with his arms, mouthing 'Close it down.' The director stepped over to the microphone, practically shoved Nessa out of the way. 'I'd like to thank the young gentleman for his question,' he said, but Luke was already striding toward the exit. Nessa excused herself and went to the bathroom. She locked herself in a cubicle and stayed there for fifteen minutes until she stopped shaking.

At her desk the next morning, Nessa opened the folder that contained the photograph of Eleanor, young and beautiful, on the hotel balcony in Nice. It was indisputable, she thought – the outline of the Chalk Sculpture seemed to rise from the photo like a hologram. She underlined something Locke had said during a conversation with a journalist in 1989 when he'd unequivocally attributed the inspiration for the sculpture to the photo of his wife. She had thought that there were many instances of Locke saying this over the years, but upon reviewing her notes, she saw that there was only the one. But one was enough, as her mother was fond of saying, mostly in an ominous way: a warning about sperm, say, or mussels that remained unopened after cooking. Nessa brought a photo of the Chalk Sculpture up onscreen. Allowing that it had no face, it was possible to argue that it both was and wasn't Eleanor Locke. Its essence lay not only in what was in that photo, but also in what had been subtracted. The missing railing opened up the void into which the sculpture reached, becoming a thing on the point of falling. But as she stared at the photo, something else settled upon her with conviction: Whatever might or might not be there of Eleanor, there wasn't one iota of Melanie Doerr.

She took out another folder on the Locke acquisition and read back over her research. Comments made by Locke that she'd initially viewed as unequivocal, now lent themselves to more than one interpretation. The academic extracts she quoted no longer had the clarity she recalled on first reading, and she found herself skipping over passages, to return to them later. She reread the transcripts of her interviews with Eleanor, alongside copies of interviews given by Locke. They were of one voice, these interviews. Sometimes phrases were repeated verbatim, like children copying from one another's exercise books. She typed 'Robert Locke sculptor' into her computer's search engine and scrolled through the results. The first four pages comprised all the usual suspects: articles and interviews she had encountered many times before. Halfway down page 5 she spotted something new: a reference to Robert Locke in the abstract of a master's thesis on Anglo-Irish literature in the twentieth century. The thesis was held at a UK university library. What Locke had to do with Anglo-Irish literature, she couldn't guess, he was never known to be much of a reader, and she suspected it was more than likely a typographical error. Nonetheless, she ordered a copy of the thesis. An automated reply said her request would take twenty-one working days to process and allocated her a transaction number.

28

Later that week, Nessa was at home, having taken a day off to clean her house. She'd been approached at work by the human resources manager, who'd pointed out that she had a lot of annual leave remaining, and perhaps it would be a good idea if she began using it up. She was upstairs mopping the bathroom floor when she heard Jennifer come in from school. There was the sound of bags being dropped on the hall floor, only today it sounded like more bags than usual, and she could hear her daughter talking to someone. Nessa went out onto the landing, to listen better. There was music playing now, but she could definitely discern a second voice, a girl's, and it sounded familiar. She abandoned the mop in its bucket of sudsy water and went downstairs.

'Hi, Mom,' Jennifer said, when her mother came into the kitchen. There sitting on a stool at the kitchen island was Mandy Wilson. *The dead arose and appeared to many,* Nessa heard Amy say in her head.

'Hello, Mrs McCormack,' Mandy said, pushing her long hair out of her face. She flushed. 'I hope you don't mind me coming over.'

She didn't expand on why Nessa might mind, but it hung in the kitchen between them. 'It's a pleasure to see you again, Mandy,' she said. And it was. Mandy was a nice girl, a genetic throwback to a grandparent, Nessa thought, because the girl wasn't remotely like her mother in temperament. Or her father either. And this would be progress to report to Ms Johnson, would it not? Perhaps it was even Ms Johnson's doing. Nessa had recently bumped into Ms Johnson in the checkout queue at Tesco, and the teacher had made a cryptic comment about how it would be good to talk some more about 'that other matter'. Nessa had said, 'Yes, of course, absolutely,' and then pretended to have forgotten something in the detergent aisle and hurried off.

'Jennifer,' she said now, 'get something for Mandy to eat,' but Jennifer had already fetched a packet of chocolate chip cookies and two cans of Coke.

The girls sat at the kitchen table and scrolled through their phones. Nessa was about to leave them to it, when Jennifer said casually, 'Luke Harkin's in town. He said he might drop in.'

Nessa had been scouring a pot and now she let it clatter into the sink. 'I didn't know you were still in contact with Luke,' she said.

'Yeah,' Jennifer said. 'We chat on Facebook sometimes.' This was delivered with a glance across the table at Mandy.

'Today isn't good, Jennifer,' Nessa said. 'I have to go out in a while. You'll have to put him off.'

Jennifer scowled. 'He's only in town today. He's staying with some relative who lives in the middle of nowhere and today's the only day she can drop him to the bus. Anyway, we can still meet him, even if you can't. We don't need a babysitter.'

'You know I don't like you having men in the house when I'm not here. When your father's not here. It isn't a good idea.'

'We're not children.'

'You're not adults either. And I have to think about Mandy's parents. What would they say? A grown man their daughter doesn't even know.'

207

'They wouldn't mind,' Mandy said quickly. 'And I do know him. Sort of. Jen gave me his email address and he helped me make a webpage for the school magazine.'

'Yes,' Jennifer said. 'And it was Luke encouraged us to be friends again, wasn't it, Mand?'

Mandy nodded. 'Life's too short,' she said solemnly. 'That's what Luke says.'

'Tell him no,' Nessa said firmly.

Mandy looked crestfallen. Nessa didn't want to involve the girl in a row when it was her first visit to the house in such a long time. She didn't want to scare her off. 'I'm responsible for you when you're under this roof,' she said, then added, more gently, 'I'm sorry, but that's just the way it is.'

She went back upstairs and sat on the edge of her bed to compose a text to Luke. She didn't wish to antagonise the boy further, but there was no way she was having him coming to her home, talking about goodness knows what with her daughter. And Cora Wilson's daughter. 'I'm sorry, Luke,' she texted, 'I know we need to talk, but I have an appointment today, so you can't come over.'

He replied almost instantly. 'I wasn't coming to see you. But hey, another time.'

She finished mopping the bathroom and went back downstairs. The girls were sitting at the table with their phones. 'I thought you'd be interested in seeing the photographs Luke took of the Chalk Sculpture,' Jennifer said accusingly. 'He's a very good photographer.'

'How do you know?' Nessa said.

'He sent me this. Look.' She held up the screen of her phone. It wasn't, as Nessa was expecting, a photo of the sculpture. It was a photograph taken by Luke the night at the Ferriters' cabin when they'd gone out on the lake in the kayaks. It was the shot of Jennifer on her own, not with her parents. She was gazing shyly at the camera, head to one side.

'Did he send you that by email?'

Jennifer shook her head. 'Instagram.'

'I snapchat him,' Mandy said, helping herself to another cookie. 'He followed me and I followed him back. Jennifer said she didn't mind.' She angled her chair so that she was facing Nessa. 'Have you been thinking any more about the Chalk Sculpture, Mrs McCormack?'

'I think about the Chalk Sculpture lots,' Nessa said. 'It's my job. Why?'

'She was on the radio again,' Jennifer said.

'Melanie,' Mandy volunteered, when Nessa looked bewildered.

So it was 'Melanie' now? 'When was this?' Nessa said.

'Yesterday afternoon,' Jennifer said, 'on the Riley show.'

'Well then,' Nessa said, 'if it's on the Riley show, it must be true.'

'You'd have to feel a little bit sorry for her, wouldn't you?' Mandy said. 'It *is* a good point she makes about the disintegration being an integral part.' This was a more persistent child than the one Nessa remembered.

Nessa was overcome with weariness. Locke's work was possibly the only topic that she'd ever felt confident claiming she knew something about. Why was she now doubting herself even in that, and having to justify herself to these kids? Why was Cora Wilson's daughter contradicting her in her own kitchen?

'Luke's really upset about it,' Jennifer said. 'He feels everything so deeply, you know?'

'How do you know what Luke feels?' Nessa said.

Jennifer's expression became defensive. 'He posted a story,' she said. 'Anyone can read it.'

'On Instagram,' she added, when Nessa looked confused. 'And you have to admit it's not a cut-and-dried case, is it, Mom? Poor Ms Doerr.'

'This isn't your mom's fault,' Mandy said. 'She has to do what the gallery tells her.'

Bless your heart, Mandy, Nessa thought, even if it wasn't exactly the robust defence she would have liked.

Mandy's phone buzzed just then. 'Oh,' she said, 'I've got to go. My mother's taking me to get my hair cut.' She must have noticed the flicker of anxiety on Nessa's face, because she added, 'I'm meeting her at the corner.'

Nessa watched Mandy pick up her bag from the hall and sling it over her shoulder. She didn't want her to cut her hair. It would, she realised, make the girl look older, make her look too much like what she was: someone on the verge of adulthood.

Everything was moving too fast. Nessa wanted to go back to the days when Mandy Wilson was just a little girl who hung out with Jennifer, when Cora Wilson was just Mandy's frumpy mother and not someone who'd slept with Nessa's husband; she wanted to go back to a time when the Chalk Sculpture featured in her life as a thing of genius and beauty, not something about which she had to argue constantly. She wanted to go back to a time when she'd never heard of Melanie Doerr; back further even than that, to a time when she had never known Stuart Harkin.

After Mandy had gone, she sat at the kitchen table beside her daughter. 'Jennifer,' she said, 'how did Luke know that you and Mandy had a . . . um . . . a falling-out?'

Jennifer coloured. 'Because I told him.'

Nessa's heart sank. 'Did you tell him *why*?'

Jennifer shrugged. 'Maybe. So what?'

'Jennifer, it's better if you don't discuss that sort of thing – private things – with strangers.'

'It's hardly a secret. Anyway, Luke isn't a stranger. Weren't you and his mom best friends?'

How far, Nessa wondered, had Luke infiltrated her daughter's confidence?

'Jennifer,' she said awkwardly, 'you know that if Luke asks you to send him a photograph of yourself, an, um . . . an inappropriate photograph . . . you should never do that?'

Jennifer grabbed her phone from the table and stood up. 'He doesn't ask me to do stuff like that.'

'Good. But if he ever does, you should say no. Because he might be trying to blackmail you. And don't look at me like that, Jennifer; it does happen.'

'Blackmail?' Jennifer glared at her. 'It wouldn't occur to you that it might be because he likes me?' She slammed the door behind her as she left the room.

After supper that evening, a supper eaten only by Nessa and Philip – Jennifer having refused to come out of her room – Nessa went for a drive, alone, to soothe her nerves. She did a loop of the city, down along the quays, across the river and out Grattan Street, Western Road, sweeping around by the university, and back over the river to Washington Street. Then she drove out to Ringaskiddy, where she parked by the pier and watched the cars driving onto the ferry. She sat by the waterside for an hour until a man working on the ferry approached her. He seemed uncomfortable as he asked if there was someone she'd like to call, or that he could call for her. He said it in a way that sounded as if he'd memorised it from a manual, and Nessa said, 'No, not all at, I'm fine, thank you, I like to look at the water,' and then she turned the key in the ignition and drove away.

211

Habit led her to choose the road she used to take on the Wednesdays she called to the Lockes. It was as good a direction as any other, she thought, and she drove on, listening to classical music on the car radio, trying not to think about her row with Jennifer. Dusk settled on the fields and ditches and she switched on the car headlights. From the ashtray in the dashboard, the little silver bird gazed up at her accusingly. She'd planned to return it discreetly on her next visit to the Lockes, but now there was no telling when that might be. It came to her as she drove that she was currently a mere twenty miles from their house; she could simply drop it through the letterbox. The lawyers could hardly take issue with that, surely. It's not as if she would be speaking to anyone. She would fold the silver bird inside a piece of paper and push it through the letterbox and then she would immediately get back in her car and drive away.

It was dusk as she drove up the avenue, and she switched off the car headlights so as not to draw attention to herself. There was no need for the Lockes to know she was here. As it turned out, Loretta's Land Rover wasn't in its usual spot at the side of the house, and there were no lights on downstairs, save for the hall. Perhaps the women were on a rare trip out. *Better again*, she thought. She found a brown envelope in the glove compartment and she sealed the piece of silver inside. Tiptoeing up the path to the porch, she put the envelope through the letterbox, listened to it drop onto the floor on the other side.

She was back in her car, about to turn the key in the ignition, when the porch light came on. *Damn it*, she thought. For a moment, she considered driving off. But the front door was already opening and someone was in silhouette in the doorway, looking down the path. It occurred to her that in her hurry to return the piece, she hadn't thought to put a note in the envelope, and felt foolish. It would look like she'd been attempting something underhanded, something grubby. The figure in the doorway shifted slightly and now that the light better illuminated it, she saw that it was Eleanor. Sighing, she got out of the car.

'Loretta?' Eleanor called shakily. 'Where are you, Loretta?'

'It's only me,' Nessa said quickly as she made her way back up the path.

Eleanor, when she reached her, was in a dressing gown and slippers. She looked as if she'd just woken up. 'You?' she said, and she blinked several times. 'What are *you* doing here?'

Nessa pointed to the envelope on the floor by Eleanor's feet. 'I took something by accident the last time I was here. I thought I'd return it. I didn't want to disturb you.' She bent and retrieved the envelope, handed it to Eleanor. 'I'm sorry.'

Eleanor turned the envelope over in her hands, frowning. Slowly, she opened it. Her eyes widened when she saw the little silver bird. She took a step backward, startled. 'I was going to drop it back at our next meeting,' Nessa said, 'but since we're now not going to have a next meeting . . .' She watched as Eleanor rolled the piece between her fingers. Though in need of a good polish, it shone dully, the silver contrasting with the black lace cuff of Eleanor's nightdress. In the glare of the porch light, Nessa thought the piece looked more like an otter, or perhaps a hybrid: a cross between a vole and a bird, its feet petering out, rootlike, into its base. It was a piece of exquisite silverwork, which, if scaled up, would bear an uncanny resemblance to Robert Locke's *Hills & Dales* series. Nessa stared, transfixed, a thought that had been fermenting in the recesses of her brain now coming into sharper focus. 'Eleanor,' she said, 'did you make this?'

Not taking her eyes from the piece of silver, Eleanor nodded.

'It's magnificent,' Nessa said.

Eleanor shrugged. 'It's nothing much. I don't know why we still have it. I told Loretta to throw that rubbish out years ago.'

'I'm very glad she didn't,' Nessa said. 'This deserves to be seen.'

'Modest' didn't readily spring to mind in relation to Eleanor, but Nessa thought the older woman appeared suddenly bashful, no longer looking at the little silver creature, but at the floor. 'I hadn't realised you were an artist too,' Nessa said. 'How come you never mentioned it?'

Eleanor shook her head a couple of times, harrumphed. She was suddenly back to her usual self. 'Artist indeed!' she said. 'I was no artist. I made things for my own amusement in my father's workshop. Trinkets, mementos, that was all. Robert was the artist, and one artist in any family is quite enough, thank you.'

Nessa reached out, touched the piece balanced in Eleanor's liver-spotted palm. 'You must see . . .' she began. How exactly could she put this? 'You must see the resemblance to Robert's work? I'm thinking of *Hills & Dales*—'

Eleanor cut her off. 'Because he also made birds? And animals? People have made the same things from the start of time.'

Nessa shook her head. 'It's more than that, Eleanor. You know it is.'

'I know that you're being impertinent.'

Nessa pressed on. 'You know what I think?' she said. 'I think you sacrificed your work for Robert's. He stole from you and you let him.'

'If I let him, then it's hardly stealing,' Eleanor said. 'And in my day, young lady, "sacrifice" was a word we reserved for men who went away to war.' She slipped the silver creature into the pocket of her dressing gown and put her hand instead on the front door. 'I think you should go now.'

'I didn't mean to upset you,' Nessa said. 'I'm just struck by how good your work is. It's such a shame that you stopped making it, such a waste.' She nodded toward Eleanor's pocket, where the outline of the tiny bird–otter bulged through the fabric. 'That – and the others too, the ones in the scullery – deserve to be seen by the whole world.'

Eleanor's gaze narrowed. '*Robert*'s work must be seen by the world,' she said. 'Isn't that what you're supposed to be about? Isn't that why our lives have been turned upside down these past months? If you are so very sure that my work is in Robert's, then when Robert's work is seen, mine will be also. Do your job right and there will be no, as you call it, *waste*.' She placed her free hand on Nessa's shoulder and with a show of strength that was surprising, pushed her out onto the doorstep. The door closed and then the porch light went off, leaving Nessa to make her way in darkness back to her car.

29

When Nessa woke Friday morning, the clock by her bedside said 8.32. Philip's side of the bed was empty. She groaned, wondering if it was too short notice to ring work and say she was taking another day off, and decided that it probably was. She jumped out of bed and began pulling on the clothes she'd discarded the night before. She grabbed a jacket from the back of a chair, checked that it was hers, and ran out the door. With as much decorum as was possible at that speed, she jogged along Sunday's Well Road, passing the iron pedestrian bridge, and along the quays into town.

Afterwards, she would think that it was just as well that she had arrived late to the gallery that morning. If she'd arrived at her usual time, Melanie Doerr might have been apprehended by someone else. Or she might not have been apprehended at all, and might simply have grown tired and gone home. As it was, Nessa was walking up the front steps when she spotted Doerr's rucksack in the foyer, thrown on the floor with a plastic bag beside it. Doerr herself was standing in the space housing the Locke exhibition, with four people around her in a semicircle. Her accented English held just the right amount of strangeness, and she had something Nessa's mother would have approved of: good posture, exaggeratedly straight, almost tipping back on herself. Today she had dressed as a guide might: a white blouse, a cravat neatly knotted, straight black trousers. From a distance, the long rectangular pendant that she wore on a string around her neck could be mistaken for a lanyard. Nessa walked over and positioned herself at the edge of the group. She stood with her arms folded, listening. Doerr's delivery didn't falter. 'Locke once spent a week in the National Library studying the camouflage of animals,' she was saying. 'He envied them their countershading, their visual trickery, the way a moth blends into the mottled surface of a stone.'

Nessa turned on her heel and went over to the information desk. 'What's going on?' she said to the woman behind the desk, who was new. The woman looked up from her computer screen. 'I presumed it was something somebody organised,' she said. 'Isn't it?'

'That's Melanie Doerr,' Nessa said.

The woman looked at her blankly. 'Is it a problem?' she asked nervously.

In her neat shirt and trousers, Melanie Doerr looked like any other tour guide. 'It's okay,' Nessa said. 'I'll deal with it.' She could see Doerr watching them as they spoke. There were now seven people in the semicircle. Nessa crossed the foyer. 'I'm so sorry to interrupt,' she said, 'I need to borrow Melanie for a moment.' She could tell from their withering glances that Doerr had given them a different name. One of the men stepped forward and pressed a crumpled banknote into Doerr's hands. She took it, squirrelled it away in her trouser pocket. Several other people had their wallets out now. 'All right,' Nessa said, 'that's it. Come with me.' She hadn't worked out what she'd do if the woman refused, but Doerr simply said, 'Allow me please to get my things.' They walked without speaking to where she'd left the rucksack and she slung it over her shoulder. The plastic bag, she carried in her hand, swinging it back and forth as she walked beside Nessa to the exit. 'I'd ask you what you thought you were doing,' Nessa said, 'except I'm not allowed to speak to you. For legal reasons.' She hesitated. 'I'm surprised you've come back here, given how angry you were the last time we spoke. I thought you were done with me.'

Melanie Doerr stopped on the front step, put down the bag. 'I never know when to give up on a thing. I never know when to forget. It's the story of my life.' She shrugged. 'Anyhow,' she said, 'did you find it interesting? My talk?'

Nessa raised an eyebrow. 'Animal camouflage? Countershading? Seriously.'

'I thought it an apt analogy.' She paused. 'I'm glad I've bumped into you. I was hoping we could reschedule our chat.'

Nessa shook her head. 'It's a bit late for that. The lawyers wouldn't like it.' She glanced at Doerr, who said nothing. 'And maybe they've got a point,' Nessa continued. 'You've stalked me at my home. You've undermined my work. Maybe it makes sense for us not to hang out.'

'I visited you,' Doerr said. 'Visiting isn't stalking.'

Nessa sighed. She had an urge to walk down the gallery steps and keep going, to turn left, right, or to cross the river, it didn't matter, she would simply keep walking, and her colleagues at the gallery would eventually notice that she had gone, would guess that she wasn't coming back. She would leave her colleagues to clear her desk. She would, in due course, send them a postcard from Wales. If it wasn't that she needed that month's salary cheque, if she wasn't still clinging to a vague and ever-diminishing hope of a bonus for the Locke acquisition, she would walk out of here right now. 'You know,' she said, turning to Doerr, 'most people would have the grace to apologise.'

'I don't like this any more than you do,' Doerr said. Her expression as she looked out onto the river was almost serene. 'I could think of other things to do with my morning. This is all down to Eleanor Locke and her fibs. And Loretta, who used to be different – better – going along with them. It's down to you shutting your mind to the truth when I know you know better.'

'You know what the strangest thing is?' Nessa said. 'I don't even care about any of that anymore. I have so much else going on right now that your hostilities with Eleanor no longer make the grade. I've stopped caring.'

'That's not true. You care deeply. Maybe not about me, but you care about Robert, about his work. I could see it in your face the first time I heard you speak about him. I saw it that day at your house when I showed you the little ones.' She touched her foot to the plastic bag on the step beside her. 'Would you like to see them again? I brought them along, in case you might.'

Nessa looked at the bag and then at Doerr, whose gaze was fixed on her expectantly. Doerr picked up the bag, seemed on the verge of unpacking it. 'I think,' Nessa said, half to herself, half to the other woman, 'we should go somewhere else to do that.'

'Back inside?' Doerr said, pointing to the gallery.

Nessa shook her head. If Doerr went back in, goodness knows how long it might take to coax her out again. 'Wait here,' she said. She ran inside and went up to the information desk again. She told the new employee to tell the human resources manager that she was taking the rest of her annual leave with immediate effect. A thought was formulating in her head. Since there was now so little of her career at the gallery left to lose, why not make one final attempt at getting to the bottom of the matter? Back outside, she glanced down the street to where a taxi was idling at the kerb.

'Come on,' she said, beckoning Doerr to follow as she walked down the steps.

Doerr halted beside the open door of the taxi. 'Where are we going?' she said.

'To my place.' Nessa settled into the backseat. 'I don't need to tell you where that is.'

Doerr hesitated a moment on the pavement. 'All right,' she said then, and she got in, tossing the rucksack and plastic bag onto the seat between them. Nessa leaned forward, gave the driver the address. She waited until they were driving down the quays before she said, 'We're going to get my car. Then we're going to drive to the Lockes'. We're all going to sit civilly around a table and sort this out once and for all.'

Doerr looked quickly left and right, as if contemplating escape. 'You told me we were going to your house.'

'And so we are. It's not a lie.'

'Huh,' Doerr said, folding her arms across her chest. 'What about the lawyers?'

'What about them?' Nessa said. 'They won't like it, but what are they going to do? Fire me? I'm going to leave anyway.'

Doerr had begun drumming her fingers on the plastic bag. She broke off abruptly and turned to Nessa. She smiled. 'I knew you cared.'

When the taxi pulled up outside her house, Nessa paid the fare and hopped out. Doerr didn't. 'Come on,' Nessa said, waiting waiting on the pavement.

'I don't know,' Doerr said. She appeared suddenly vulnerable. 'I'm not sure that this is the right thing to do.'

'Welcome to my world,' Nessa said.

The driver turned around to stare. 'Are you getting out or what?' he said.

Nessa reached into the car and dragged out Doerr's ruck-sack and, more carefully, the plastic bag. She gave the bag the gentlest shake – she didn't entirely trust that Doerr was being honest about the contents. Whatever was in the bag made no sound to give itself away, but it was possible that everything was swaddled in towels, as before.

With a loud, exaggerated sigh, Melanie Doerr climbed out of the taxi. The driver threw Nessa a sympathetic glance as he drove off. Nessa pointed to her own blue Cit-roën, parked by the kerb. 'Hop in, I'll put your things in the boot.'

'I'd rather keep them with me, thank you.' Doerr stashed her belongings on the floor by her feet.

They left the city using the same route Nessa had driven so many times over the previous months, the same route she had driven the night before. She was reminded of a genre of books popular when she was at school where the beginning of the story was always the same, but the ending depended on what options the reader chose along the way. She had never liked those books; they made her feel complicit whenever something bad happened.

Doerr looked out the window for the first twenty minutes.

'Would you like the radio on?' Nessa said, because the silence was uncomfortable.

Doerr shook her head. 'Do they know I'm coming?'

'No. They don't know I'm coming either.'

'Eleanor won't like it. She never liked people arriving unannounced.'

They drove in silence for another mile. 'Perhaps they won't be in,' Doerr said.

'Perhaps. But it's not like they ever go anywhere.'

'It's been such a long time,' Doerr said, as they were passing Innishannon. 'I don't remember these roads, or perhaps we never came this way.'

Nessa glanced across at her. 'You know the area?' She had no idea what, if anything, she could believe from the woman.

'I spent time here, remember?' Melanie Doerr said. 'The summer of 1973.'

The year Locke had begun work on the Chalk Sculpture. But then, Doerr would have known that, could employ her knowledge to serve whatever story she chose to spin.

'You'd have to wonder about the artistic value of what the gallery is doing,' Doerr said. 'I mean, quite apart from what is being done to me. I don't wish to be difficult, I can see that you're sad today. If you'd like to tell me what's distressing you, I'm considered a good listener, anyone who knows me will tell you that. But I'm not sure all this posthumous excavation is worthwhile, trying to pin down Robert's work, like children playing at pinning tails on horses.'

'Donkeys,' Nessa said. 'It's Pin the Tail on the Donkey.'

'See?' she said. 'You always have to be right. Robert never trusted academics, you know, called them the devil's fire shovellers.'

Nessa laughed. 'He accepted enough money off universities during his life.'

'He was right to take their money,' Doerr said. 'The less they have, the less harm they can do. Better that Robert spent it on a nice bottle of Rioja.'

'Or a crate of it,' Nessa said, Robert Locke not being known for stopping at one bottle.

They drove deeper into the countryside. Every so often Doerr marvelled at some plant or other in the ditches, before lapsing again into silence.

Nessa decided a more direct approach was necessary. 'Did you tell Luke Harkin that Robert Locke kept diaries?'

'The boy messaged me, asked me if Robert had kept any. I told him that he was in the habit of keeping notebooks, which to all intents and purposes were the same as a diary. It's hardly the name on the cover of a thing that determines its nature.'

'I was granted access to all his papers,' Nessa said slowly. 'Or at least all of them that are known to exist. You must believe me when I say that there is nothing approximating a diary.'

'I rarely saw him without a notebook in his hand that summer,' Doerr said.

'Perhaps he liked to look busy.'

'Perhaps Eleanor destroyed them because she didn't like what she read.'

'Do you have proof of that?'

Doerr sighed. 'No. But once, when I asked him what he was writing in the notebooks, he said that he was writing about me, about the work I was doing.'

'Did he ever let you see them? Or give them to you to read?'

Doerr shook her head. She turned away to look out the window once more and there was suddenly so much sadness in her face that Nessa decided to change the subject. 'Tell me again how you came to know the Lockes.'

'It was Robert that I knew first. I think I explained that. I met him up North at an artists' colony a year before I came to Cork. I was working in housekeeping at the colony, but I had the evenings off. We wrote to each other afterwards, simple letters about art and books and the ideas of the time, the kind of letter anyone could read.'

'Did he write back?'

'In the beginning, he always wrote back.'

'Did you keep the letters?' She tried to keep her voice neutral, but the thought of a previously unseen trove of letters by Robert Locke was enough to make her want to pull the car onto the shoulder and take this woman next to her by the throat and throttle her until she handed them over.

'I kept them for years and then later, when I got older and got a bit of sense, I burned them.'

'You *burned* them?'

'Yes.' Then, as if to change the subject, she said, 'I'd forgotten how beautiful it is here, so wild, so unspoiled.'

Nessa gripped the wheel tighter. She thought that she would never forgive the loss of those letters – if, of course, they had existed in the first place. She cast a sideways glance at Doerr. 'I expect it was dark the night you came down here with your letter for Loretta,' she said. 'I expect that's why you don't remember how beautiful it is.'

Doerr's expression clouded. 'Yes,' she said, turning to the side window. 'It was dark, and I had my eyes closed pretending to be asleep, to stop the driver talking.'

Nessa didn't like to think how much that taxi ride might have cost. 'Why didn't you just post it?'

'It didn't seem right to consign a communication like that to the post, not knowing when or if it might arrive.'

She tapped Nessa on the shoulder, startling her and causing her to swerve. 'Don't do that,' Nessa said when she'd brought the car back onto its own side of the road, 'you'll cause an accident.'

'Don't expect me to be nice to them,' Doerr said.

'You haven't exactly been nice to me. I've no expectations that you'll be nice to anyone else.'

'Huh,' Doerr said. 'You're not exactly charming yourself.'

They were close to Tragumna when Doerr leaned forward in her seat, pointing animatedly to a tiny side road. 'This way, this way,' she said.

Nessa brought the car to a stop on the shoulder. 'That's not the way,' she said.

'It is. That's the way we used to go. A shortcut. I remember the first time Robert drove me to the top of that road and I saw the sea from there.'

The lane branched off the main road, leading in the general direction of the Lockes' house. It was possible that it was an alternative route, though Nessa doubted that it was shorter. 'Did the taxi go that way?' she said.

Doerr waved a hand dismissively. 'I told you,' she said, 'it was dark that night. I don't know what road we took. But I remember this was the way Robert brought me. And anyway, it's not like we have to be there for a particular time. It's not like they're expecting us.'

Nessa pulled back onto the road. 'I'm going to take the road I know,' she said. 'I didn't come all this way to get lost. After we've all had our chat, we can go home any which way you like.'

30

When Nessa parked outside the Lockes' house, Doerr bent to rummage in her rucksack. She upended it and shook half the contents onto the car floor – travel guides, a packet of wipes, a sweater, a hairbrush, several lined notebooks, and a box of whole-grain crackers – until she'd made enough room to shove the plastic bag in. She stepped out of the car, slipping the rucksack onto her back. She stood looking at the house. When Nessa went to stand beside her, she saw that tears were streaming down her face. Doerr tut-tutted, embarrassed, and drew her sleeve quickly across her cheeks. 'They'll never let us in,' she said.

'They will,' Nessa said. 'They'll let us in and we'll sit down together and have a reasonable discussion.'

'Huh,' Doerr said, 'that woman never had a reasonable discussion in her life.'

'Which one?' At that stage Nessa wasn't sure that she'd have applied the word 'reasonable' to either of the Lockes.

'I meant Eleanor,' Doerr said. 'I used to have some wonderful conversations with Loretta. That all stopped, of course. But we used to talk once. We talked about what she'd do with her life; Loretta had plans for a life once. I feel sorry for her, her life wasted like it was, but then I think about how she denies ever knowing me, the barefaced lie of it. The Loretta I knew wouldn't have been capable of lies.'

Nessa's phone rang. When she saw that it was Luke Harkin, she dropped it back in her handbag, unanswered. Melanie Doerr had her back to the house and was pointing to a distant spire, saying something about its history, but Nessa was hit by a wave of panic. The dazzling sea and the silver light on the horizon acquired an apocalyptic tinge.

Doerr darted suddenly into the middle of the garden, where the wet, untended grass reached above her ankles. 'Look,' she said. She stooped to pick an unusually shaped mushroom. She waved it at Nessa. 'We used to gather these, Loretta and I. We'd get up early in the morning and fill whole baskets.' She bent to pick another. They were morels, stubby, with brown vaulted caps.

'They mightn't like you picking their mushrooms,' Nessa said. 'I think you should stop.'

Doerr ignored her. She gathered up the ends of her blouse to serve as a basket, exposing the pale skin of her stomach. Inside Nessa's handbag, her phone pinged – Luke, presumably, leaving a message. Why was he contacting her? she wondered. To arrange to call round? To berate her? Nessa glanced in at the studio where the Chalk Sculpture stood, majestic, and felt like a ghost gazing in on her old life. She turned to Doerr to say something, but stopped when she saw the expression on her face. Doerr's attention was on a different window. Loretta was in the porch, her face pressed to the glass.

Doerr seemed dazed, rooted to the spot. She was still carrying the morels in her blouse, the white cotton streaked with mud and a strip of greyish stomach on display.

'Throw those things in the grass,' Nessa said. 'You can't go in like that.'

Loretta opened the front door. Her cheeks had a purplish tinge. 'How dare you,' she said to Nessa, 'how dare you bring that woman to our home.' There was no doubting her anger, but she delivered the words quietly, almost in a whisper.

'Lotty,' Doerr said, 'look what I found. I haven't picked mushrooms since I left this house. Remember how we used to go out in the mornings . . .'

Loretta came down the path toward them. She struck at the outstretched blouse, knocking the mushrooms to the ground. One rolled in a half circle, another broke into pieces. 'We went mushroom picking once,' Loretta said. 'Once. Do not make me out to be your long-lost friend. We are not friends.'

'I thought you didn't know her.' Nessa matched her voice to Loretta's, low and hushed. 'And now you're telling me you went mushroom picking together?'

'Once,' Loretta said, 'we went once. And I only remember because there was such a fuss afterwards. She' — she inclined her head toward Doerr — 'had picked pookapiles and puffballs, didn't know the difference.' She jabbed a finger at Nessa. 'You!' she said. 'I was about to call you. What on earth were you thinking of, coming here last night?'

'Can we talk inside?' Nessa said.

'She can't come in,' Loretta said. 'My mother won't stand for it.'

'Tell her why,' Doerr said.

'Because you're a lying thief, come round sniffing after money.'

It had begun to rain, a half-hearted drizzle. 'I don't care what your mother thinks,' Nessa said, 'we're going inside.' The words took her by surprise — it was the first time she'd displayed such defiance to Loretta. The feeling it brought was not unpleasant.

Loretta seemed caught off guard by the sudden forthrightness. As they went to walk past her into the porch, she took

Nessa by the arm. 'Give me a moment to settle her for a nap. I'll give her a cup of tea and a sleeping tablet.' She glared at Doerr. 'You ruined our lives once,' she said, 'and not content with that, you've come back to do it again, to hurt my mother in what may be her final weeks.'

'In that case, she won't have to suffer the hurt for long,' Doerr said. 'Not like me, left to hurt for years.'

Loretta turned to Nessa. 'I'll be back out presently,' she said. 'Go wait in your car.' She paused on the porch. 'This may take a while. Sometimes my mother can be slow to take her naps. She might notice that it's early.'

The rain had become heavier, but the day wasn't cold, and the interior of the car was humid and airless. Nessa put down a window and fiddled with the radio until she found a music station. Then, fearing Eleanor might hear the music, she switched it off again. The women sat in silence for a while. Nessa thought that she should ring Jennifer to check what her plans were for the afternoon – she hoped they didn't involve Luke Harkin. 'Excuse me,' she said, taking out her phone, 'I need to ring my daughter.'

She got out of the car, careful to close the door quietly. Hunching her shoulders against the rain, she sheltered beneath a tree as she listened to the phone ring out. She returned the phone to her bag and got back in the car.

'Your daughter. Is everything okay with her?' Doerr asked.

Nothing is okay with her, Nessa thought. *Nothing is okay with any of us.* 'She's fine,' she said, keeping her eyes on the windshield.

'You know, we follow each other on Facebook, Jennifer and I.'

'What?' Nessa turned to face her.

'Yes. Although we don't have much to do with one another. But I enjoy the photos she posts of Bailey.'

'Bailey . . .' Nessa repeated faintly.

'We discovered each other through a mutual Facebook friend. The young Harkin gentleman, as it happens,' Doerr said.

Nessa thought she was going to be sick. 'Jennifer doesn't tell me who she hangs out with on Facebook,' she said. 'She knows that I don't like her spending time on it.'

'If I had a daughter, I wouldn't like her being on Facebook either. But what can you do?'

'The Harkin boy. And Jennifer. What do they talk about?'

Doerr shrugged. 'Films, Bailey, choir.'

Nessa didn't realise she'd been holding her breath until she released it. 'Is that all?'

'He posts often about the Chalk Sculpture. That was how we came to each other's attention. He sends me private messages; he's quite an intense young man. He offered to design a poster and make a podcast. I think he must have qualifications in that area. He describes himself as a supporter of my cause.' She laughed. 'It's strange to have acquired a "cause" at this hour of my life. Sometimes it occurs to me that my cause might do better without the assistance of that young man. He's too excitable, I think. And too angry. I think your daughter might do better with friends her own age, girls her own age.'

Nessa glanced at Doerr, then quickly looked away again. Was the woman hinting at something? She fixed her gaze on the windshield. She wasn't comfortable with her daughter and Luke exchanging confidences. It was unlikely to end well. She would take Jennifer aside as soon as she got home, would attempt to persuade her not to have anything more to do with Luke Harkin. How exactly she would broach this, she didn't know, but it would have to be done.

'Jennifer seems a nice young woman,' Doerr said. 'Innocent. I was like that too when I was her age. I was still like that when I was a good deal older.'

Nessa switched on the windshield wipers, took refuge in their rhythmic squeak. Here was Melanie Doerr, she thought: intelligent, handsome, in good health, a woman who, as best she could tell, was without dependants and had financial means. And she was wasting her life, waiting in a car in the middle of nowhere, fighting with the family of a man who may very well have slept with her occasionally, but who hadn't let her existence encroach upon him in any meaningful way, who hadn't thought fit to acknowledge her, allowing for the sake of argument that some acknowledgement may have been warranted. Robert Locke had been dead for close to twenty years. At what point was it too late to say to someone, *He's just not that into you.*

She jumped when Loretta tapped on the car window. 'You can come in now. I had to give her two pills. I hate doing that, but I can't take the risk of her waking up.'

They were on the porch when Nessa noticed that Melanie had brought her rucksack with her. She raised an eyebrow, but the other woman wasn't meeting her gaze. They went through to the kitchen, where Loretta motioned them to sit at the small table. Melanie appeared nervous. She took the chair farthest from Loretta. 'It's strange to be back,' she said, setting the rucksack on the floor beside her.

Loretta was clasping and unclasping her hands.

'Loretta,' Nessa said, 'why did you tell me that you didn't know Melanie?'

Loretta cleared her throat. 'If you cast your mind back,' she said, 'I think you'll find that I said I didn't remember any person by the name of Doerr. That remains correct. She didn't call herself that back then.'

Nessa could feel her temper rising. 'You're fucking with me, Loretta,' she said, 'you're wasting my time. Again.' She turned to Melanie. 'You too.'

'Oh now,' Melanie said, 'oh now.'

Loretta spoke first. 'It's grubby,' she said, 'for her to appear out of the woodwork like this, thirty years on when there's money changing hands. It shows a lack of class, though I suppose we're not allowed say things like that anymore. Imagine if everyone who'd ever known my father started laying claim to his work. The whole thing is ludicrous. That sculpture is of my mother at the Hotel Negresco.' She looked at Nessa pleadingly. 'We've talked about this,' she said, 'you *know* this. Everybody knows it.'

'Can you imagine what it's like for me to be back, Lotty?' Melanie Doerr spoke softly. 'I came to put the record straight. It's not about the money. I've probably spent more money these past weeks than that sculpture is worth. It's hardly his finest hour.'

Loretta flinched. 'So you're an expert now?' she said.

'You were always jealous of me, Loretta.'

'Don't flatter yourself! What would I be jealous of?'

'Of the life I was going to have. Of my closeness to your father.'

Nessa had put up with enough. She wanted to be done with all this and get home. She had family matters to attend to. Perhaps Jennifer merely saw Luke Harkin as the brother she'd never had, but there was too much of his father in the boy for Nessa's liking. At the same time, she had a wish to rehabilitate herself in Luke's esteem, if only in memory of Amy. 'Melanie,' she said, 'were you and Robert lovers?'

Loretta's hand went to her throat. Her expression was one of disappointment rather than anger.

'I'm sorry,' Nessa said, 'but we've wasted enough time.'

'Like I told you, I met Robert in Inishowen in 1972,' Melanie said. 'We wrote to each other, off and on, for a year, and he invited me here as his student.'

'You took advantage of my mother's trust and hospitality,' Loretta said. 'You took advantage of me, pretending that we were friends.'

'We *were* friends, Lottie,' Melanie said. 'But how could I tell you about me and Robert? You were too young, and he was your father. I wasn't entirely honest with you back then and for that I'm sorry, but I was twenty-one years old and in a foreign country. My position in the household was precarious.'

'I've no wish to hear your excuses,' Loretta said. 'What is it that you want?'

'I want you to stop telling lies,' Melanie said. 'I want what's mine: the Chalk Sculpture.'

'It's not hers,' Loretta said, turning to Nessa. 'It had nothing to do with her. It's evident that he worked from the photo of my mother. He's on record as saying that.'

Melanie bent and unlaced the boot on her right foot. Slowly she removed her sock. She pushed back her chair and stood up. Balanced on one leg, she extended her foot in the direction of Loretta. Nessa leaned across the table to look. Doerr's foot was webbed, the two smallest toes fused together. 'The foot was the first thing he carved of the Chalk Sculpture,' she said. '*My* foot. All that gibberish about Huxley amphibian influences was invented by the critics. Robert went along with it; it made it all sound more intelligent than it was.' She remained standing, absentmindedly wringing her sock in her hands, twisting it the way a distressed Victorian lady might twist a handkerchief. 'I want to see it,' she said. 'I haven't seen it – not properly, not in the flesh – for so long.'

She didn't wait for Loretta to say yes, but walked barefoot out of the kitchen and down the hall. Nessa noted that Loretta's disappointment now appeared to have been replaced by fear. They got up from the table and followed Doerr to the studio. Her walk was uneven: one booted foot, one bare webbed foot. It could have been a transcendent moment, muse and sculpture reunited under one roof, but in the studio that day, the light tamped down by the persistent rain, Melanie looked like what she was, an aged woman in a mud-streaked blouse, her hair frizzy from the rain, her exposed foot looking grey and mottled and very human beside the ethereal magnificence of the stone. She stood very still beside it for a moment and then she stepped away. The Chalk Sculpture had a way of humbling people.

Nessa had hung back in the doorway of the studio, beside Loretta. Melanie turned and pushed past them hurriedly. 'Excuse me,' she said, 'I must fetch something,' and they watched her hobble up the hall.

Loretta swore under her breath, a mild oath, but it was the first time Nessa heard her utter any kind of profanity. 'Do I have to trail her all over the house?' she said. 'Am I reduced to performing the duties of a security guard in my own home? What on earth possessed you to bring her here?' But already Melanie was returning down the hall, on the point of breaking into a run, the rucksack over her shoulder. She got down on her knees in front of the Chalk Sculpture and took out the plastic bag containing the miniature carvings. Each one emerged with a smattering of white dust. It was painful for Nessa to see these things, which might or might not be the work of Robert Locke, abused in such a fashion, their heads banging off each other, the ones that had heads, because some had been decapitated, whether by accident or design, and others were missing limbs. Without saying a word, Melanie arranged them in a circle around the base of the sculpture. Loretta had grown completely still, apart from her breathing, which had become more pronounced, her chest rising and falling beneath her cashmere sweater. When the last of the little maquettes was in place, Melanie turned to the two women. 'Let's play a game,' she said. There was an edge to her voice. 'Guess which are his and which are mine.'

It was a sordid game, in bad taste. And yet . . . Nessa found the temptation almost too great. Would she know? Could Melanie even be trusted to know, with all the pieces mixed together for so long, battered to the point where they might, literally, be unrecognisable? And if she did know, would she tell? Nessa took a few steps into the room. She crouched low beside the Chalk Sculpture, noticed the quickening of her pulse that always happened when she was near it. At first glance all the pieces seemed to have been carved in the same general style. On closer inspection, in juxtaposition with the mother sculpture, some seemed more like legitimate offspring than others; oddly, it was the pieces that were less like the Chalk Sculpture that held a strange familiarity. She experienced a tug when she peered at them that she couldn't explain. There were nine little creatures in total, all of them maimed to varying degrees. Five she would categorise as having emanated from the same hand as the Chalk Sculpture. The other four didn't share the same likeness, but felt known to her in a different way. As she continued to observe them, a strange dichotomy presented itself: the more distant cousins, the ones that chimed least with the Chalk Sculpture, were the ones that resonated most strongly with the work of Robert Locke in his middle years.

31

'Do you see?' Melanie said.

Nessa swallowed. She opened her mouth to say something, closed it again. At that moment, she didn't know what to think.

Loretta was less circumspect. 'I have no intention of playing your silly games,' she said. 'If any of those are my father's, I suggest you leave them here with the rest of what belongs to him, and go.'

'These ones,' Melanie said, and she began to circle the sculptures, 'are mine.' She touched the heads of five of the tiny white figures. 'See how they resemble their mother.' She turned to Loretta. 'The others were made by your father. He never worked with maquettes, but I did, and when I persisted, he threw some together to please me. See how he has infused their little necks with the intimation of a curve. I was never able to manage it.' She rubbed the Chalk Sculpture's arm, gently, as if in apology, the way one might rub the arm of a child who was sick. 'But this, flawed as it is, is mine. Or ninety per cent of it is mine; the other ten per cent is Robert's.' She bent and ran a finger along the carved foot with its exquisite toes and nails. 'The foot was the first thing Robert carved of the Chalk Sculpture,' she said. 'It's also the only thing.'

Nessa looked at the Chalk Sculpture. She looked at the little maquettes, their different parentage more obvious now that she saw them clustered together around their mother. 'Why didn't you come forward years ago?' Nessa said. She fully expected Loretta to throw them out at any moment.

'Because nobody tried to take it from me until now. I always meant to come back for it someday. And I liked to hear it lauded as the masterpiece of Robert Locke. The praise that sculpture got! If it had been put out under my name, nobody would have paid it any attention.' She turned to Nessa. 'I thought you knew,' she said. 'I thought you knew but were averting your eyes for your own purposes. After all, what gallery would pay money for a sculpture by Melanie Doerr? I thought, "She's the expert, she has surely read Robert's diaries, she must know."'

'There are no diaries,' Loretta said. 'My father didn't believe in them.'

'Yes . . . well,' Melanie said. 'Robert is the only one who knows for sure about that.'

'The Chalk Sculpture achieved fame a long time ago,' Nessa said. 'And Robert has been dead years. Why wait so long to claim it?'

'It had come to mean something to people, especially to the women who got pregnant. I've seen their photos on the internet, bouncing their little Chalk Sculpture babies on their knees. Imagine how they would have felt when they discovered that it wasn't after all the work of Robert Locke.'

Nessa raised an eyebrow. 'You do know that the Chalk Sculpture didn't make them pregnant?' she said.

Doerr's mouth set in a tight line. 'Who is to say?' she said. 'The doctors think they know everything, but there is so much not yet understood about the connection between mind and body. I've read the studies in the medical journals. Fertility may be affected by stress, anxiety; the Chalk Sculpture gave those women hope when the obstetricians gave them nothing. So what if it acquired a reputation beyond what was proven or earned? That's the way the world works, is it not?' An edge had crept into her voice. 'It suited everyone to pretend the sculpture was made by Robert. It suited even me for a while. He promised me that people would know the truth in time, that he was writing it all down.' She gave a short laugh. 'That seems to have been a joke at my expense, the way much of Robert's life was a joke at other people's expense.'

'Many artists have assistants,' Loretta said. 'I often think my father should have made more use of them.'

'You watched me working on it, Loretta. You used to sunbathe in the front garden just to spy on us.'

'So now I'm a spy?' Loretta said. 'For sitting in my own garden?'

Nessa turned to Loretta. 'Did you see her working on it?' she asked. Loretta ignored her.

'It unnerved me,' Melanie said, 'to know that you were watching us. I had to hang drapes on the windows, even though it spoiled the light, because I hated so much being watched. I used to get up early in the morning to work while you were still in bed.'

'Whenever you drew the curtains in the studio,' Loretta said, 'I used to think that you and my father were making love. I used to run to my room and put a pillow over my head in case you made any noise.'

Melanie shook her head. 'We never made love in this house,' she said. 'It was one of his rules. That should have been a warning to me, because he would happily fuck me behind a sand dune, or in the car down a lane.'

Nessa waited for Loretta to interrupt, but she didn't.

'I gave him an ultimatum once,' Melanie continued. 'That he make love to me in this house or not make love to me at all. I lasted two weeks and then I couldn't stand it anymore, I had to give in.'

'Did Eleanor know?' Nessa said.

'About me making the Chalk Sculpture? Or about me sleeping with her husband?'

Loretta shook her head. 'You didn't make it,' she said, her voice little more than a hiss.

'I saw the way she looked at me over supper the first evening I arrived,' Melanie said. 'She must have had her suspicions before. I'm not so naïve as to believe I was the first. Robert was a busy man when he wasn't working. But she only began to hate me properly when she found out that we were working together. That was something none of his other women had been granted. I think she was more angry about that than about the fact that he might be sleeping with me.'

All the time Doerr was speaking, Nessa was looking at the Chalk Sculpture, taking apart grain by grain everything she'd ever thought she knew about it. It was not, after all, Locke's exploration of the amphibious nature of human existence. It was a piece of work by a young student he'd taken advantage of, a deception he'd been happy to feed for his own glorification and private amusement.

'But I didn't lose Robert because of Eleanor,' Melanie said. 'I lost him because of this.' She slapped the rump of the Chalk Sculpture, slapped it so hard it wobbled. 'Up until then, I think Robert believed that I had some covert talent that had not yet come to fruition, that there was greatness in me, it was just buried very deep down. Perhaps he thought that if he fucked me enough it might become dislodged and would surface. I do think he believed in the sacramental nature of his fucking. When he saw that I wasn't good enough, he lost interest.'

Loretta had angled herself slightly away from both of them, and was looking out the window. 'Is there a need to be so foulmouthed?' she said, almost under her breath. Then, a little louder, and still without looking at the other women, she said, 'My father was kind enough, or foolish enough, to encourage you, to give you a chance. As you have admitted yourself, you weren't good enough. Everything about that sculpture is dependent on the carving of the foot.'

'Not everything,' Nessa said. It had been left to her to defend the sculpture. Neither Melanie nor Loretta was going to come to its aid. All the time she was listening to Melanie, it was as if two separate parts of herself were vying for the upper hand in their reaction. There was the art historian, excited, mesmerised by all that was being revealed. And there was the employee of now dubious standing who would be faced with presenting an update to the director and to the board. Might it be suggested that she should have known before? Looking at the little creatures now – the little Lockes, the little Doerrs – it was easy to imagine how someone might argue that yes, she should. Yet Melanie Doerr, at twenty-one and in love, had been so under Locke's spell that his influence had muddied the waters. It was as if two hands had held the one chisel. Nessa decided that she was not to be blamed, though the likelihood was that she'd be blamed anyway. It would be a mainly private embarrassment, confined to the small circle of art historians and curators who were her peers. Doerr would no doubt be the focus of an article or two, photographed standing next to the Chalk Sculpture in her blue mohair coat. A few short weeks ago, the very idea of this would have consumed Nessa entirely. Now it paled to a mere inconvenience, when compared to the larger and more personal threat to her happiness posed by the prospect of Luke Harkin spilling the beans to her husband, and grooming her daughter. She was reminded of the message waiting on her phone.

'You knew about this, Loretta,' she said. 'You lied.'

Loretta shook her head. 'I never misled you,' she said. 'Not deliberately. There were a few things here and there that my mother was unable to be precise about; it's only to be expected at her age. She did the best she could. And nothing has changed.' She gestured to the Chalk Sculpture. 'It is my father's vision, carved under his direction, in his studio. It's based on a photo of my mother, his wife. It is my father's sculpture.' It was enunciated so clearly, so deliberately, that she must have been turning it over in her head, preparing it, while Melanie was talking. It might be that she'd been preparing it for years.

'The sculpture was always mine,' Melanie said. 'When it was finished, it was to be put on that little beach down there.' She pointed out the window. 'We'd paced it out, measured where the tide came in, where the spray would hit it. We talked about how it would wear away, distort, each passing month.'

There came a rare sound then, the sound of Loretta laughing. 'Could you be any more deluded?' she said. 'It was never going to be put on the beach. How could it even be got down there, for a start? What were you going to do – roll it?'

Nessa looked out across the field of reeds and long grass that sloped to the shore. Loretta had a point.

'Huh,' Melanie said. She'd adopted the exaggeratedly straight posture that Nessa had observed at the gallery earlier, the slight backward tilt. She clasped her hands in front of her, tightly, and even from some feet away, Nessa could see the whiteness of her knuckles. 'It was to be put on the beach,' Melanie said. 'But Eleanor sent it away when Robert refused to carve a face on it. You know that very well, Loretta.'

Another laugh. 'Is that what he told you?' Loretta said. 'He had it taken away to a friend's farm because he needed space here.' She spread her arms to encompass the room. 'Once he'd finished a thing, that was it for him. It was on to the next. The sculpture was only in his way.'

A floorboard creaked overhead. 'Oh, dear God,' Loretta said, and she ran out to the hall. Nessa followed her, but Melanie Doerr remained behind in the studio. Eleanor, in her bathrobe, had made her way to the top of the stairs. She was gripping the banister with both hands, doing an odd sideways shuffle as she edged herself down. Her robe was blue, quilted, tied around the waist with burgundy cord, and she wore slippers, not the terry-cloth sort, but ballet-style in pale gold. Her hair had come loose from its French twist to hang untidily to one side. 'Stay where you are, Mother,' Loretta said, and Nessa had never heard such panic in her voice. 'Don't move.'

Eleanor nodded at Nessa. 'What's she doing here again?' she said.

Loretta had scaled the stairs in a few strides and was now by her mother's side. Nessa glanced back into the studio, saw Melanie frozen to the spot in the middle of the floor. 'Who else is here?' Eleanor said. 'Who is it that you're smirking at?'

Nessa hadn't realised that she was, in Eleanor's words, 'smirking'. It was a thing that happened when she was nervous. 'Nobody,' she said.

'Come on,' Loretta said. She put one arm around her mother's waist. 'Let's get you back to bed.' With her other hand, she attempted to loosen her mother's grip on the banister.

That was the moment Melanie chose to retreat farther into the studio, instinct kicking in, perhaps, in the form of an urge to put more distance between herself and Eleanor. As she stepped backwards she knocked over one of the little maquettes, sent it clattering sideways to collide with another, which also toppled. When they stopped rolling across the studio floor, there followed a second of silence akin to that described by survivors of bombs and other explosions. On the stairs, Eleanor sucked in her breath until both her cheeks were hollow pits.

'Mother,' Loretta said pleadingly.

Eleanor shook off her daughter's hand. 'Who is here?' she said. 'Who have you brought to our house, Loretta?'

Nessa waited for Loretta to rescue them from the situation, but Loretta seemed to choose that particular moment to give up. She abandoned her attempt to steer her mother back to bed. 'I didn't invite them,' she said, 'I didn't know they were coming. They just turned up.' She looked down at her feet, like a girl waiting to be scolded.

Eleanor leaned her weight onto the banister. She was no more than three or four steps from the top, and she shouted down at Nessa. 'Who have you brought with you?' she said. 'Is it that fat man from the gallery?'

Nessa glanced quickly at Loretta, but she was still staring at the floor resignedly. 'No,' Nessa said. 'He's not here.'

'Well, who *is* here?' Eleanor said. 'Is it the solicitor? If it's the solicitor, I'll speak with him myself. I'm perfectly capable of attending to my affairs, in spite of what some people try to tell me.'

Loretta spoke again, tremulously. 'Why don't I take you back to your room, Mother? The solicitor isn't here, but I'll call him this afternoon and arrange for him to come tomorrow.'

'But who . . .' Eleanor said.

Melanie Doerr walked out into the hall. She didn't meet Nessa's eye as she passed her and she didn't say a word until she had reached the foot of the stairs. 'Hello, Eleanor,' she said.

Eleanor seemed to deflate. She collapsed forward, onto the banister. Loretta let out a small cry, put an arm around her mother's shoulders, tried to lift her. 'What is she doing here?' Eleanor said. 'Where has she come from? I thought she was gone.' She sank down onto the step. Nessa started to climb the stairs to see if she could help. 'Get out,' Eleanor said, 'I've put up with enough. Get out and take that . . . that . . . *thing* with you.'

Loretta looked at Nessa. 'It's better if you go,' she said. 'The doctor says she mustn't get overexcited. Her heart isn't up to it.'

It was only when she heard a door slam that Nessa realised Melanie had already gone. 'Goodbye,' she said, raising her hand in an awkward wave. It was hardly an appropriate leave-taking, in the circumstances, but neither of the Locke women appeared to hear her. She battled an urge to sneak one last look at the Chalk Sculpture and its various offspring – 'last' because there was no telling what Loretta might do with them after she left. Even as she fled, she couldn't help picturing how they might look in an exhibition space, the text of the card she would affix to the wall, how the photos should pick up on the hollow in the skull of the littlest one, the texture of the roughness of where an arm had been hewn off, or a leg lost.

32

Melanie Doerr was in the front garden, at the end of the path.

'It was stupid what you did in there,' Nessa said, walking past her to the car. 'Showing yourself, frightening Eleanor like that. It was cruel. You could have stayed quiet.'

'Or stayed away,' Doerr said. 'You were the one who brought me here.' She opened the passenger door and sat in. 'I wasn't going to hide like a small child,' she said. 'I was not going to be afraid of her. Or lie.'

'You didn't mind going along with Robert Locke's lies,' Nessa said.

'With that, it was not so much a question of lying, as of releasing the least amount of information necessary to achieve our purpose.' She glanced at Nessa. 'I was sure that you knew. I thought we were both engaged in the same pretence, but to different ends.' She sighed. 'Now I'm wondering what Loretta did with her father's notebooks. The rest of them, I mean. The important ones. I know they must exist.'

'What am I going to do?' Nessa said, more to herself than to Doerr. The acquisition could not go ahead, that much was clear. She could say goodbye to what hope remained of her bonus. If the Lockes, all of them, had been circumspect with the truth about the Chalk Sculpture, who could guarantee the provenance of the other pieces in the catalogue?

Her phone beeped and when she checked it she saw that it was another message from Luke Harkin. She stared at the screen, contemplating whether or not to click on the message.

'Is everything okay?' Doerr said.

'Just my daughter,' Nessa said, starting the engine. 'Letting me know she's at a friend's house.' She had no intention of explaining her entanglement with Luke; it was enough to have spent the past couple of hours mired in the quagmire of Melanie Doerr's past, without adding to it with her own.

'Your daughter sounds like a thoughtful girl,' Doerr said. 'A friend of mine has a teenager and already this year they've been to the police station three times.'

'Do you have children, Melanie?'

Doerr shook her head. 'No,' she said. 'The time for that has come and gone. I confess it sometimes struck me as strange that the Chalk Sculpture, *my* sculpture, was conjuring up babies, when I didn't have any of my own. Sometimes that made me angry.'

'Did you ever marry?'

'I was married for a few short and sweet years to a lovely and much older man, who has since passed away. I took his name, Doerr; my own name was Petrovic.'

Nessa put her foot to the accelerator, and they drove down the potholed road.

Melanie was silent for a moment. 'There is one thing, and one thing only, that I've been untruthful about,' she said eventually.

'Go on,' Nessa said. Whatever it was, she would do precisely nothing about it, she decided. Today's visit had been ill-judged. The Lockes' solicitor was probably already on the phone to the gallery's solicitor.

'Robert wouldn't have objected to the preservation of that sculpture,' Doerr said. 'If he were alive, he'd probably be lapping up all the attention. He got that block of stone cheap, from a friend. He wouldn't have trusted me with marble, he'd have considered it a waste. That's why it's carved in soft stone.'

Nessa whistled softly. 'You've changed your tune,' she said. 'What was all that fuss about allowing it to disintegrate?'

'It's a monument to my foolishness.'

'You were young,' Nessa said, 'not foolish. At least no more or less foolish than the rest of us. And your work – the Chalk Sculpture – is good; there's something ineffable in it. Rage, maybe. Or desperation.'

'Love too,' Melanie said. 'You don't seem keen to acknowledge love, I notice.'

She would not be drawn into a discussion of love. 'Locke didn't lose interest in you,' she said. 'He was jealous of you. It's why he carved that foot so elaborately, why he made it like the foot of some other creature entirely. He was trying to prove something.'

'No,' Melanie said. 'The foot was his reprimand. I was always ashamed of that foot, and he knew it. When I was a child my mother made me hide it always; it was considered a mark of bad luck. I was never allowed to remove my socks out of doors. The foot was his way of punishing me.'

'For what?'

'For not being good enough. For disappointing him.' She paused. 'For being pregnant.'

Nessa turned to her. 'You were pregnant?'

'Four months gone when I left that house.'

Nessa waited for her to volunteer more but she didn't. After they'd driven a few hundred yards, and when Melanie still hadn't said anything else, Nessa said, 'In that case it was pretty insensitive of him to use that photo of his pregnant wife.'

'I was the one who had the idea to make her – the Chalk Sculpture – pregnant. He fetched the photo of Eleanor outside that hotel when I ran into difficulty with the proportions. I won't pretend that I was pleased – what young girl would be? His wife's photo taped to the studio floor, looking up at me. The photo was from sixteen years earlier, but I remember thinking, from the look on Eleanor's face, from the way she was staring at me, that it was like she'd been waiting for me, as if she'd known I'd be coming someday.'

Yes, Nessa thought, the Chalk Sculpture was indisputably infused with the pith of Eleanor Locke, in her prime.

As if she'd guessed what Nessa was thinking, Melanie said, 'She made her way into the stone after that. I couldn't keep her out. He put her in. That damn photo. Maybe it was his way of telling me something. His way of saying that he wasn't going to leave his wife.'

'Did he send you away, or was it Eleanor?'

'Robert arranged for me to go to Liverpool, to a woman he knew over there, a Mrs Calder. Looking back, I think she must have been one of his old lovers. She made the appointment, took me to the clinic. I never once had a conversation with Eleanor about it. But then, Eleanor had never spoken to me much at all, apart from finding fault. It was Loretta I relied on for company. She was good company back then, believe it or not.'

They had reached the main road, the vista of sea before them. 'Did you have any contact with Robert afterwards?'

'We spoke by telephone in the first few days after I went to Liverpool. I think he probably wanted to make sure that I'd actually gone through with it. I stayed with Mrs Calder for a couple of weeks and then I got a job sewing, making alterations to clothing. He'd given me enough money to go to Liverpool, but not to come back.'

'Bastard.'

'Yes, perhaps, though he never had a lot of money to give to anyone. It was Eleanor's family who paid for that house, he told me that several times.' Melanie seemed about to say something else, then stuttered to a halt. She tried again: 'He did love me, you know.'

How enormously we delude ourselves, Nessa thought. 'You could well be right,' she said, 'I'm no expert on love.' She decided not to tell Melanie that it was Locke's family that had the money, not Eleanor's. Locke, his older brother having died young, had inherited the sheep farm that he promptly and discreetly sold. A distant relative of Locke's had, reluctantly, divulged this to Nessa during her research. Locke himself never discussed it publicly.

On the journey back, Melanie looked out the window, commenting occasionally on some landmark or other, or a flower or tree that caught her attention. When they reached the outskirts of the city, she said, 'So you've never seen anything that Robert wrote about me? Nothing at all?'

'No,' Nessa said. 'I'm sorry.'

Melanie was quiet for a moment, and when Nessa glanced sideways at her, she saw that she was crying. Melanie took a handkerchief from her sleeve. 'Loretta burned everything,' she said, wiping her eyes. 'She must have. There was a time when I would not have expected it of her. But now . . .' She shrugged.

Nessa tuned the radio to a music station. While she waited for the traffic lights to change, she said, 'It's going to be difficult to establish that you own the Chalk Sculpture. The evidence is against you.'

Melanie nodded. 'So my lawyer tells me.'

She didn't speak again except to direct Nessa to the B & B when they reached St Luke's.

33

When Nessa got home to Sunday's Well that afternoon, the first thing that greeted her as she stepped into the hall was the smell of something burning, something more complex than blackened toast because there were hints of herbs in there too. It was a sound that registered next, the sound of her daughter crying. She opened the door to the living room. Jennifer was on the sofa beside Philip. He had his arms around her and she was weeping loudly, her shoulders convulsing. The sudden shock of it: her child, hurt. As she crossed the room she thought, *If she's crying with that much force, at least she can't be ill, or not too ill*, because it was a hearty wailing, and as she reached her daughter, she detected a hint of anger.

She wondered if Luke, piqued that Nessa hadn't returned his call, had phoned Jennifer, explained to her exactly what sort of person her mother was.

She sat on the other side of Jennifer and began to stroke her hair. 'What's the matter, sweetheart?' *Please, God, let her not be pregnant.* The thought came unbidden. But Jennifer wasn't pregnant.

'I won't go,' she said, raising her face, streaked with tears, to her mother, 'you can't make me.'

'I thought it was a good time to tell her,' Philip said. 'She was complaining about school, and I thought it might cheer her up.'

'I wasn't complaining,' Jennifer wailed, 'I was *saying*. Saying isn't complaining.'

'Is this about Wales?' Nessa said, trying to keep the relief out of her voice.

'I'm going to stay here and live with the Sullivans,' Jennifer said. 'You can go if you like.'

Nessa pushed a strand of hair from her daughter's face. 'There's no need to be like that about it. We haven't even talked it through properly yet. You're not giving it a chance.'

'How could you decide this without telling me?'

Nessa sighed. 'Because sometimes adults have to make hard decisions. There are a lot of reasons why this makes sense right now.'

'You're running away from people, aren't you?'

Nessa flinched, but their daughter was looking, not at her, but at Philip.

'No,' he said, 'I'm doing this because I want a better life for you and for your mother. For all of us as a family.'

'You owe people money,' Jennifer persisted. 'Don't try and deny it. I'm not a child. I know.'

Was this true? Nessa wondered. Did she know? They'd made a point of not discussing financial worries in front of her, but she was a smart kid.

'Nobody's running away from anything,' Philip said. 'We'll have another chance in Wales, that's all. A better chance. More time together as a family. And yes, the money matters. Don't you want to have nice things?'

'I'm going to miss my friends,' Jennifer said.

How ironic, Nessa thought, that just a few short weeks ago she might have taken solace in this assertion that her daughter had friends.

'When I was your age,' Philip said, 'there was a boy in my school who moved to Canada with his family. His best friend went with them for three months to help him settle in.'

Nessa didn't like the idea of Mandy Wilson coming to live with them for three months. That was presuming Mandy was back to best-friend status. Perhaps it would be the Sullivan girl.

Jennifer's expression brightened. 'I suppose we could go for a short while,' she said. 'On a trial basis.'

'If you don't like it, we'll come back,' Philip said. 'I promise.'

If she got away from here, if she survived all this, she would never come back, Nessa thought. But time enough to face that further down the line. She would concentrate on getting her daughter to Wales first, deal with the rest afterwards.

Jennifer stood up. 'I'm going to ring Deirdre.'

'Who?' Philip said.

'Deirdre Sullivan,' Jennifer said.

'Maybe we could keep the news to ourselves for a while,' Nessa said. 'There are a few people your father and I need to tell first.'

'I don't keep secrets from my friends.' Jennifer picked up her phone from the coffee table and ran upstairs.

Was it the Sullivan girl who had told Ms Johnson about them? Nessa wondered. And would the girl have to have her own room in their house in Wales?

Philip touched her shoulder, gave a wan smile. 'I'll go check on dinner,' he said, getting up.

'I'm guessing it's too late for that.' The smell of burning, which she'd temporarily forgotten about, had worsened. 'There's shepherd's pie in the freezer.'

She remained in the living room, gazing out the window at the deadheaded flowers in the front garden. She'd thought she might feel stirrings of nostalgia for them, now that her time here was drawing to a close, but she felt only indifference. She hadn't planted them, it was Philip's mother who'd done that; she hadn't even been that dutiful a caretaker.

She went upstairs to their bedroom, taking her phone with her, and went into the ensuite bathroom. Luke had left a curt message, asking her to ring back.

He answered on the second ring.

'I'm sorry I couldn't call you earlier,' she said, 'I was at work. I had someone with me.' Silence. 'You were looking for me?' she said.

'That day in the gallery,' he said. 'I didn't mean it when I said . . . well, you know, all the stuff I said about you. The things I read out. The names I called you.'

'Don't, Luke,' she said.

'I was upset. I'd only just found out about you and my dad. I hadn't had time to process it. Whatever you might have done, I don't think my mother would have liked me to speak to you like that.'

'Listen, Luke, it's okay . . .'

'And I shouldn't have given you a hard time at that lecture at the gallery. I let myself down. I let my mother down.'

'There's no need to apologise,' she said quietly, 'I'm the one who should be apologising to you.'

'There's something I want to ask you,' he said.

'Go on.'

'It's about the Chalk Sculpture,' he said. 'I have a theory. I've been looking over the photographs I took and I made a few notes. I'd like to show them to you.'

She wondered if she should tell him what had transpired at the Lockes' house earlier: how she no longer needed a theory because now she was in possession of the facts, how it looked like Melanie's version of events was true after all. But it seemed wrong to tell this boy when she hadn't yet had a chance to tell the director or the board.

She took a deep breath. 'Thank you, Luke,' she said, 'but it's okay. I have all the information I need at present.'

'How . . . how can you say that?' he said. 'Don't you even want to know what my theory is?'

'Luke,' she said, more firmly. 'I think you've developed a fixation about the Chalk Sculpture. You need to let it go.'

There was silence on the other end of the phone. '*Fixation* . . . ?' he said eventually.

It had been a poor choice of word, but there was no undoing it now, so she pressed on. 'Yes,' she said. 'Listen, Luke, I know things have gone badly for you here, and I'm sorry for what's happened. But we can't change the past. We can't allow ourselves to be crippled by it either.'

Neither of them said anything for a moment.

'I'm going to go back to Manchester,' he said. He sounded tired. 'I'm going to look for a job. Find a place to live.'

'I think that's for the best,' she said. 'Maybe you'll go back to university?'

He didn't say anything to that, and she imagined him on the other end of the line, shrugging his shoulders, scowling. *An intense young man* – Melanie Doerr's pronouncement in the car earlier came back to her, and with it a reminder that Luke Harkin was Facebook friends with her daughter.

'Luke . . .' She took a deep breath. 'This is slightly awkward, and I don't want you to take it the wrong way, but I know you've been in contact with Jennifer on Facebook.'

There was silence on the other end of the line. 'It's nothing personal,' she continued, 'it's just that her father and I don't like her spending too much time online. It distracts from her study. So if you don't mind . . .'

'Of course,' he said, 'I understand.' He hung up before she could say anything else.

Perhaps it was a mistake to have mentioned Jennifer, she thought, lying back against the pillows, her phone in her hand. She hoped he hadn't taken it the wrong way. But she was the child's mother, it was her duty to see to these things, wasn't it?

34

On Monday morning, Nessa stayed in bed until Philip and Jennifer had left the house, then got up and went downstairs. All weekend she'd mulled things over in her head and now she'd come to a decision. She opened her laptop and typed an email, brisk and matter-of-fact, to Henchy at the gallery. She typed that Doerr might, at a minimum, have collaborated on the Chalk Sculpture; that if the acquisition was to proceed, then it should proceed with caution. She suggested that a review by an independent expert might be beneficial at this stage and gave the names of three people who might be suitable to undertake that task. She offered her resignation, saying that the time had come for her to move on, and pressed Send. Then she went back upstairs and crawled under the duvet.

Jennifer texted mid-afternoon to say that she had choir practice after school but would be home for supper. Nessa saw that her daughter's music folder was on top of the TV cabinet in the living room, where Jennifer had tossed it when she got home from the last practice. If she was working at the gallery, Nessa would have had no choice but to leave her daughter's forgotten belongings where they lay, and the girl would have to manage without them. But today, suddenly, she had all the time in the world, and she was glad to have an excuse not to take out the vacuum cleaner. She got in her car, taking the folder with her, and drove to the school. The hanging baskets by the entrance were loud and triumphant, pansies and geraniums spilling from them in long trails of abundance. She parked and, tucking the folder under her arm, walked to the music hall. The sound of Gilbert and Sullivan wafted out to greet her, *H.M.S Pinafore*, she thought, because wasn't that the chorus from 'Let's Give Three Cheers for the Sailor's Bride'? Nessa smiled, imagining the response if any young woman from that choir had the temerity to announce to her parents that she was marrying a sailor. There was unlikely to be much cheering. She knocked on the door of the music hall but the singing continued at full scale and no one answered. She considered pounding harder on the door, but decided instead to go in. She was met by a familiar sea of blue uniforms, a homogenous mass of young womanhood. It always took a moment before her eyes adjusted and she was able to pick out her own daughter. Ms Prendergast, the music teacher, turned and smiled. 'Girls, girls,' she said, 'why must you keep doing this to your poor parents? Which one of you forgot your folder today?'

Nessa's eyes scanned the rows. It would be so much easier if Jennifer stepped forward.

'Come along, girls,' the teacher said, 'who is it? Surely you recognise your own mother!'

This provoked a ripple of laughter, just as it was dawning on Nessa that her daughter was not in the group. She turned to the teacher, who was beaming good-naturedly, pleased at her own joke. 'I think I must have made a mistake,' Nessa said. 'Sorry to interrupt.'

'But who are you looking for?' the teacher asked, puzzled.

Nessa wanted to disappear into thin air. 'Jennifer,' she said, 'I'm looking for Jennifer McCormack. But I think I've made a mistake.'

'Oh,' the teacher said, and she stopped smiling. 'I see. Yes. Well, Jennifer *used* to be part of choir. And I must say I would be glad to have her back, because she has a very fine voice. Very fine indeed. But hockey has surpassed choir in her affections, I'm afraid. She has returned to her first love.' Giggles from the group of girls, the laughter more nervous this time.

'I forgot,' Nessa said, feeling her cheeks burning under the eyes of her daughter's classmates. 'She told me that, but I forgot.'

'That's quite all right,' the teacher said. 'So that your journey hasn't been entirely in vain, perhaps another of my girls is without a folder today? Girls? Anyone? Spare folder?'

There was a general shaking of heads, a staring at feet. 'Okay then,' the teacher said, raising her baton again. 'We won't keep you any longer, Mrs McCormack.'

Nessa went back to her car, puce-faced. She was shaking with humiliation and rage. Jennifer had gone too far this time, how dare she put her mother in a situation like that? The embarrassment quickly gave way to dread. If Jennifer wasn't at choir practice, then where was she? She wasn't with the Sullivan girl, that much was certain. Nessa had picked out Deirdre's face in the choir lineup. Deirdre would likely know where Jennifer was, of course, but Nessa could hardly go back in there and haul her out to ask her. She considered for a moment, attempted to steady her nerves.

Wherever Jennifer was, Jennifer's phone would also be; it was surgically attached. It was an expensive model they'd bought her for Christmas and Philip had downloaded an app that allowed its whereabouts to be traced if lost. Jennifer was always losing phones. Now Nessa went online and keyed in her daughter's phone number, waited for the software to work its magic. The app turned and spun and then it told her that the phone was currently in a building halfway down Oliver Plunkett Street. Nessa threw her own phone onto the passenger seat beside her and started her car.

There was a coffee shop favoured by teenagers at the point indicated on the app. Having parked once more, Nessa walked toward the café, then stood across the road staring in. It was crowded and there were young people milling about in groups, so that at first it was difficult to get a clear view. Then two young men moved aside and she saw her: Jennifer, sitting at a table, a latte in front of her. She wasn't alone; beside her, talking with great animation, his arms in motion as if to lend emphasis, was Luke. Nessa didn't bother waiting to compose what she might say. She crossed the road and strode into the café, directly to their table, and stood there with hands on her hips. She saw the look of horror that crossed Jennifer's face when she glanced up and registered her mother's presence. 'Go and wait for me outside, Jennifer,' she said. 'I'll be out to deal with you in a minute.'

Jennifer opened her mouth to protest.

'Now, Jennifer! Please,' Nessa said. 'Don't make me say anything else.'

Sullenly, Jennifer got up. 'Why aren't you at work?' she said. Before Nessa could answer, she rolled her eyes at Luke, mouthed, 'Call me,' and left.

Luke rose as if to leave also. 'Oh no you don't,' Nessa said.

He frowned. 'I'll go if I like, or I'll stay if I like,' he said. 'You can't stop me.'

'You wouldn't believe how well versed I am in stopping people,' Nessa said. 'Didn't I tell you not to contact my daughter?'

'You told me not to Facebook her,' he said. 'Something about your family internet usage policy, if I recall. You never told me not to have a coffee with her.'

'She's sixteen, Luke.'

'And?'

'Can't you find someone your own age to hang out with?'

He flushed. 'I'm not some dirty old man.' Behind them someone loaded a dishwasher, a clattering of cups and plates.

Luke looked toward Jennifer, who was waiting on the pavement outside. 'At least someone is interested in hearing what I have to say.'

She hoped he meant about the Chalk Sculpture.

'If my mother was here, she would stand up to you,' Luke continued. 'My mother would speak out for Melanie Doerr.'

'Grow up, Luke,' she said, exasperated. 'If your mother was here, she'd have bigger things to worry about than Melanie Doerr. And don't flatter yourself that Melanie needs your help. Melanie is more than capable of speaking for herself.'

'But you don't listen to her, do you?'

'That's not true,' she said, though she experienced a niggle of guilt as she said it. 'I do listen.' She paused. 'As it happens, I'm of the opinion that there may well be a lot of truth in what Melanie says.' There was no need to tell him precisely how much truth.

His eyes widened. 'So you believe her now?'

Nessa sighed. 'Yes,' she said, 'I believe her.'

Luke's elation was almost childlike. She was reminded of the boy they'd met that first night at Katherine's cabin, intense but charming, laughing with Jennifer as they pushed their kayaks out onto the lake. 'So you're going to give the sculpture back?' he said.

'It's not that straightforward, Luke. You know that.'

'But it's hers. You've just said that she's telling the truth. You have to give it back.'

She became aware that other people in the café were listening. 'It's not solely my decision,' she said, lowering her voice. She thought of the email tendering her resignation. 'In fact, it's not my decision at all.'

'I don't understand,' he said. 'If you believe it's hers, then you *must* give it back. You're hardly going to let the Locke women keep it?'

'There are procedures to be followed,' she said. 'It's not that simple . . .'

He ran a hand through his hair. 'I don't believe this,' he said. 'I really don't believe it. You think you can get away with anything.' He pushed past her toward the exit. When he reached the door he turned to her and said, 'It's not right that my mother was told everything, but your husband still thinks you're some kind of saint.' Then he set off down the street.

When Nessa got outside, she looked left and right for Jennifer, but her daughter had gone. Luke, head down, hands in his pockets, was disappearing into the distance.

35

She waited until she got home to ring Philip. Jennifer was home before her and was upstairs in her bedroom, crying. Nessa knocked on her door. 'I hate you!' Jennifer shouted. 'I am never going to speak to you again. How could you do that to me?' Nessa tried the handle but it was locked. Sighing, she went back downstairs, dialled Philip.

'Hey,' she said when he answered.

'Hey yourself,' he said. 'Are you in town? I'm just about to go grab a sandwich, if you feel like joining me?'

He was mostly upbeat these days. When they spent time together, he no longer gave the impression that he was dutifully attempting conversation. And now she was about to put a spanner in the works, just when they were starting to make progress.

She could no longer manage Luke Harkin on her own. Things were deteriorating too quickly. She needed Philip to talk to him – to talk to Jennifer also – and before that could happen there was a particular conversation she had to have with her husband. Luke Harkin was angrier with her now than he'd ever been. And if he was any way inclined to share the sordid news of how she'd betrayed Amy, he would surely avail himself of the opportunity once Philip contacted him, if only in self-defence. All she could do, she thought, was to defuse the story by telling Philip before Luke did. But she needed to have Philip to herself when she confessed. A bustling pub wouldn't do. 'Thanks,' she said, 'but I can't come into town. I have a mountain of laundry to get through.'

'Leave it,' he said. 'Get Jennifer to do it.'

She took a deep breath. 'Why don't you come home instead?' she said. 'I'll make sandwiches. Maybe we can go for a walk somewhere. Or a drive.'

'Okay,' he said doubtfully.

'I'll see you at home,' she said. 'In about an hour? We can decide where to go then.'

'Is everything okay, Nessa?' he said.

'I just need to talk to you about something.' She hesitated. 'It won't take long.'

'You haven't changed your mind about Wales, have you?'

'Nothing like that,' she said, and before he could ask anything more, she said, 'See you soon.'

She stood very still after returning the handset to its cradle. Where, she wondered, would be considered a good place to break it to one's husband that one had had an affair? She made coffee and went back out to the garden, but there was no warmth in the day and the buzz of a hedge trimmer on the other side of the fence kept breaking into her thoughts. She was about to reveal herself as a cheat, and not only that but someone who had cheated on her best friend. On beautiful dead Amy. But better that Philip heard it from her than from Luke. And it had to be soon, because she and Philip needed to plan how best to keep Luke and Jennifer apart. She went into the kitchen and made two perfunctory cheese and tomato sandwiches. It wasn't as if they were likely to be eaten. She would ask Philip not to tell Jennifer. It would serve no purpose to have her know, and if she could manage to keep her daughter away from Luke Harkin until he went back to Manchester, it just might be possible for Jennifer never to find out.

Luke knew nothing of the one night she'd spent with his father at the ten-year reunion in London. So there was no need for her to tell Philip about that. But as she wrapped the sandwiches in foil, she thought that she might as well decommission all the artillery in the possession of the Harkin men. She would be honest with her husband, totally honest. It was what he deserved. She would come clean, get it over with; what had happened at the reunion was one night, years ago now, that meant nothing. And it paled in comparison to what she'd absolved Philip of concerning Cora Wilson.

The place she chose for their conversation was tucked behind a warren of city back lanes, a small square of prettily overgrown wasteland. Sometime in the past, mounds of builder's rubble had mossed over, forming small, flower-dotted hillocks that provided a vantage point from which to look out over the city. To the north, one could glimpse Hollyhill, where the Wilsons lived. It would be useful to have it in their sight line, she thought. It would serve as a reminder in case Philip decided to get all holier-than-thou. He could hardly portray himself as whiter than the driven snow with Cora Wilson's house staring back at them.

When he arrived home, he dropped his briefcase in the hall without saying anything. He didn't ask her again what it was she had to say to him, and they barely exchanged a word until they reached the green area. A cat wove in and out of the high grass at the edge of a copse of beech trees, and Nessa waited to see if there might be a human accompanying it, but there wasn't. She climbed to the top of the nearest hillock 'and gestured to Philip to join her. He groaned as he sat down next to her. 'Old age,' he said. 'This sort of thing used to be easier.'

She gave a wobbly smile. 'Yes,' she said, 'but I wouldn't go back. To being young, I mean. Would you?'

'Why not?' he said.

'Young people are so foolish, aren't they?' she said. 'And self-destructive.'

'Is this about Jennifer?' he asked. 'Has she done something? Is that why you need to talk to me?'

'Yes and no,' she said slowly. 'I sense her spinning away from us, Philip; I don't seem to have charge of her anymore. And I'm worried. So yes, this is in part about Jennifer. But . . .' She sighed. 'It's also about something stupid I did. In my defence, it was a very long time ago. It's something that goes back to before I even met you, Philip. Most of it, anyway. But I wanted to tell you all the same. If we're going to make a new start, I want you to know everything about me.'

'Okay,' he said uncertainly.

She took a deep breath. 'There's something I never told you about me and Amy,' she said. 'It's not that I was in any way obliged to tell you. But I've decided that I want to.' She paused. 'I wasn't always a good friend to Amy.'

'You were her best friend, Ness.' He shook his head. 'You need to stop beating yourself up over Amy. What happened to her had nothing to do with you. We've been through this before. You know, maybe this is something you should talk to the counsellor about.'

'I never got over Amy dying,' Nessa said. 'I tried to put it out of my head, but she was always there.'

A short distance away, a man with pruning shears was taking cuttings from shrubs growing wild outside the walls of the old convent. He chose that moment to turn around, and seeing them, scuttled off as if he'd been apprehended in the middle of a bank robbery.

'Amy had a boyfriend when we were in college in London,' Nessa said. 'And the boyfriend and I, well . . . we got together when we shouldn't have.'

She allowed a gap for him to say something. She had intended to attempt a quip – *We weren't exactly playing Monopoly* – but something in Philip's expression stopped her.

He frowned. 'You must have been really into the guy to risk Amy's wrath,' he said.

What was the right answer to that? she wondered. Neither a yes nor a no would cast her in a particularly good light.

'Was it a one-off?' Philip asked.

'This was back before I met you, remember,' she said lightly. 'I'm not sure that it matters.'

'You can't leave me with half a story,' he said. 'Was it a one-night thing or not?'

'It lasted a number of months. I ended it once I learned that Amy was pregnant.'

'Pregnant?' Confusion flickered across his face.

'Yes.'

'Pregnant with Luke, or was this a different . . .'

She nodded. 'With Luke.' This was proving even more difficult than she had imagined.

'So your affair was with Stuart Harkin?' He stood up.

'Yes.' She patted the grass beside her. 'Sit down please, Philip.'

He ignored her and instead made his way down the slope, slipping and sliding. When he reached the bottom, he stood with his back to her. 'You and Harkin,' he said, swinging around. 'I can't believe it. Him of all people.'

'I thought you liked him,' she said. 'You got on well enough when you met him at Katherine's place.'

'I tolerated him,' he said. 'If I'd known . . .'

'We all make mistakes, Philip.'

'I wish you'd taken that line when you found out about me and Cora. *I* had an affair for a few months and you're still making me pay for it.'

So you think you're *the only one paying for it?* she wanted to say. *You don't think I might have paid for it more? Or our daughter?* 'That was completely different, Philip. You're not comparing like with like.'

'Aren't I? It sounds similar enough to me.'

'You and I didn't even know each other when I was in college. I didn't owe you anything. You have no right to police my behaviour from back then. You have no right to judge.' She wondered now if perhaps it might not be such a good idea to confess what had happened at the reunion.

'But you owed Amy something,' he said. 'Amy had a right, didn't she?' His voice had risen, and she feared that someone passing might hear them. She scrambled down the slope to stand beside him.

'Yes,' she said. There was no point being defensive. She would take her punishment and get it over with. 'Amy was the innocent party and she got hurt. Like I got hurt when I was the innocent party and you had an affair with Cora Wilson.'

'Maybe it's karma,' he said.

'What are you saying? That I deserved to be cheated on?'

'What goes around comes around,' he said. 'That's what my mother used to say.' He shook his head. 'Stuart Harkin,' he said. 'What were you thinking, Nessa? If it had been with a better class of guy . . . I don't see Stuart and myself in the same league exactly. I find it hard to imagine you and him . . .'

Then don't try, she wanted to say. *Don't imagine.*

He was staring at the ground. 'You could at least have told me before I met the guy. I bet he was having a good snigger behind my back that night at the lake.'

'No,' she said quickly, 'it wasn't like that at all.'

'Why are you telling me now, Nessa? This is what I don't understand. After all this time, when you never said anything before.' His expression darkened. 'Has something happened?' he said slowly. 'Have you started seeing Harkin again? Is that what this is about?'

'Philip!' she cried. 'How can you say that?'

'You slept with him before. Why wouldn't you do it again?'

She wiped a tear from her cheek with the back of her hand. 'Don't,' she said. 'You're being cruel. Do you know how much I've hated myself for betraying Amy?' There was no way on this earth that she was going to tell him about the night of the reunion now.

'Why this sudden interest in being honest?' he said. He loaded the word 'honest' with sarcasm.

'Because Luke found out,' she said miserably.

'How?'

'Aunt Gretta told him.'

'Gretta knows too?' He swore. 'Am I the only idiot who didn't know about this?'

She shook her head. 'Amy kept a diary. Aunt Gretta read it. Gave it to Luke.'

Philip took a couple of steps away from her. He stood looking out at the city, his hands in his pockets. He muttered something under his breath that she didn't catch.

'Jennifer doesn't know,' she said. 'Please don't tell her.'

'What do you take me for?' he said, turning around. 'Do you know what it would do to the child to learn something like that about her mother? I wouldn't do that to my daughter.'

The disgust on his face made her cheeks burn with shame, but sparked anger too. 'You have no cause for complaint,' she said. 'You are not the wronged party here. I'm telling you so that you don't hear it from Luke.'

He put his hands to his face for a moment. When he took them away, he said, 'What will we do if Luke tells Jennifer? Should I speak with him, head him off at the pass?'

'Actually, I think you need to speak with him anyway.' She cleared her throat. 'He's been spending a lot of time with Jennifer lately. Even though I've warned him about it. She sneaked off to meet him today, telling me she was at choir practice.'

Philip swore under his breath. 'I knew he was trouble,' he said. 'That first evening at the Ferriters', I said that he was too old for her.'

'You need to tell him to stay away from Jennifer,' she said. 'He won't listen to me. I'm worried that he's using her as a means of getting back at me. You need to talk to him and you need to do it quickly. And then we have to figure out how to keep her occupied and out of his way until he goes back to Manchester.'

He held her gaze. 'Anything else I should know?' he said.
She shook her head.
'No other surprises? That's it?'
'That's it.'
He sighed. 'All right,' he said. 'I need some time to get my head around this.' He set off on his own, across the green.

36

The following morning Jennifer pleaded flu. 'I can't go to school,' she mumbled from beneath the duvet, 'I'm too sick.'

'Are you really sick, or is this to do with yesterday?' Nessa asked, sitting on the edge of her daughter's bed.

'You embarrassed me,' Jennifer said. 'I'm going to be the laughing stock of my whole class. I can't go in.'

Nessa sighed. She wondered what part of yesterday her daughter considered the most embarrassing – her mother's appearance at the music hall, details of which had no doubt filtered through by now, or her mother's showdown in the café with Luke Harkin. Her anger at Jennifer had dissipated since the evening before; her daughter was sixteen, naïve; it wasn't her fault that she had become a pawn in someone else's game. 'Why don't you rest for the morning and we can see how you're feeling later?' Nessa said. She went out of the bedroom, pulling the door closed gently behind her.

Philip wasn't awake yet. He'd come home in the early hours of the morning and gone straight to the spare room, knocking over a potted plant on his way. A scatter of dry soil across the hall tiles had greeted her when she went downstairs in the morning. She hadn't managed to sleep herself. She'd lain awake, tossing and turning, wondering if she should go to Philip, but deciding that he was unlikely to be sober enough to register her presence.

Through the kitchen window, she could see Mrs Moriarty from next door at the far end of her garden, giving the stray cats she tended their breakfast. Nessa made a pot of coffee and drank it sitting at the table. There was an immense loneliness to being in the house knowing that her husband and daughter were both upstairs and that, assuming that they did surface, neither of them would wish to speak to her. When the silence of the kitchen got to be too much, she turned on the radio, and when that didn't help she got Bailey's lead and went out, walking all the way down to the Lee fields and out along the floodplains, nodding at the other dog walkers, offering sympathetic smiles to the parents chasing toddlers. Once she reached the end of the path, and when there was no one else in sight, she let Bailey off the lead and watched him race along the edges of the riverbank, his belly and paws thick with mud, barking in delight, calling her to follow him.

Back home at noon, she washed Bailey down with a hose in the back garden and topped up his water bowl. Upstairs, the door of the spare room was open. Philip had gone. The bedclothes lay in a rumpled heap on the floor, as did several towels. Putting her head around Jennifer's door, she saw that her daughter was asleep, or at least she didn't stir when Nessa softly called her name. Deciding to let her be, she went downstairs and checked the kitchen table in case Philip had left a note, but there was nothing, no sign that he'd had breakfast either. She would have to talk to him again today about having a word with Luke Harkin and with Jennifer, but better to let his head clear first. To keep her mind occupied, she repotted some shrubs, then heated up a carton of soup and ate it in the back garden, Bailey slumped at her feet, pleased at having her to himself for the day. Having sat down, she found that exhaustion began to catch up with her. She went back indoors and, not bothering to undress, took a sleeping pill and climbed into bed.

When later she woke, the light in the room was dim and she was momentarily puzzled to find herself in bed, fully dressed. Surfacing from the fug of sleep, she peered at the alarm clock. 7 p.m. She sat on the edge of the bed while she got her bearings. The house was quiet. Philip hadn't come home, then. She crossed the landing and knocked on Jennifer's bedroom door, but there was no answer. The room, when she peaked in, was empty. Perhaps Jennifer was downstairs with her headphones on. But no, there was only Bailey, lying on his mat by the back door. He jumped up and wandered over to lick her hand. She took her copy of *Flight of the Doves* from its shelf, but gave up after a couple of pages. She stretched out on the sofa in the living room. She wondered how much food was in the pantry, considered if she should go buy groceries. She checked her phone. No word from Philip or Jennifer. No more messages from Luke either; at least that. Philip she would have to allow to come round at his own pace, but she rang Jennifer's number and left a message. When there was still no sign of Jennifer by 8.30 p.m., she tried ringing her again and then she rang the Sullivans.

'We haven't seen her today,' Mrs Sullivan said. 'Is she missing? Deirdre said she wasn't at school today.'

'Not missing, no. Just crossed wires, I expect. She's probably at Helen's.' Helen was a name she'd heard mentioned once or twice in the context of hockey.

'Helen's gone to athletics trials in Limerick.'

'That's fine. I'll ring around. Sorry for disturbing you.'

'Jennifer hasn't been at our house since last Tuesday.'

As if Nessa were the sort of parent who mightn't have seen her daughter since then. 'Thanks for your help,' she said, and hung up.

She rang Philip next, steeling herself for the onslaught. Since they'd started counselling, he'd been conscientiously taking her calls, but this time it went to voicemail. It was only to be expected, she thought, considering their conversation of the evening before. Plus, he must be badly hungover. *Calm down*, she told herself. Jennifer was sixteen; in other parts of the world, perhaps even in this part, children that age were working forty-hour weeks, raising kids, crossing state borders on their own. Nessa dialled her daughter's number again and left another message. Then she went upstairs, showered, and got into her pyjamas. When 10 p.m. arrived, she carried a chair out to the hall and stood on it to take the tape from the home security system. It was one of the old-fashioned kind, with a tape for every day of the week, though they always let theirs tape over. Not much happened in Sunday's Well. She slotted the tape into the VCR player in the living room and sat down on the floor to watch.

She fast-forwarded past the mundanity of traffic passing by on the road, Mrs Moriarty on her way to the shop for her daily paper, Mrs Moriarty on her way back. She sent the tape forward, stopping and stuttering, speeding through hours of footage in which nothing happened except the tedium of cars and pedestrians passing the front gate, and still Jennifer didn't come out of the house. When the tape reached 4.54 p.m., a car pulled up outside the house and parked half in, half out of a space, its rear jutting out into the street. It was a Volvo, just like the one Katherine Ferriter drove. It stayed like that, partly on the pavement, partly on the road. Mrs Moriarty must have been going demented behind her net curtains.

Then there was Jennifer, pixelated and grainy, running down the path, stopping halfway. The window of the Volvo wound down and Jennifer turned on her heel and

273

went back into the house. Nothing happened on the tape for five minutes, except that a small traffic jam formed on Sunday's Well Road as motorists slowed to edge around the Volvo. When Jennifer reappeared a few moments later, she had a bag with her. She climbed into the passenger seat, and as the Volvo reversed out onto the road, Nessa saw that it wasn't driven by Katherine Ferriter, but by Luke Harkin. He sped away, clipping the wing mirror of Mrs Moriarty's Fiat.

She switched off the VCR and automatically reached to stroke Bailey, who was curled at her feet. She tried to think what to do. She dialled Philip's number. 'Call me, please,' she said when it went to voicemail. It was only after she'd hung up that she realised he would probably interpret that as her attempt at an apology. She rang Luke next, but he didn't answer. She paced up and down the living room. She tried Jennifer again, and when there was no reply, she rang Katherine Ferriter.

'Katherine,' she said, 'is Jennifer with you?'

'I'm sorry, who's this? Oh, it's you, Nessa. Hi! Jennifer? No, she's not here. Why would she be?'

'Is Luke there?'

'No.' This more cagily.

'He came to our house while I was out today and took Jennifer away in your car. Why did you give him that thing, Katherine? He can't drive it properly.'

'I lent him the car to do some sightseeing,' Katherine said. 'He's flying home tomorrow from Cork Airport and he's overnighting at my place. He said he'd like to go to the beach, and that he wanted to call on your friends, the Lockes, to take more photos. I didn't see any harm in it. He didn't mention anything about Jennifer.' She paused. 'And he does know how to drive. He has a licence. I wouldn't have given him the car otherwise.'

'I think I'm going to have to ring the police,' Nessa said.

'That's probably best,' Katherine said. 'I would if I were you. I feel responsible for giving him the car. I'm sorry. I'd no idea he'd arranged to see Jennifer.'

Nessa tried Jennifer's number one more time, then, feeling nauseous, she punched the number for Emergency Services into her phone. She was about to hit Dial when the phone rang.

'You were looking for me?' Philip said brusquely.

'Yes.' She cleared her throat. 'Was Jennifer in touch?'

'No. Why?'

'It's just that she's not home, and I think she went out with Luke Harkin. Without permission. And it's late.'

He swore under his breath. 'For God's sake, Nessa. Luke Harkin? So much for your plan to keep them apart. Did you ring her?'

'Yes, I rang her, Philip. I rang her lots of times. But she's not answering. Maybe you could try. She's always more amenable to talking to you.'

'I hope we're not going down that road again, Nessa. It's been a long day. I've already taken all I can for this week, to be honest.'

'No,' she said quickly, 'that wasn't what I meant, but it's worth seeing if maybe she'll pick up for you.'

'I doubt it, but I'll try.'

When her daughter rang five minutes later, Nessa could hear a rattle of voices in the background. 'Mom, I will never, ever forgive you if you humiliate me,' she said. 'I'm out with a friend. Since when is that a crime? Dad says you're going to call the police. What do you want the police for?' She started to say something else and there was the sound of a toilet flushing.

'I didn't catch that,' Nessa said. 'What did you say?'

'You can't stand to see me happy. Just because you're unhappy, you want everyone else to be too. You haven't got a clue. All the other girls at school have been going with boys since First Year. You're making me go to shitty Wales, just because your life is messed up.' In the background, Nessa could hear the soothing murmurs of young women.

'Calm down, Jennifer. Of course I want you to be happy, I'm your mother. But I'm worried about you. Luke Harkin is a lot older than you. And I hope he's not drinking, if he's driving.'

Jennifer sighed. 'He's having a Coke, okay?' A pause. 'Anyway, I'm not alone with him.'

'Who else is there?'

'Just a friend. Luke is taking us to see the sculpture, the one your gallery is trying to steal from the old lady.'

'She's not an old lady, she's fifty-eight. And the gallery isn't stealing it.'

'Whatever.'

Was that a slight slurring? 'Jennifer, have you been drinking?'

'Can you stay out of my life? Can you please do that? I don't want to talk to you. I only rang you to stop you making a fool of yourself.'

Nessa decided to attempt a compromise. 'It's too late to go bothering the Lockes at this hour,' she said. 'I don't know what Luke's thinking. Why don't you stay where you are, enjoy yourself, and I can swing by in an hour and bring you home.'

Another sigh. 'I told you,' Jennifer said – Nessa could imagine her daughter rolling her eyes, a bevy of teenage girls gathered round, rolling their eyes in solidarity – 'we're going to see the sculpture. Luke rang ahead, we have an appointment. We're leaving now. It's, like, *totally* not too late. I'll be home later, okay? And if you ring the police, I swear I will never, *ever* speak to you again.' She hung up.

Breathe, Nessa told herself. She wondered if she should ring the Lockes to see if Jennifer's story checked out, and apologise for her daughter arriving at this late hour. But she'd had no further contact with Loretta since the day she'd arrived on her doorstep, unannounced, with Melanie Doerr. She could hardly pick up the phone and call her now. She would drive to the Lockes' herself, she decided. Luke and Jennifer would make it there ahead of her, but she would wait in the driveway until they came out again, and then she would calmly assert herself – there would be no scene – and she would take her daughter home, as she was perfectly entitled to do.

She'd almost reached Skibbereen when her phone rang. She had to look twice at the name that flashed up on the screen. It was a name that hadn't appeared on her phone for a long time. Cora Wilson. Her hands shook on the wheel and she pulled over onto the hard shoulder. She watched the phone as it rang out and Cora's name faded away. Immediately it began to ring again. She would have to answer it. Something was very wrong if Cora Wilson was calling her.

'Hello,' she said, attempting to keep her voice steady.

'This is Cora Wilson.' Silence. 'Please don't hang up,' Cora said. 'I wish I didn't have to ring you and I know you won't want to speak to me, but I don't know what else to do. Mandy is missing. And I'm wondering if she might be with Jennifer.'

37

The small roads looked different in the dark. Twists that she knew so well in daylight ambushed her now. When she drove into the Lockes' driveway, there was Katherine Ferriter's Volvo in the space where Nessa usually parked. The lights were on in the studio, and from her car she could see the Chalk Sculpture, and a young girl with a short dark bob who could well be Mandy Wilson with a new haircut. And there was Loretta, stooping low. But where was Jennifer? Nessa was getting out of the car when the front door of the house swung open and her daughter appeared in the porch.

'Mom!' Jennifer shouted. 'Come in here. Quick!'

Nessa started hurrying up the path, then came to a sudden standstill. Through the studio window, she saw that Eleanor was stretched out on the floor, unmoving, with Loretta and a young woman who was indeed Mandy Wilson bent over her. 'Hurry, Mom, please,' Jennifer said. She ran down the path and, grabbing her mother's hand, pulled her toward the house.

Inside, Loretta was crouched over her mother, crying, while Mandy Wilson, who had taken a first aid course, administered CPR.

'What happened?' Nessa said. 'Have you called an ambulance?'

'Yes,' Jennifer said. She knelt on the floor beside Mandy. 'Is she okay?' she asked, but her friend didn't answer, just continued to pump Eleanor's chest with her hands. Loretta was weeping silently, every so often touching a hand to her mother's forehead.

'What happened?' Nessa asked again.

She noticed Luke in the corner of the studio. He was twisting something in his hand that looked like a chisel. He appeared dazed, confused, like a bystander who had happened upon the scene of an accident. In that moment, he didn't look much older than the two girls. Then, as if coming round from an anaesthetic, he began to blink and, slowly, his head turned to the window. Nessa heard then what he must have heard: the sound of sirens approaching.

Loretta was holding her mother's wrist, searching for a pulse. 'Help me,' she pleaded. As Nessa bent to take Eleanor's wrist, Mandy Wilson caught her eye and gave the tiniest shake of her head, before continuing with the CPR. Nessa felt for a pulse. Nothing. She put a finger to Eleanor's neck – no flicker there either. There wasn't a mark on her. In her nightclothes, she looked like she could have been asleep.

Outside, the Volvo threw up a spray of gravel as it roared off, Luke hunched over the steering wheel. There was a glimmer of blue lights among the trees fringing the lane – the ambulance, Nessa supposed – but the lights seemed to hang there, rather than advancing. Then there were people on foot in high-vis jackets with stretchers, running up the path and in through the still-open front door, mercifully taking charge. One of them lifted Loretta to her feet, while the others tended to Eleanor. Another crunch of gravel and the Volvo reversed back into the driveway, driven now by a Garda. A squad car followed, and behind that an ambulance. There was no sign of Luke.

The studio was suddenly crowded with people. Robert Locke's desk was commandeered by the paramedics, who pushed aside the chisels Nessa had spent months so carefully labelling, and laid out their medical devices. The driveway was ablaze with headlamps and flashlights. Jennifer went outside and sat on the grass beside the fuchsia hedge. Nessa followed her; her daughter was right, of course – better to give the paramedics room to do their job; at least Mandy had enough medical know-how to be of assistance. Jennifer began to sob. All the self-assurance she'd displayed earlier had deserted her. Nessa stroked her daughter's hair. 'Are you going to tell me what happened?' she said softly.

Jennifer rested her head on her mother's shoulder. 'Is she dead, do you think?'

'I don't know,' Nessa said slowly. 'It might be that she's had some kind of turn.' She paused, debating whether to go further. 'She's very old and she hasn't been well for a while.'

In the studio, paramedics were lifting Eleanor onto a stretcher. As they moved to angle it out of the room, one of them, a large man, backed into the Chalk Sculpture. It rocked on its base; it tilted. As if in slow motion, Nessa watched it, waiting for it to tilt back again. It was like one of those dreams she sometimes had where she was frozen and couldn't scream, couldn't even speak. The Chalk Sculpture toppled to the floor. Nessa jumped to her feet, raced across the grass to the window. 'Oh, shit, Mom,' Jennifer said, scrambling up after her. They stood together with their faces pressed against the glass. Inside, the paramedics were shouting instructions to one another, but they didn't delay for more than a second. The white chalk dust had not yet finished settling on the floor when they appeared in the doorway and Eleanor was stretchered into the ambulance. The noise of the crashing sculpture had not woken her, and yes, 'woken' was the first word that came to mind, because she still looked merely asleep. At least there was no sheet over her head, Nessa thought, surely that was a good sign? Loretta was helped into the back of the ambulance and the doors were closed. Nessa went slowly into the house, afraid of what she might see. 'It's only a statue, Mom,' Jennifer ventured, following her.

The Chalk Sculpture lay on the ground, mostly intact save for one arm that had snapped off and rolled a few feet away from the torso. Nessa crouched beside it. A Garda and Mandy Wilson were surveying the damage, and goodness, Nessa thought, how grown up that girl seemed tonight, and it wasn't just the new haircut. Jennifer and Mandy hugged as if they hadn't seen each other for years. She really should ring Cora Wilson, Nessa remembered now, but she could not keep her eyes away from the Chalk Sculpture. She traced a finger along the floorboards, then brought it to her face, inspecting the coating of white dust. 'Did somebody do something to Eleanor?' she asked. 'Did Luke do something?'

Jennifer shook her head. 'She just fainted, Mom, I swear. Nobody touched her, nobody even . . .' The rest of her words were drowned out by the siren of the ambulance as it pulled away. The Garda stood on the porch waving it off, speaking into a walkie-talkie, sweeping her flashlight up and down along the hedgerows. Nessa stood up, dusted off her hands. 'What happened, girls?'

Jennifer spoke first. 'Luke said we should write an investigative feature for the school magazine.' She gestured to her friend. 'Mandy's editor this year. Luke said it would be good if we worked on it together.' She looked uncomfortable. 'He said somebody needed to do something about it . . .'

'Go on,' Nessa said.

'The plan was, we'd show up. We'd ask the Lockes some questions, and Luke would take some more photos. Mandy and I with the Chalk Sculpture, Mandy and I with the two old ladies, Mandy and—'

'Did Loretta let you in?' Nessa said. 'Or was it Eleanor?'

Jennifer and Mandy exchanged glances. 'Actually, Loretta said we couldn't come in,' Jennifer said. 'She told us she didn't do interviews. I said, "Well, actually, you did some for my mother . . ."'

'Oh, Jennifer,' Nessa said, shaking her head.

'Yeah, I know. Then she asked if you were my mom and I said yes, and then she said we should be ashamed of ourselves, which I thought was, like, harsh, you know? And then she went back into the house and switched off the porch light and left us outside in the dark.'

'Jennifer and I wanted to go home then,' Mandy said. 'We actually said it, didn't we, Jennifer? We said, "Luke, let's go home."'

Jennifer nodded. 'But Luke said he knew a way in round the back. He said Eleanor was different, that she would talk to us once we explained things. We just had to bypass the other lady and get inside.'

'Luke was – is – on the side of Ms Doerr,' Mandy said, 'the woman who says she owns—'

'I know who she is,' Nessa said. It was sharper than she'd intended, and she flashed Mandy an apologetic smile. 'I'm sorry,' she said, 'it's been a long day.'

'We walked around the back,' Jennifer said. 'We had to climb over a gate and I snagged my jeans, and we could hardly see in the dark, and there were nettles, and ugh . . . Anyway, the back door was locked.'

'We thought since it was out in the country it might have been unlocked,' Mandy said. 'Country people leave their doors unlocked all the time.'

'But then Luke pushed the door, hard, a couple of times and . . . um . . . it opened.' Jennifer swallowed. 'So we went in.'

Nessa looked around to check if there were any police within earshot. There was only the Garda in the driveway, the high-vis reflectors on her uniform like beacons across the grass.

'Luke went in first, obviously,' Jennifer said. 'Then Mandy. I was last. I was a big coward.'

'No,' Mandy said, 'you were smart.'

'I was a coward,' Jennifer said miserably. She looked at her mother. 'Luke told Mandy that it would be something she could look back on when she was older and be proud of. He said the story might be picked up by real newspapers. He told her it would make things better at school after, you know, that thing with her mother.'

'I see,' Nessa said.

Jennifer's hand flew to her mouth. 'Sorry, Mom, I didn't mean to talk about Mrs Wilson . . .'

'It's okay,' Nessa said. 'Really, it doesn't matter. It's not important now.'

'But when we went in the house,' Jennifer continued, 'we only got as far as the kitchen. The woman was there, the younger one, shouting about calling the police.'

'We wanted to leave then, didn't we?' Mandy said.

Jennifer nodded. 'But Luke pushed past the younger old lady . . .'

'Loretta,' Nessa said, 'her name's Loretta.'

'Well, anyway,' Jennifer said, 'he ran down the hall to here' – she gestured around the studio – 'and Loretta followed him. Then Eleanor came down the stairs shouting "Who's there?" Luke went over to the bench and picked up a chisel. That's when Eleanor fainted.'

'Or whatever . . .' Mandy said glumly.

The policewoman put her head around the door. 'We're going to secure the property now,' she said, 'so if you wouldn't mind stepping outside . . .'

Mandy's phone rang as they were leaving the house. She began talking animatedly to someone, her mother presumably, before bursting into tears. Nessa was about to go to her, but Jennifer got there first, put an arm around her friend's shoulder. Mandy said a sniffled goodbye to her mother, slid her phone back in her pocket. They were standing in the high grass, trampling the leaves of the wild rhubarb plants. The garden looked smaller tonight, the house more ordinary. Nessa gazed in through the window at the studio. If you ignored the sculpture lying on the floor, it could be any old room. A spell had been broken.

'You'll be able to fix it,' Jennifer said. 'I saw a thing on TV about a statue in Greece, a really old one, and they glued it.'

'Whoever will be fixing it, it won't be me,' Nessa said.

As they drove down the lane, Jennifer, clinging to Mandy in the backseat, began to cry. 'It's all my fault,' she said. 'That old lady could be dead and it's my fault.'

'Mine too,' Mandy said loyally.

'You wouldn't even be here if it wasn't for me,' Jennifer said. 'It's totally not your fault.'

'Whoever's fault all of this is,' Nessa said, 'it's not yours. Either of you. If you hadn't gone with him, he'd have gone on his own.' In the rearview mirror, she saw Jennifer wipe her nose on her sleeve. She opened the glove compartment and found a box of tissues.

'Thanks, Mom,' Jennifer said. She blew her nose and passed the box to Mandy. 'I couldn't believe he was interested in me,' she said. 'It was too good to be true. He was so good-looking and no one else has ever been interested in me. I should have known there was something up.'

'You are *way* too good for him,' Nessa said. 'He doesn't deserve you. And I don't expect he knew what he was doing. He wasn't thinking right.'

They drove to Bantry Hospital because Nessa thought that someone should be there for Loretta. Mandy sat on a plastic hospital chair, swinging her legs and scrolling through her phone. Her mother was coming to collect her, she'd informed Nessa. 'I can drop you home,' Nessa had said, but Mandy quickly, as if she'd been warned, shook her head. 'No,' she said, 'it's fine. Mum's on her way.'

'Will Luke go to jail?' Jennifer asked.

'I don't know,' Nessa said. 'He didn't do himself any favours by disappearing like that.' Luke's attempt to flee across the fields had left him with a broken ankle and a multitude of cuts and bruises. He was currently on a gurney outside the emergency room, waiting to be seen. Nessa went again to the nearest nurses' station to inquire about Eleanor. 'Are you family?' a nurse said kindly. 'I'm afraid we can only speak to family.'

There was no sign of Loretta. As they were preparing to leave, Nessa looked down the corridor and saw Cora Wilson hovering around the vending machine. The women stared at each other for a moment, neither of them approaching the other. Cora took a tentative step toward them.

'Mandy,' Nessa said quickly, 'your mother's here.'

Mandy picked up her bag. 'Thank you,' she said to Nessa as she pulled on her coat, 'and sorry. About everything.' Cora had halted a few feet away. Nessa looked at her and then turned and went into a nearby bathroom. She stood in front of the mirror, gripping the sink. She splashed water on her face, winced at how drawn she looked. When after a few minutes she ventured out, Cora and Mandy had gone.

38

When Nessa went to the gallery to fetch her things, she found two empty cardboard boxes waiting on her chair. She began to gather her mugs and potted plants, her makeup and spare tights. There was a letter marked 'Personal' unopened on the desk. It was from a woman in Inishowen whose family Locke had stayed with for a number of weeks in 1972. Nessa reflected on the date, calculated that it was when Locke had disappeared for those six weeks that Eleanor had so often complained about. The correspondent enclosed a photo. It was of half a dozen ruddy-faced men with net-roughened hands, Locke in their midst. She was surprised to learn that Locke had been a sculptor, the woman wrote. She had thought he was a poet, because he wrote a love poem for a girl in the town, which caused something of a scandal as it was presumed he was a Protestant. They'd no idea that he was married. The love interest had kept the poem, and the woman enclosed a copy. The woman wrote that she knew nothing about poetry, but she knew she didn't like this poem, she'd never thought it any good. The fact that Locke was really a sculptor rather than a writer explained a lot, she said. The poem was in Robert Locke's handwriting. It was not addressed to Melanie Doerr, who had also made Locke's acquaintance during his time in Inishowen, but was titled simply 'For Máire'. When Nessa began to read it, she recognised it as 'Wild Nights' by Emily Dickinson.

The English literature thesis that she'd requested some weeks previously was also waiting for her. Curious, she turned to the index, located the page containing the reference to Robert Locke. It was not, after all, a typo. It was a photograph of Locke pictured with the writer William Trevor who, in his youth, had also practised sculpture in England. The focus of the thesis was Anglo-Irish literature of the twentieth century, and Locke had achieved inclusion only in his capacity as one of Trevor's acquaintances. There was no indication of where the photo had been taken, but in it, Locke and Trevor were clearly in their middle years. Standing slightly apart from the two men, looking self-consciously at the camera, was someone captioned as *Unknown Woman*: Melanie Doerr. Nessa sighed and closed the thesis, placed it in a tray for filing.

A week after Eleanor's funeral, Nessa got a phone call from Katherine.

'I still have some of Jennifer's belongings that were left in the Volvo that night,' Katherine said. 'Maybe we could meet for coffee and I can return them to you. I'd meant to ring you before now, but there's been so much going on.'

She sounded tired. 'Sure,' Nessa said, 'but why don't I come down to the cabin? You've already been inconvenienced enough.'

'No,' Katherine said quickly, 'it's fine. No need for you to come all the way down here. I have to go to the city anyway. Why don't we say Brookes café on Grattan Street, maybe Friday morning at eleven?'

On Friday they talked a little about Lough Hyne, and about the cabin, and Nessa asked after William, who was keeping well, Katherine said, but was busy, and didn't get to the lake as much as he'd like. Jennifer's belongings were contained in a black tote bag that Nessa hadn't seen before. The price was still on it – Penneys, €8.99

– and she wondered that Katherine wasn't wearing surgical gloves to handle it, before scolding herself silently for being so ungracious.

There was an unmistakable clink as the bag was passed across the table. 'I didn't know what best to do,' Katherine said. 'I thought about taking the bottles out, so as not to upset you. Goodness knows, you've enough to be upset about lately, but then I thought I'd be hiding something from you, and I didn't want to do that.'

Nessa peered into the bag, saw two small bottles of cheap vodka. 'You did the right thing,' she said. 'Thank you. I'll speak to Jennifer about this.' She didn't like to think about what else might be in the bag.

As if she'd read her thoughts, Katherine said, 'I didn't go through Jennifer's stuff, it was just that I couldn't help noticing the bottles . . .'

'I understand,' Nessa said, 'it's fine.' There was silence for a moment, apart from the hiss of a coffee machine, the shriek of a small child being divested of a ketchup bottle.

Katherine told her that Luke's broken ankle was healing well. 'Stuart came to take him home,' Katherine said. 'They stayed with us in the cabin for a couple of days. They're gone back to Manchester now. I thought that you might like to know.'

'I thought Luke was on bail?' Nessa said. 'Wasn't he charged with breaking and entering?'

'He was, but then Loretta decided to withdraw the charges.'

'That was good of her. I'm not sure I would have done the same in her position.'

'I think she felt sorry for him,' Katherine said.

Neither of them said anything for a moment.

'I heard that you stood bail for him,' Nessa said.

Katherine, uncomfortable, nodded.

'I feel that I should have been the one to do that,' Nessa said. It had occurred to her at the time that it was the kind of thing a godmother might do, but when she contacted the Garda station, they told her it had already been taken care of.

Katherine frowned. 'Why you?'

Nessa shrugged. 'I don't know. I feel guilty, I suppose. I was the one who introduced him to the Lockes. My daughter was there too that night.'

'If we're going to go down that road,' Katherine said, 'I was the one who introduced him to you. And they went in my car.' She shook her head. 'I'm remembering that day we bumped into each other in the mini-mart,' she said. 'God, it seems like a lifetime ago now! You were so hesitant when I invited you to the cabin. And I thought it was because I'd caught you off guard.' She paused. 'I'd never have asked you to meet him, or Stuart, if I'd had any idea that . . .' She trailed off, stared glumly into her coffee.

She knows, Nessa thought, *she must know*. She imagined Stuart and Katherine sitting up late into the night at the cabin, and Stuart, in thrall to Katherine's basic decency, confessing, recounting in all its ugly detail the story of his and Nessa's affair, their betrayal of Amy. Stuart who had sung Katherine's praises even before she'd taken him in for the second time, driven him back and forth to the hospital to see his son. Of course he'd told her, and why should it matter now, when almost everyone who was involved in any real way – Amy, Philip, Luke – already knew? As best Nessa could tell, Jennifer did not know; it seemed that Luke had not told her, and for that at least, she was grateful. It should not matter in the greater scheme of things that Katherine knew, but Nessa found that it did. She was engulfed by a sense of shame, and dropped her gaze to fidget with her napkin.

'Luke never had any intention of hurting Eleanor,' Katherine said. 'He was very fond of her, actually. He wanted to go to the funeral, but I advised against it. I wasn't sure how Loretta would take it.' She reached across the table and touched Nessa's arm. 'He didn't do anything to Jennifer either, you know that, don't you?'

'He hurt her,' Nessa said. It came out in a choked whisper.

'I expect she feels betrayed, and yes, that does hurt.'

Was she imagining it or was that a flash of anger on Katherine's face?

'You've always been a good person, Katherine,' she said. 'I don't think I ever gave you credit for that. I wasn't too nice to you when we lived together in London, but you never held it against me.'

Katherine looked away, out the window. She shrugged. 'We were just kids then,' she said.

Perhaps it wasn't too late to start again with Katherine, to pick up where they had left off all those years ago, but as mature grown-ups now. She would like to have Katherine to share things with, the way she used to with her sister, before her sister moved away. The way she used to with Amy.

'Kids or not, you were always there for Amy when she needed you,' Nessa said.

Katherine turned back from the window. 'Amy needed a friend,' she said. 'I'm not sure I was friend enough. I feel like I let her down.'

'No, I was the one who did that,' Nessa said quietly.

Katherine looked miserable. She squeezed Nessa's hand briefly. Then she reached for the bill. 'I'd better get going,' she said.

'No, let me pay, please,' Nessa said. 'It's the least I can do.' As if the price of two coffees equated to all the suffering she'd caused, she thought, as she went to the register.

Katherine stood to put on her jacket, fixed her scarf. 'Thank you for the coffee,' she said. 'And the best of luck with Wales.'

'Maybe we'll catch up when I'm back for Christmas or New Year,' Nessa said.

The expression on Katherine's face was unreadable. 'I'm not going to be in Cork as much from now on,' she said. 'I'm looking at spending more time with William in Dublin, especially during the winter. And we'll probably go skiing for New Year. But I'm sure our paths will cross again.'

Nessa wondered if Katherine might invite her for another of her suppers, but as the seconds passed, it became clear that Katherine wasn't going to. They parted with the unspoken understanding that they would recede quietly from each other's lives. As Nessa paid, she watched Katherine cross the car park and get into her Volvo, her walk still neat, still confident. Nessa was going out the door when the waitress called her back. 'You forgot something,' she said, holding up the black tote bag. The bottles clinked. 'Thank you,' Nessa said quietly, not meeting her eye.

39

Wales was a strange country, full of contradictions. There were days when she thought that even the air smelled British, other days when for a second she forgot that she was no longer in Ireland and thought that she was back in Cork. There was a river near the new house and in the mornings after breakfast she walked the bank with Bailey. She tried to confine her thoughts on these walks to whatever book she was currently reading. She steered clear of books about art; she tried not to think about anything she'd left behind. It was, she told herself, what she'd brought with her that mattered. When she was a child, Nessa had a record player and had listened to 'Puff, the Magic Dragon' and nursery rhymes on LPs or 45s. Sometimes, because the records were badly scratched, the needle would skip. And sometimes she would lift the needle herself, even though she wasn't supposed to, and jump over a song she didn't know. She'd ruined an LP her sister got as a Christmas present by doing that, though she had never owned up to it. These past weeks in Wales, it felt like someone had lifted the needle of her life and set it down again in a place where she recognised the lyrics. She went for walks alone; she had sex with her husband. There was an old mill in the Welsh town that Philip said would make a good gallery space. He had a new Welsh friend, a builder, who believed that the yard behind it was ripe for development, and knew a man who could arrange the finance. Nessa already had a name for it: *Cariad*, the Welsh translation of Amy, meaning 'beloved'.

Philip arrived home from lectures one evening in September, saying, 'You've got a new fan. There's a postgrad student who would like to meet you.'

'What would an architectural student want with me?' she said.

'He's not one of my students, he's a doctoral student in art history. I got talking to him in the common room the other day. By which I mean he talked at me for a full twenty minutes, once he realised I was married to you. He's researching the life and work of Robert Locke.'

'God help him,' Nessa said wryly.

'He's a nice lad. A bit on the serious side. I had to tell him that you'd meet him to get him to shut up.'

The student, whose name was Dylan, arrived by bus on a crisp afternoon in late September. Nessa met him at the bus stop. They bought hot chocolate and took the public footpath by the river. Dylan had sandy hair that flopped onto his forehead, and glasses. His jacket and briefcase looked like they might have been nicked from his dad, and he held the case out stiffly from his side as he walked, as if he wasn't used to carrying one. They stopped at a table in a picnic area.

'I couldn't believe my luck when I learned you were living here,' he said. 'I'm familiar with your work. Only last week, I was discussing an essay of yours with a group of first years.'

Praise had always made her uncomfortable. 'My husband tells me you're researching Robert Locke?' she said.

They talked then about Locke, and Melanie Doerr, and about the Chalk Sculpture. 'I'm no longer involved,' she said. 'I understand that it's in something of a limbo. The matter's for other people to decide now.'

'But what do you think?' he said. 'Do you believe that Doerr made the Chalk Sculpture?'

She thought at first of deflecting the question, but then she said, 'Yes. Yes, I do. I believe that it is fundamentally hers in premise and design and execution. Apart from the foot. The foot is Locke's toddler-esque egotistical tantrum. Quite a genius tantrum, of course. Probably up there with his best work.'

'You know, Locke was quite a hero of mine,' Dylan said. 'Now I have to recalibrate how I feel about him.'

Nessa smiled. 'You and me both.'

'Were you aware of his foray into literature?' Dylan asked.

'Is this about a poem?' Nessa said. She braced herself for a rerun of the Emily Dickinson plagiarism.

'A short story, actually. Just the one.' Dylan sounded apologetic, as if he were personally responsible for Locke's lack of literary output. 'A friend's grandfather used to run a journal. He knew Robert Locke. They'd lived near each other in Cambridgeshire for a time. Whaley is the man's name. The journal stopped publishing decades ago, but he kept all the correspondence in his attic, boxes and boxes of it. He brought me up to see it. He told me that Locke had once submitted a story to the magazine. It caused a bit of awkwardness between them, because it wasn't any good, it was maudlin and sentimental, and Whaley couldn't publish it.'

He clicked open the locks on his briefcase. 'I brought you a copy.'

She took the pages he handed her. 'Do you mind if I read it now?' she said, but she was already halfway down the opening paragraph.

'Please do,' he said. 'As you see, it's quite short.'

When she got to the end, she placed the pages face down on the table.

'What do you think?' he said.

She made a face. 'Grim.'

The story was about a Scottish boy, aged ten, who'd taken a neighbour's puppy and pushed it down an abandoned mine shaft. The neighbour's child came along, a girl aged six, and on hearing the dog whimper, climbed down the mine shaft to try and save it. The mine was full of water, the story went, and the little girl got into difficulty. The boy ran to fetch his older brother, who managed to save the girl, but was himself drowned, along with the dog. The young boy was praised for having had the wit to run and raise the alarm. He never told anyone how the puppy got down the mine shaft.

Dylan reached again into the briefcase and took out a bundle wrapped in tissue. It was a collection of blue copy books.

'What are these?' she said, her pulse quickening as she picked one up.

'They're drafts,' he said. 'All of the same story, with little variation. He must have known it by heart by the time he was finished. The same thing over and over again, like *Groundhog Day*.'

She thumbed through page after page of Locke's spidery scrawl. All those times Locke had told Melanie Doerr that he was writing her story – *their* story – when it was a different story entirely that had preoccupied him. That summer in 1973 when he had relinquished the chisel to her, this was the story he had been concerned with telling, writing it over and over again, as if by doing so he could change the narrative. Loretta had not burned the notebooks after all. Loretta had most likely never even seen them.

'I wish I could leave them with you, but they're on loan,' Dylan said apologetically.

She became aware that she was holding the notebooks tightly to her chest. 'I understand,' she said, handing them back. 'Anyhow, I've stepped away from all that now.'

As she watched him put the notebooks back in their tissue paper, she asked herself what she would tell Melanie Doerr. Did Melanie have a right to know? Did she deserve to know, or would it be kinder to not tell her, to allow her to continue to think that Locke's mind had been consumed with her all that summer, so very sure had she been of his love?

Nessa wasn't privy to the negotiations that took place after Eleanor's funeral between Loretta Locke and Melanie Doerr. Months later, the Chalk Sculpture finally went on display in the gallery, but without the severed arm. 'Let the damage show,' Doerr said, in an email to Nessa. 'Let nobody try and fool themselves.' Now that the Chalk Sculpture was no longer reaching for something that wasn't there, it looked less like it was toppling, steadier now that it wasn't leaning into dead space. When Nessa asked why the piece remained attributed solely to Robert Locke, Melanie replied that she felt bad about what had happened to Eleanor, and had no wish to be in dispute with the dead. 'Or with Loretta,' she added. Nessa wondered if now would be the time to tell her about the notebooks. The words were on the tip of her tongue, but something stopped her.

Melanie's name did end up alongside Robert Locke's after all, albeit inscribed on a small brass plate that acknowledged her as a benefactor of the gallery. The laminated text on the wall beside the sculpture said that Locke's work was unrivaled among his generation for its honesty, uniqueness, and independence of thought.

At the October midterm break, Mandy Wilson came to visit. She was old enough to fly unaccompanied, and so there was no awkwardness about who else might have to travel with her. She arrived with an armful of exquisitely wrapped gifts. At the airport, Nessa watched the two girls hug each other and shriek and giggle. Later, at home, when she was walking Bailey, she happened upon them sitting together on a fallen log near the river. Jennifer had a colourful journal in her lap and was writing in it, her tongue tracing back and forth over her lip in concentration.

Nessa stopped in front of them. 'What's that?' she said.

'A diary,' Jennifer said. 'It's a present from Mandy.'

For a fleeting second, Nessa thought that she might grab the diary from her daughter and throw it in the river, put it beyond use. But she gathered herself and smiled. 'That's nice,' she said. And then she tugged at Bailey's lead and they walked on.

Acknowledgements

My thanks to:

My editors – Kate Medina and Erica Gonzalez at Random ʿuse, Mark Richards and Becky Walsh at John Murray – for all their help, patience, and positivity during the years when *The Art of Falling* was taking shape; my amazing agent Lucy Luck at C&W, who read umpteen drafts of this novel and made inspired suggestions; my writing group members: Barbara Leahy, Marie Gethins, Marie Murphy, John Mee and David Brennan for their friendship and support and for making me a better writer; Listowel Writers Week and Noelle Campbell-Sharpe for time spent writing at beautiful Cill Rialaig; the Department of English UCC, where I was lucky enough to be Writer-in-Residence in 2018; the community of readers and writers at Fiction at the Friary, Cork, and especially my friend and co-founder Madeleine D'Arcy; Nuala O'Connor for the writing workshop at Waterford Writers Weekend in 2012, where the 'Chalk Sculpture' first sparked into life; artist Siobhán Rea whose work inspired Luke's 2.17 project in this novel; Declan Meade and the Stinging Fly Press for having faith in my writing when I was just starting out; the Munster Literature Centre for their support and encouragement over the years, and especially for those workshops in 2010–2011 led by Lory Manrique-Hyland.

My thanks to John and our children, Ellie, Áine and Rory, for everything – you are the most supportive family a writer could wish for!